EKAKI

THE GIRL WHO SAW FATE

EKAKI

THE GIRL WHO SAW FATE

HARSSH SINGH

NU VOICE
PRESS

First published by NU VOICE PRESS 2024
An imprint of Hubhawks Pvt. Ltd
www.nuvoicepress.com

ISBN: 978-81-970218-8-6

Typeset by Saanvi Graphics, Noida
Printed at Nutech Print Services - India
Published by Nu Voice Press

Dedicated to Pritpal Kaur.
Miss you Mamma,
Everyday.

DISCLAIMER

This book is a work of fiction.

Although it has been inspired by historical events, all the names, characters, businesses, places, events, and incidents in this book are the product of the author's imagination and have been used in a fictitious manner.

Any resemblance to actual persons, living or dead, or actual events is purely coincidental.

"I thought I could organise freedom.
How Scandinavian of me."
Bjork Gudmundstodir
'The Hunter' – 1998

"After great trouble for humanity, a greater one is prepared, the immortal ruler."
"Asia will bow before this conquering scholar."
– Nostradamus (Q 46, Century II;
Q 75, Century X)

Author's Note

The origins of this book are humble. I suppose the inspiration came to me when a delayed Howrah Express stalled at the Asansol station for three hours. It was 10 p.m. and the platform was deserted. I stepped out, wanting a break from the book that I was reading called *Conversations with God* by Neale Donald Walsch. It's a book where a writer engages in a dialogue with God.

In the book, it was said that human beings *choose* the kind of life they are going to live, even before they are born. It confused me and got me thinking.

If immortal souls arrive at this earthly plane and experience life in all its splendour and all its misery "by choice," then why would they choose to come again? Haven't they already experienced what they came for? Why do we have eight billion fractured souls roaming this planet in fear and anguish?

It all comes down to the moment of death.

Don't ask me why I came to that conclusion! There is nothing logical about this so-called soul searching. We're not going to get scientific answers on it anyway.

The moment of death is the key. If you die at peace, then there is nothing more to acquire. That doesn't mean that your life has been perfect and your relationships were loving and generous. It just means that at the end of it all, you have made peace with what happened to you. You are done with *this* life.

Long after the train drew out of Asansol station and led me towards Howrah, this thought remained with me.

Many years later, I read an article about how the deaths in the twentieth century were estimated to be 123 million. The twentieth century would be the bloodiest century that humans had known.

Now you must be thinking that I have Thanatophobia (yes, it's a word, I checked!). I don't; I assure you that my obsessions are far less morbid.

So first, I wrote a short story about God preparing to receive 123 million souls and I imagined how buried God would be under the paperwork. God would need help from a staff, maybe? Angels?

I imagined that there would be these angels roaming the earth, in human form, here to help us in our moment of departure and to ease us through to the other realm. These angels, as it always happens, would be bloody confused as to what they're doing here and what they should do next. Amidst their own existential crisis, they would be dealing with wars and revolutions as well as with their family and love affairs.

This book is the origin story of one of those angels—Ekaki, a solitary angel.

My grandparents lived in Calcutta in an old British area. They were aristocrats who would take me to British styled clubs where we would be served prawn cocktails (yuck!) by waiters wearing pristine white gloves. You couldn't walk into The British Club in shorts and flip flops, which was my summer uniform. You had to dress up formally or you were sent home. The rules were strict. There, in The British Club library, ironically, I read about the Pahartali European Club in Chittagong, which had the sign outside—"Dogs and Indians Not allowed."

A book about the Indian martyrs had a short terse passage about Pritilata Waddedar, a twenty-one-year-old philosophy graduate who led fifteen armed revolutionaries into an armed attack at The British Club on September 24th, 1932. The attack was a disaster and Pritilata was shot in the hip. To avoid being questioned when captured, she consumed cyanide.

Nobody knows what actually happened that night and why the attack didn't go down as it was planned. And nobody knows much about Pritilata, except that she was inspired by the Rani of Jhansi and she was a master of disguise. She was the second inspiration behind this novel.

I have no explanation to why these two inspirations merged, and became a fast-paced supernatural novel about birds dying, black magic, history, and freedom. All I knew was that I wanted to write something that I could see in my head, as actual scenes in a movie.

I had two rules. Rule number one was that I would write first and read later. I would not edit or read the manuscript till I was done with the whole novel. The second rule was that the book had to be action-oriented. I had to show and not tell. Somewhat like the thriller and horror movies that I have loved. After all, I am an actor.

And because I am an actor, all of it was written during shoots and theatre performances and rehearsals. I have written parts of this book in dingy make up rooms, sitting at the back of taxi rides to the location, and sometimes even hiding under a table at a shoot where I knew it would be an hour before I would be required on sets. I used to put on headphones, slid under the table and wrote for an hour. I loved every minute of it. I hope you do too.

Harssh Singh

Prologue

Jatinga Valley.

When birds come here, they simply stop flying.

They fall.

Every year. Hundreds.

At the foot of the Himalayas.

Five hundred miles from Shillong where people come.

To siesta throughout the summer and leave in August.

There is a forest, deep in the mountains.

Two rivers flow through this forest.

The rivers never meet.

Khasi people have lived there for centuries. By themselves.

They say, that only a few hundred live there, spread over the mountains.

They pray to a goddess.

They are ruled by their mothers.

They know about the voice.

The trees talk, the caves whisper, the wind murmurs,

And the birds listen.

They listen from thousands and thousands of miles away.

And then they come here to die.

During the monsoon months,

on moonless nights,
when the fog hangs over the trees like the whites of waves over a dark ocean.
The birds fall out of the sky.
Hundreds of them,
Dazed or dead.
They hit the trees, roof tops, clouds, the bamboo sticks – sometimes each other
And they plummet.
It's as if they are misled to death. Or Mis 'voiced'.
One day, they say.
The voice will fall silent.
They will listen no more.
They will stop dying.

10th August 1925

My name is Rewa.
I am eight years old.
This is my diary.
My Baba's name is Dabir.
My Amma's name is Kakoli.
My younger brother's name is Tuku.
My younger sister's name is Kantha.
They all live in a house.
I live in a cage in the house.

15th December 1925

I like this new cage which Baba got me.

I can finally stretch my legs in the cage now.

The previous one was too small. I couldn't even straighten my legs in it to sleep. This cage is tall and I can even stand in it. Tuku saw my new cage and ran inside before I got in and Amma got angry with him. She dragged him out and tossed my mat and sheet on the cage floor. Then I got in and Amma locked me inside the cage.

I wondered why Tuku didn't have to live in a cage. Then I realised.

It must be because of the people that I have killed.

13th February 1926

I had that nightmare again. The same one—every time.
The monster is at the door.
I see the night sky.
The green door in a hut is pushed open.
And in the silhouette, I see
the monster, the devil.
Every time, I hear women scream in terror.
As he enters the room, I hear another wailing.
Then I see, two men fighting for their lives.
One of them is my Baba.
I don't know why that dream terrifies me every time.

10th April 1926

Thakurma—my Amma's Amma is not nice to me. She pokes me with a stick in the cage and tells Amma to throw me out of the house. Thakurma doesn't like my notebook and my pencil.

"Who teaches an 'animal' to read and write?" she asked Amma. Amma usually slides the food under the bars of the cage, but this evening, Thakurma hurled the food at me through the bars. It splattered all over the cage. I ate it off the floor.

She grabbed my hand when I tried to pick up a morsel that had fallen outside the cage.

She went back to her village that evening with Thakurda. Both the husband and wife looked at me in disgust.

11th April 1926

The first death that I remember

"Thakurma is dying!" I shouted. "I saw it."

Amma threw hot water at my cage and ran out, screaming for Baba. He came in, looking at me, as I grovelled on one side of the cage. I repeated, "Thakurma is dying. She is burning. Her hair is burning. It smells bad."

"She can only see fire all around."

"She's choking and her eyes are hurting so much. They're bleeding."

I began to choke.

"Her skin is peeling off in the fire!"

I was screaming like Thakurma.

I was shaking and I began to vomit all over the cage. I began hitting my head against the cage to make the pain stop. I wanted to stop seeing her skin get brown and wrinkle up like paper because of the fire.

Baba ran and shut all the doors and windows of the house while I screamed and screamed and screamed. And then I fainted.

When I woke up, there was vomit on my saree and in my hair, mixed with the blood from my forehead.

Baba went to Thakurma's village to find out what happened. It took him a whole day to discover that Thakurma was fine.

Amma was very angry.

15th April 1926

Thakurma died today. Her house caught fire. Thakurda was not at home. They say they could hear her blood curdling shrieks from a mile away, as she was burning inside.

I don't understand how I saw and felt it all, four days ago.

Did I kill Thakurma?

1st May 1926

Baba read me a poem from a book:

'Where the mind is without fear and the head is held high.

Where knowledge is free, where the world has not been broken into fragments by narrow domestic walls.'

He explained to me what it meant.

I was locked in.

He was sitting on a chair, staring at me through the bars of the cage.

12th May 1926

The second one to die

Shah Jahan came to fix my cage today. He is a carpenter.

One of the bars in the cage had come loose. He was loud and his laughter echoed in the courtyard.

It was so strange.

I liked it.

The sound.

I was tied to the charpoi with a rope, inside the house. Baba had left the cage in the courtyard and gone to work. I heard Amma tell Shah Jahan that the cage was for the animals which Tuku likes to catch.

Shah Jahan burst out laughing. I crawled to the door and peeked. He saw me and laughed again.

"And who might this be?" he enquired,

"The one who catches the wild animals?"

Amma looked furious because I was seen. I tried to duck back inside but he looked kind. He came up to the door and petted me.

Then he died.

I saw it and felt it again.

A big branch from the tree fell on him. He looked up as it came crushing down. The branch pierced his right eye. I felt some liquid squish out of my eye and I began to scream, and scream and scream. Then, I fainted.

Amma and Baba were fighting about me when I woke up. The cage was fixed and Shah Jahan was gone. I was back inside the cage. Amma saw me stir and she stopped mid-sentence. I heard what she had said to Baba.

"Get rid of her."

She was talking about me.

13th May 1926

Amma was angry.

Shah Jahan came to our house again with an old man. The old man stroked his long beard and spoke nothing. He was wearing a green cloth over his head like a scarf. He just kept trying to peer at me and I kept retreating to the farthest end of the cage. Shah Jahan wasn't laughing. He was looking at me kindly. Both his eyes were fine. He was absolutely fine. He was alive. I don't know what is happening to me.

I haven't killed him.

It must have been a dream.

19th May 1926

Rukaiyah said, "Shah Jahan is dead."

Rukaiyah sells fish to Amma. They've been having weekly gossip sessions in the courtyard for a year. She has never seen me or asked about me earlier. But today she did.

I guess Shah Jahan must have told the whole village about me.

I had bathed and was clean. I had my ragged saree on and was perfectly still in the cage so Rukaiyah sat across the room and stared at me curiously while talking to Amma. She spoke about me as if I didn't exist. She didn't ask me a single question or address me at all.

She told Amma, "Shah Jahan died yesterday when a branch had fell on him in his own courtyard while he stood smoking a beedi."

I thought that a wooden branch falling on a carpenter was a funny coincidence. I began to laugh. Rukaiyah shrieked and ran out the door. Amma sat there, staring at me.

Then I realized, I had killed Shah Jahan as well.

It made no sense.

20th May 1926

I'm writing this, seated on a luggage cart driven by a horse.

Baba is driving the cart in the middle of the night.

Earlier this night, we all left that house and are going away. Now all our belongings are on three carts. I am in the first cart, and the other luggage is piled up on top of my cage. My cage is covered with a blanket so no one can see me. I am allowed a lantern to write.

Baba said we have to move because of Shah Jahan and his old, bearded medicine man.

I killed Shah Jahan.

I killed again. I liked him.

He was funny and kind and I killed him.

Baba didn't say anything but I know that's what he thinks. That's what they all think.

26th December 1927

Today was a special day.
Baba took me out of the cage.
He held me in his arms.
He said that I will never have to live in the cage anymore.
He held me in his arms. He touched me.
Amma stared at me and Tuku smiled, but they didn't hug me.
He held me in his arms, and yet I didn't kill him.
Maybe I don't kill everyone I touch.

1ST January 1927

I caught Amma's saree this morning from my cage.

I said, "Amma, I didn't wish for Thakurma to die. I just saw it in my head.'

I began to cry. Amma looked scared. She quickly pulled her saree and hurried out of the room.

I wanted to tell her not to be afraid of me. But I couldn't.

I am afraid of myself.

15th April 1928

It's been two years since Amma spoke to me.

Since the day Thakurma died.

Two years.

24th February 1929

Today Baba brought me out into the courtyard. I thought he was going to put me back in a cage again. But, he didn't.

Baba told me that I am strange. He wanted to say I'm a freak, but he didn't say it. Not at first.

He told me that I have a strange power. When I touch someone who is about to die, I can see their deaths in my head.

I do not kill them.

I just see what is going to happen.

I can see the future, but only deaths.

I already knew that. I told him that if Amma had believed me that day, Thakurma might still have been alive. Baba was not pleased to hear that.

Baba said, "Death is destiny. You are a freak, not God. You can't change death. Only God can change death. If you try to interfere with God's plan, the world will explode."

When I asked if we could have saved Shah Jahan or Thakurma, he angrily replied, "Don't be arrogant."

I got scared. I didn't want to be in a cage again.

25th February 1929

Each time I touch someone and I 'see' their death, it feels as if lightening has surged through me. My head hurts like someone has held it in a grip so hard in the back, that my heart will burst out from my ribs in front of me. My knees buckle. I feel that the earth is shaking and my head hurts like someone has held my head in a grip so hard that tears stream down from my eyes. My throat chokes so hard. I cough and cry at the same time.

I see how they're going to die and I see when and where.

26th June 1929

I love rain.

Since it's raining today, I am allowed to run around in the courtyard by myself. I'm hidden from the direct view as the walls are eight feet high, and no other houses are around.

Even the courtyard door is kept unlocked.

Sometimes I am allowed to run in the forest, but not for long. I have to be close enough to hear Amma or Baba call me so that I can run back. I cannot respond with a shout. No one must hear me or see me.

But I am free to run around in the courtyard.

23rd September 1929

I miss talking to Baba but he has been missing for over a month. Nowadays he disappears a lot, sometimes for days and weeks.

Amma received a letter from him today. I thought she'd be happy but it made her angry. She slapped me six times today but I did not cry. Tuku tried to take my diary and I began to scream. I shrieked like I do when I get the 'visions'. He threw the diary back at me and Amma slapped me. Tuku stood there, watching.

I wish Baba was here. Amma is not mean to me when he is here.

I liked it when Amma had gone away for a month.

26th September 1930

I was punished this week.

I was tied to the charpoi for the entire day and I was not fed.

I had been wandering around in the forest and I didn't hear Amma call out for me. When I got back, Amma was furious. She tied my hands with a rope and tied the rope to the charpoi. Baba left for work the next morning, and was gone for five days. So then, the punishment was extended. I was kept tied and not fed for three more days. When Baba returned, I did not complain to him.

When Amma had gone, I was treated well. I wish she would go away again.

12th December 1930

Tuku told his friends that I am a retard. I was spotted by a villager last week and since Baba wasn't there, Amma didn't know what to say. And when they came to our house and asked her about me, she told them that I am a crazy fourteen-year-old girl—a retard, violent and prone to fits. They all mumbled and quickly wandered away when I came to the courtyard. Now they stay away.

Finally, I can roam around the forest and nobody bothers me. I met some old men, shuffling back to their cottages in the night.

I met the beggar and gypsy women who would be leaving Chittagong when the rains end. They'll go to Dhaka or Calcutta to be beggars there. I touched all of them.

I saw two more deaths.

I got so sick that I felt I was going to die.

2nd January 1931

I am getting used to my 'visions'.

Earlier, I used to faint when I had these visions. The dizziness wouldn't go away for an hour. I would feel like someone had pierced the back of my neck with a spoke. My eyes felt like they would fall out of my face. I used to chant over and over, "Please stop! Please stop!" Last week when I was waiting for the gypsy women to die, I was banging my head against the wall to stop the pain. But even after I cut myself above the right eye, the pain didn't subside for hours.

I lay on the floor of our tiny kitchen, right next to the earthen pots and the dirty floor mats, rolled up like a spool of thread, my head in my knees and my hands clasping my head and neck. I was curled into a ball, moaning and begging to God for the torment to end.

"Why me? Why must it be me?"

The fifth one to die was just a child.

Shanta's baby. Only a few months old.

Shanta rushed through the door with the baby in her hands when I was in the courtyard. Grabbed my hand and made me touch the baby. I pushed her away and ran inside. The baby died in his sleep that night.

How did she know about me?

The sixth death was Shanta.

1st October 1931

The Seventh One

Rattan was a lanky boy, with patches of white skin all over his elbows, face, and his back.

He was the ugliest thing I had ever seen.

He followed Tuku home while I was in the courtyard. The door had been left open for Tuku. I stepped out into the courtyard and Rattan jumped at me and grabbed me from my waist from behind. I shoved him off and ran inside the house. He stood there laughing.

The next day he beat Tuku in school and told everyone in the village that Tuku had a monster sister, locked up in his house.

About fifteen children showed up around the house. They wouldn't dare enter the courtyard or scale the eight foot wall, but they climbed all the trees, overlooking the courtyard and hung on the branches, throwing things at me and chanting—

"Chagulle baccha pagol."

It means that this goat's child is crazy.

For some reason, they found it really funny.

Rattan was the loudest to chant and laugh. I had no time to react as they had already seen me and started chanting.

Eventually they left.

When I went inside the hut, Tuku was crying, his head in Amma's lap and both of them were looking at me accusingly.

Now the whole village knew.

4th October 1931

I sneaked out of the hut at dusk and crept into the village. I had never been on my own before I hid in the bushes and trees, crawled and crept, making sure that no one saw me. I knew if Amma called and I didn't respond, I would be punished but I had to see it with my own eyes.

When I finally reached the village square, I covered my head and face with my ragged saree and I sat against a wall with a clear view of the village marketplace and the mango tree. No one noticed me. The kids played around. My heart was pounding, I had never been around people.

Rattan, I saw him in the crowd of kids, with the white patches on his face and skin. He was laughing.

His face and back were dripping with sweat.

I glanced at the sky and noticed a kite, a minute before the rest of the kids did. I saw it float down and settle on top of the mango tree.

Rattan, being the tallest, jumped up the branches and began to climb the tree, as the other kids pranced about the tree shouting instructions. He was quick and strong. He managed to reach the kite in a few minutes. Another roar came from the watching kids, this time celebratory. Rattan began to climb down but the string in his right hand.

I got up to get a better view.

A branch cracked and Rattan tumbled down, his dhoti got caught up in the branch and trapped his legs for a second, before he toppled and landed on his head.

I heard the soft cracking sound of Rattan's neck.

This was the first death that I had seen with my own eyes and not just in my head.

I walked back home and slept.

5th October 1931

Once more, stealthily, like thieves in the night, we're leaving behind our home. This time, it was our home only for a year.

Baba, Amma, Tuku, Kantha, and I will be gone from this place in an hour.

I will miss our hut, the garden, and the deserted path next to the forest.

It's a very cold night. When I breathe, I see fog coming out of my mouth.

My hand trembles when I write this.

I am alone in the courtyard with the lantern, as my family is packing inside. Kantha is crying and Tuku is sulking. They don't want to move again.

The next morning, when the villagers will wake up, and come to our house, it will be empty and no one will know where the whole family disappeared.

Amma, Tuku and Kantha blame me.

Because Rattan is dead.

Because they know I killed Rattan.

CHAPTER I

The Village Without A Name

It was an unnamed village.

In the middle of a dark, moonless night, the family of five entered the village. They got off a boat and traipsed past the ancient temple. Four silent men, their faces covered, carried all the luggage from the boat. One man lit his torch on fire and led the group slowly through the forest. The children stared at the abandoned temple in awe as they crept by.

Three hundred years ago, a King had no access to stone so he burnt sand, terracotta. He built temples made of clay, *poramatir.* Of the many that are scattered through Bengal, one terracotta temple, still breathes near this village. Barely.

It's forgotten by its brothers and lives lonely and derelict— covered by a thick, green, tropical forest on the banks of the river, nine miles away from Chittagong, next to this unnamed village. Overgrown trees claim ownership of its once-sacred structure, and its stone marketplace—now obscured by neglect.

Up till a century ago, it had a commandant priest, a community, a marketplace. The King and his dynasty are long gone and despite all his prayers, the gods and the devotees have long left the temples too. No one knows what happened and where they went.

Many say that this was the first stop for travellers before they breached the river and saw Chittagong, but no one alive remembers that time.

Only the boatmen know how to spot the temple and can see the *shikhar* from the middle of the river.

Within this forsaken village, which itself has forgotten its name, approximately forty families make a living in the sprawling, overgrown terrain. The landless farmers, exist sub-humanly because they know of no other existence. Occasionally, a lone individual leaves his family and goes to the city to make a living. Either his family dies waiting, or if they are lucky, they abandon their shacks and move to the city with him. They never come back and are never heard of again.

A year ago, one of these shacks was taken up by a new family. Whispers spread like wildfire through the community.

Has someone returned?

No, they're new, they moved in. And built big walls around the shack.

Where did they come from?

No one knows.

It's a peculiar family.

A man of words and letters, they say.

From Calcutta?

No one knows.

In the house lives his uneducated wife.

His son plays with our children but says nothing about his family or his sisters.

Why did they build walls around the shack?

Where did they come from?

What are they hiding?

They wonder.

The older daughter is a mad girl?

The man, is a phantom.

He shuffles down the forest when it's still dark and takes a boat to Chittagong early in the morning.

He comes back late at night, sometimes he doesn't come back for weeks.

His wife guards the mad girl. His younger daughter helps around the house.

The son went to the school a few times, but now the school building is abandoned, because there are no teachers.

A few months ago, the mad girl was seen. She was seen running through the forest screaming. No one went to her rescue.

She is a petni.

28th February 1932

The forest was my solace. In the depth of the forest, I scream at the skies and beg God to save the people that I would see dying. It had almost become a ritual.

There used to be hope.

I made a decision today.

Starting now, when I get a vision, I will wait.

I will not hope and I will not pray.

I will wait to hear about Tutul's death.

28th February 1932

Young and beautiful Tutul.

The only girl in our village who was kind to me. She must have heard about the 'mad girl' so she climbed our tree and jumped over the wall into the courtyard. I was hiding behind the door, alone at home. I was terrified.

Tutul grabbed my hand and pulled me into the sunlight to look at me. She lifted my chin, smiled kindly, put a sweet in my hand, and jumped back across the wall.

She should not have grabbed my hand.

1st March 1932

The eighth death

Yesterday, Tutul was standing by the riverside, the water swirled around her ankles. Suddenly, as her mother watched, Tutul slipped into the water and was swallowed by the river. "They found her body an hour later, with her saree tangled up in the weeds of the river," Amma told Kantha. "Tutul was floating face down in the water. She was only fifteen years old."

"Kantha, be careful," Amma said seriously. "There are poisonous snakes in the woods near the river."

But I know that it was no snake.

It was the boy, Gablu.

He had been loitering around Tutul for a couple of weeks. Yesterday evening, he had called Tutul behind her hut.

I know what he had made her taste. Something mixed in those betel leaves. She ate that and was about to follow him into the woods.

But then, Tutul's mom called her to help her carry some things to the river boat. By the time they reached the river, Tutul became dizzy. Whatever was in those betel leaves was too strong. I saw Tutul slip and disappear into the water.

Gablu will never know that he was the reason Tutul was gone. He will now transfer his attention to Anandi.

Tutul is my eighth death.

I wept for the friend that I never had, the friend I had met just once.

I have not told Baba about Tutul.

I don't want us to move again.

3rd March 1932

A spectral weight hangs over me. Dates, time, and places etched in my mind.

I feel the terror and helplessness of the dying and the dead.

Their pain courses through me, flooding my heart, my head, my eyes, my throat, my limbs, and my stomach until I feel like throwing up.

I share their last agonizing moments again and again.

I die like them.

I die with them.

CHAPTER 2

Peelo: Day 1

It was a sunny afternoon. Rewa was sitting in the courtyard. A spell of rain had washed the forest down, and muddied the path leading up to the house with big walls. It was still cloudy. Rewa heard the footsteps approaching. The shoes made a squelchy sound in the puddles, instead of a swishy sound—they must be wooden shoes and not *chappals*. The sound was light. Rewa guessed that it was a woman.

She expected the woman to hurriedly pass by, as most people avoided the house, but the footsteps marched right up to the door. There was a sound of someone almost slipping on the two stones close to the door—a gasp as the woman steadied themselves. Two more steps and then, there was a knock on the padlock. Rewa scrambled from the courtyard into the house as Amma walked towards the door. As she opened the door, Rewa knelt under the window and peeked out to see who had come.

A young woman.

She was dark skinned, thin, not very tall but long limbed, with really long arms. Her hair, black and oiled, was tied up in a bun behind her head. Her eyes were big and brown. They slanted back towards her ears. She was wearing a beautiful brown saree and a blouse which covered her arms with a white frill.

She said her name was Peelo and that she was Baba's friend. Her voice was calm and warm. Rewa thought Amma stiffened as she could feel it.

"Dabir isn't here," Amma said.

Peelo looked confused for a second.

"When did he leave?"

Amma felt like she didn't need to reveal this to a stranger.

"This morning," she said flatly.

"And I don't know when he will be back."

The woman at the door smiled almost sympathetically.

"Can I get some water?" she asked.

Amma hesitated and then looked towards the window of the house. Rewa got the hint. She scrambled under the charpoi and lay still.

The two women walked across the courtyard into the kitchen. Amma was silent and unwelcoming. Peelo did most of the talking.

"I didn't know your house is so far from the river. I almost got lost in the forest and then, the rain has made the path so slippery and muddy."

Amma handed her a glass of water.

"Would you like a cup of tea?" Amma asked, but her tone was anything but inviting.

Peelo shook her head, and handed back the glass.

"I was returning from the..."

There was a pause.

"I was returning to the city, when I thought I should take Dabir with me. I have a boat waiting."

"Well, he left early this morning."

Amma stretched out the mat for Peelo to sit on. They sat down. Amma spoke impatiently.

"He's been leaving early the last few days. Last month, he was gone for two whole weeks. I didn't know where he was at all."

Peelo sensed that Amma was looking pointedly at her for answers.

"Well, we work together at a school. I'm sorry but I don't know anything about all that," she said kindly. "He's an amazing artist and everyone loves him. But I wanted to discuss about Tuku, your son right now."

"Why?" Amma sounded rude.

Peelo was unfazed.

"Dabir says that Tuku isn't serious about education at all. He said that there is no school here..."

"There is one up the hill," Amma interrupted.

"Which stays shut most of the time because there are no teachers." Peelo tried to touch Amma's arm.

"Think about sending him to Chittagong. It will be good for him. I will make sure he is taken care of."

Rewa shook her head as she lay under the charpoi. Tuku, her little vagabond brother, would never go there if he could help it. He would rather wander around and play with his friends in the woods or by the river and Amma wouldn't care about school. Rewa was sure that Amma was not literate. In fact, Amma resented that Rewa could read, write and do basic arithmetic, even better than Tuku. What Amma didn't know that Rewa was better at mathematics and science than Baba himself.

It suddenly began to drizzle and Amma hurried out to pick the washed clothes from the courtyard. Rewa lay quietly, waiting for Amma to come back. She heard no sound from the kitchen and sneaked a look from under the charpoi and froze.

Peelo was in their bedroom.

She was looking around with a wistfulness on her face.

The room wasn't much to look at from inside. A tiny, low-roofed room was so small that Rewa would take only twenty-seven steps, toe to heel, to walk across the room, wall to wall. There was a charpoi which Baba slept on and the three floor mats were for Amma, Tuku, and Kantha. Kantha's broken wooden toys were always strewn around the floor.

Rewa was not allowed to touch her toys and she didn't have her own toys. Ever.

Peelo was touching the walls, running her hands through the clothes hanging on nails on the mud walls. She opened the wooden cupboard and as she tried to close it, the broken door hung on its hinges. She picked up one of Baba's books and touched it. Her fingers caressed the top of the page which had his name printed in Baba's handwriting. Peelo put the book back and smiled at other papers and crumpled clothes thrown untidily in the cupboard.

By the corner, next to one of the windows, was Rewa's area which was cordoned off from the rest of the room. Torn old sarees hung on thin brown ropes to segregate the space from the rest of the family. A small rectangle of separation existed, marked by a mat on the floor. The whole area took Rewa nine steps toe to heel from the wall to the rope on one side.

Rewa lay under the charpoi, observing Peelo. She looked bright and clean. The room smelt fresh. Her clothes looked soft. Rewa had never seen such nice clothes before.

She was the most beautiful woman Rewa had ever seen.

She was looking curiously at Rewa's space, when she turned and saw Rewa under Baba's charpoi. For a second, they both looked at each other in shock, and then she smiled.

"Hello."

Rewa quickly dragged herself out from under the bed and scrambled to a wall covering her head, face, and arms with her tattered saree. She didn't want to be close enough to be touched.

"My name is Peelo. Dabir didn't tell me he had such a beautiful daughter. That's so strange. He mentioned Tuku, and Kantha, but not you. What's your name?"

After a moment's hesitation, she replied, "Rewa."

"How old are you, Rewa?"

"Fourteen."

Looking surprised, Peelo said,

"Oh, so you're the eldest one?"

Rewa nodded.

"Tuku is twelve and Kantha is seven."

Peelo smiled.

"You're so beautiful," she said.

Rewa felt like cold water had been splashed on her back.

"Such long black hair and you're quite tall for your age, aren't you?" she continued. "You're fairer than Tuku and Dabir too."

She edged closer and Rewa retreated further into a corner. Just then, they heard Amma scuttling towards the house. Before Rewa could say or do anything, Peelo quickly took her arm and put a small crumpled piece of paper in her hand and squeezed it shut with her other hand.

"Give this to Dabir and don't tell your Amma," she whispered urgently.

In a second, she was back in the kitchen.

Peelo had touched Rewa.

17th September 1932

Peelo will die. In seven days.

I know the time and the spot where it will happen. I know who the killer will be.

I know what Baba will say.

"Nothing can be done. Nothing should be done. Death is destiny."

But this is different.

Peelo is different. Peelo should be saved.

Peelo is in love with Baba,

And she will die, saving him.

But I cannot warn her.

If I save Peelo–if I stop her death somehow, heavens will fall, the floods will storm the entire village, everything will be swept away into the river, and everyone I know will die.

That's the punishment for one moment of my sympathy.

No. Peelo has to die and I have to let her die.

I must not do anything.

Just seven days and it will be over.

Peelo will be gone, but everyone else will be safe.
That's how it is and that's how it has always been.
Nine people. Eight are dead.
The ninth will die on 24th September 1932.
My name is Rewa. I will have seen nine deaths
and I am only fourteen years old.

CHAPTER 3

It Begins...

The note in Rewa's palm remained crushed there as she writhed against the wall. Only when she heard Peelo leave and heard Amma come back to the kitchen, did she hide it quickly in her blouse.

She didn't think of reading the note.

Baba didn't come back home till late in the evening. Tuku and Kantha came back from their wanderings in the forest as the sun was setting. Kantha was quickly scolded and put to work by Amma.

"Go pull the water from the well, you good for nothing girl! Then clean the rice, wash it and set it up for dinner. Do not step on those clothes. They have to be put to dry again. It kept raining all day."

Then Baba walked in. Rewa watched him quietly from the window. He came into the courtyard and stared towards the hut. He looked sad as if he didn't want to come in. He looked up to the sky, in the moonlight, Rewa thought how fair he was, so unlike the rest of us. He would have been handsome, except for the fact that he rarely smiled.

Dabir.

My Baba—his name means teacher. That's what he does in the city.

My baba is a tall man who walks with a slight stoop because he sits and writes so much.

Baba says he's 43 years old and still doesn't need any spectacles to read.

Baba speaks English, Bengali, and Urdu fluently.

If you heard him speak you would think that he wasn't from Bengal at all.

My baba has the most alive eyes—sharp, and sometimes scary.

All three children ran out of the house to greet Dabir. Tuku and Kantha avoided Rewa as they hugged him.

Dabir looked tired and dirty. He had ink stains on his hand and his clothes. He took his bag off his shoulder and then removed his faded shirt. He kept both of them on the floor. He bent over and rummaged around in his bag and took out two small balls of faded newspaper.

He kept the first ball on his bag.

The second ball, he gave to Tuku and Kantha. They grabbed it and ran back to the house, tittering.

The one on the bag was for Rewa.

Rewa stepped up to talk about Peelo.

But Amma came out and began to collect Baba's stuff.

Amma picked up his shirt and his bag, leaving the one newspaper ball on the floor. Then, they both went inside.

Rewa picked up the newspaper ball. She smiled.

Shaundesh... from the city.

Dinner was a noisy affair.

Rewa sat inside. In the bedroom, in her corner.

The rest of the family spread out some mats on the kitchen floor, talking and eating together. When they finished, Rewa got up and went to the kitchen to eat whatever was left over.

She didn't mind that. A couple of years ago, she had been fed in the cage. This was better.

She still remembered those days.

The feeding—three times a day and the bathroom—three times a day. Amma or Baba would open the cage and lead her to the bathroom outside the house. Mornings and evenings would be bath time while Amma or Baba stood guard outside the door. It was Baba who had insisted that Rewa should be treated better and after quite a few arguments with Amma, the door of the cage began to be left unlocked. Then, she was allowed to step out of the cage as and when she wanted.

And finally, one day, the cage was gone.

But Rewa was still not allowed in the room with the family at meal times.

Once they finished dinner, she went to the kitchen but Rewa could barely eat, she was too anxious. She would wait till study time to talk to Dabir.

Every night Dabir and Rewa had study time, alone in the courtyard, under the light of a kerosene lamp. In the last four years, Dabir had taught Rewa how to read and write—Hindi, English, Bengali, History, and Maths.

The lessons were meandering monologues, which tailed off into rants, about freedom and revolution. But Rewa loved them all and she was a fast learner.

When the rest of the family laid out their mats to sleep, Rewa lit the oil lamp in the courtyard, went to the box under Dabir's charpoi and pulled out her books.

Baba came out, a few moments later, with another book in his hand. Rewa had spread all her books, waiting.

"Geography," he showed her a tattered book.

"You must know all about where we are and what all is there in our great country."

She was finally alone with Baba.

"Baba! I got *the sight* again today."

He froze and looked at Rewa. Then, he saw the house where the family was getting ready to sleep inside.

"No, not them, Baba. It's Peelo."

"What?" His face went red.

"Peelo, your friend from the city. She came today in the afternoon and left you this note."

Rewa placed the note on the floor. Through years of practice, she had learnt to never hand things to anyone.

Dabir quickly picked up the note but didn't read it. He stared into the night, breathing hard.

"When?" he asked quietly.

"September 24th. In the night."

He put his head in his hands and groaned.

He stayed like that for a couple of minutes and then he nodded to himself.

"Rewa, It's time."

"For?"

"You to know the truth about you and about me."

CHAPTER 4

The Man With The Light Eyes

Nine miles away to the east, across the swollen Karnaphuli river, in the heart of the 'British area' in Chittagong, Richard Henley, the Mayor of the city, paced in his study, fuming.

His anger intensified with each glance at his desk. Two pamphlets were kept there. They weren't identical. The pamphlets were laden with 'Anti British Propaganda'. Though, he couldn't understand everything that was written on the pamphlets, the language was mostly Urdu, but it had bold, English phrases like:

> If the British are good for us, why are we hungry and naked?
> Do not be tools at the hands of the British. Save your country.
> Kill the British, Save your sons.
> If we are savages, then show them how much.

These were different from the pamphlets he had seen strewn around in the last few months. These were hand painted and carefully designed, like a painting. They were elegant. The calligraphy was slanting and though it featured at least three languages—Bengali, Urdu, and English, the writing was uniform and beautiful. These were works of art.

What made Richard angry was the fact that he had found these pamphlets in *his* car, pushed in through the windows, while his car was parked at 'The British Club'. They had not been in the car earlier, so someone had sneaked into the parking area, found his car and shoved the pamphlets in.

Richard had been in a good mood.

After a nice drink with members of the British Chittagong Business Council, a few of them had supper together. Then, by 10:30 p.m. when the chauffeur brought the car up the driveway to take him home.

That's when he found the pamphlets in the car.

This was unacceptable. No Indian was allowed within miles of The British Club, unless they worked there. Yet someone had managed to sneak in and distribute these rather aggressive pamphlets. These pamphlets were meant for the "natives" and someone had the gall to deliver them to The British Club. *They* were mocking the British now.

He summoned Davon and waited.

Davon appeared in five minutes. He slid into the room, and stood still by the window. He always came in from the garden, never the front door. People rarely saw him come and go.

"Yes sir?"

He enquired in his polished accent. His voice was deep and his words were measured. He always spoke that way, as if talking too loud or too much was a waste of resources.

Richard pushed the two pamphlets across the desk. Davon walked up to the desk and picked up one of the pamphlets. Richard observed Davon.

Davon was a tall good-looking Indian man in his mid-thirties, with a wide forehead, a trim muscular body, cropped hair, greying on his temples and strangely, light eyes for someone so dusky. He was always clean shaven and crisply dressed. He always wore dark safari suits which fitted him well. He never wore a colour that would be showy. He looked solid and powerful. Like a bodyguard should.

In the last seven years, Richard had really used that power and expertise, especially when someone needed to be threatened, punished or when some information needed to be coerced out of someone. Davon could get anyone to do his bidding by simply fixing his hypnotic gaze onto the person. If needed, he could be violent, ruthless, and brutal.

"Well?" asked Richard, after Davon had been staring at the pamphlet for a while.

"Is this different? Davon?"

Davon was still reading the pamphlet, his brow furrowed.

"It is."

"Does it say anything different than the other ones?"

"No, but it's...," he replied hesitantly.

"More threatening?"

"More confrontational."

"There's no date?" asked Richard, as he grabbed one of the pamphlets and examined it again.

"No."

"Who are they?"

"The New India Revolution Army!"

"Suraj Roy's group?" Richard's concern heightened.

"Yes, Suraj Roy's group and others," Davon confirmed.

"They're planning something in Chittagong?"

"I think so."

"What do you mean?"

"I'm not sure. They've been active near Calcutta and Bihar, but last four months have been quiet. I assumed they've been hiding in the mountains, but then this. This pamphlet seems more aggressive than all their last few ones over the years."

"Should we be worried?"

Richard turned to Davon.

Davon kept poring over the pamphlet.

There was something about it that he couldn't quite put his finger on. He rubbed the beautifully designed border with his thumb.

Richard saw Davon's eyes go wide suddenly.

"What is it? What happened?" Richard asked

Davon didn't answer for a minute. He was breathing hard.

"Nothing! It's nothing. I need to be..." He paused. Hesitating, he continued, "I think I recognize this artist's work, but I can't say for sure... Let me find out. Where did you get this?"

Richard sat down heavily in his chair.

"At The British Club, in my car. In the parking lot."

Davon understood why Richard was angry.

"I'll look into it right away."

They heard a noise by the door.

Mrs. Henley, the Mayor's wife stood by the door, wearing a dressing gown, barefoot. She was swaying, a whiskey glass in her hand, her shoulder length blonde hair was messy and her green eyes were blood shot.

As she stepped into the room, her robe slipped from her shoulders to reveal a small, overweight woman having gone to waste. She stank of whiskey and damp sweat. Davon stepped back to place himself away from the light in the room and Richard sighed as Eleanor stumbled into the room.

"Aah! The wonderful team is right here. Both of you. What gossip from around the city do you bring, oh faithful servant?" she said to Davon as she fell into the chair in front of the desk. Richard stood behind, but made no move to help her.

Davon said nothing.

The glass spilled some whiskey on the carpet and Davon respectfully retreated even further to one side of the desk, his eyes down and hands behind his back in submission, holding both the pamphlets away from her gaze.

"Who is plotting against the great Empire?" she slurred. "Who dared to trouble the great Mayor of Chittagong?"

"Off with their heads!" Eleanor shouted suddenly.

"Throw them in with the rest of the natives, now why don't you Richard?"

"What crime did they commit this time? Spit on our royal car? Make loud speeches? Of course, they must be punished. Nothing can happen in this city without your permission, isn't it?"

Richard and Davon exchanged a resigned look.

They had seen and heard this, a thousand times before.

"Nothing escapes the two of you," she laughed.

"And yet you have found nothing. In seven years, you have found nothing!"

Richard dismissed Davon with a slight nod of his head and Davon made to leave the room.

"Oh, Running away from me? You cowardly piece of dirty Indian shit!"

She tossed the glass at Davon and missed him by a mile as it fell on the carpet—whiskey and ice spilling out.

"Tell me, where he is. Where is he? I know that you know. I know. Tell me!"

Richard made another sign to Davon to leave the room.

She was now rolling on the floor as Davon left the room, shutting the door discretely behind him.

Richard Henley, current Mayor of Chittagong, was loved by the businessmen in the city and the port, and hated by the revolutionaries. Forty-two years old and considered one of the most powerful and charismatic men of the British Empire in India, he sat down next to his drunken wife, as she rolled on the floor moaning and cursing, and for the first time that night, he allowed a tear to fall down his cheek.

Twenty minutes later, Davon was now outside The British Club across the street from the driveway, staring at the big sign hung outside, next to the gate—

"Dogs and Indians Not allowed."

He grimaced because he knew that on various occassions, the rule had been bended. Last year, Sir Simon from London had been allowed to take his pet poodle inside for a dinner.

Only those natives hired by The British Club as waiters, or cooks or parking valets, were allowed inside the premises, but that too, after severe background checks. The irony was that everyday, their comings and goings were checked by the security service, also comprising of Indians. The security must have lapsed, one of the staff must have placed the pamphlets in the Mayor's car. Whoever he was, needed to be found tonight.

The British Club was one of the three most prestigious clubs in Chittagong. There was the Daka Club which was the newest, built in 1911; there was the European Club which was built in 1893. The British Club, built in 1825, was the oldest and the most exclusive club for the Europeans. It was described as "An oasis of calm in a frantic city, with several acres of lawns, tennis courts and reading rooms." It was situated on the west bank of the river, on sprawling green hills.

Two of its main features were the boathouse by the river and the stone path leading up to the main building on the east side. The river ran wide near The British Club and with monsoon in swing from May to October, was always overflowing, sometimes even flooding the boat house. The British loved their boat rides from The British Club.

The second feature was the acres of manicured lawns separating the building from the city on the west of the building.

A mile long driveway from the gate to The British Club house building made sure that the noise and hustle bustle of the city never reached the guests inside. A stone wall, ten feet high surrounded the entire premises, giving the impression of a fortress, when one drove up to the gate.

There was another smaller staff gate to The British Club, far away from the Main gate. A kilometre long winding road from this gate to the kitchen was used by 'Staff and Supplies'. This road winded through the lawns. The gate had only two guards mostly.

Only the 'natives' used this road.

At around 11 p.m., Gautam was cycling down this road, from The British Club to the staff gate. Thirty years old, thin and skinny with long oiled hair in oversized 'sahib' clothes, a loose *bushirt* and pants. The clothes he wore were three sizes too large and faded from being washed a hundred times.

It had been raining on and off all evening, Gautam was used to riding in the rain. His bicycle didn't have a head light and the road was dark, but he wasn't bothered.

He had cycled down this road every day for the last seven months. He knew every pothole, every stone and every turn of the road.

Gautam delivered laundry every day to The British Club. He was able to pile over thirty clean tablecloths and waiter uniforms on the back of his bicycle, tied with a rope to the carrier and another twenty clean tablecloths tied on the carrier placed on the front handle. The clothes would pile up almost to his chin, and they were heavy. He had never dropped any of his luggage and the clothes had never been delivered dirty. His delivery for the day was done and he was speeding down the road, when he skidded and almost fell. He swore and stopped in the dark to steady his breathing.

It was Gautam, who had put the pamphlets in the Mayor's car. Gautam was a member of 'The New India Revolution Army'. Of course, no one at The British Club knew. He had been 'assigned' the job of delivering the laundry at The British Club.

An hour ago, he had parked his cycle close to the Mayor's car and slid in the two pamphlets. He had looked around to check if anyone had seen him. The parking lot had been empty.

Then he had walked his bicycle to the kitchen door and delivered the freshly washed tablecloths. The British Club laundry manager and Gautam had counted the number of tablecloths and signed the register.

Now Gautam was on his way back to the city.

He was worried. He was sure he should not have put the pamphlets in the Mayor's car. He had not approved of the idea.

This would warn the British.

At the New India Revolutionary Army meeting last night, he had said so to Dabir, but Dabir had insisted and Gautam never questioned Dabir.

Eventually everyone at the printing press had been convinced by Dabir.

Now that it was done, Gautam still felt uncomfortable about it.

What if they started raiding the city?

What if they increased security?

We should have kept a low profile till the 24th. But it was too late now.

It took another twenty minutes for him to reach the main city and another fifteen minutes to Chakma.

Chakma was a ramshackle, unplanned, and overcrowded slum area in the heart of Chittagong. A labyrinth of thousands of houses, shacks, tiny basements, rooms, shops and tiny factories.

Gautam and his comrades of the New India Revolutionary Army had been living, hiding, working in Chakma as servants, maids, cycle mechanics, rag pickers, you name it—for over a year now. Their real identities hidden.

It was midnight but Chakma was crowded and buzzing. Hundreds of people, thousands—walking, squatting, sitting, lying down, spread on the street, sleeping wherever they could spread their legs, oblivious to the other men. Bodies living over other bodies—smoking, chatting, spitting, eating.

If they stepped on sleeping bodies no one complained, they just adjusted and continued to sleep.

This nightly ritual unfolded every night in Chakma, the most densely populated area in the city where millions lived in poverty and squalor.

Gautam walked his cycle down the dirty lanes and found his way to the little window at the bottom of a two-storey building, no different from thousand other such buildings. He parked his bicycle and knocked on the window. The lady who opened the window, handed him a *patra,* a huge banana leaf with simple rice and fish curry on it. Gautam took the packet and found a place to squat close to window. He spread the patra on the floor between his legs and began eating with his hand.

A few seconds later, he noticed an old man, with light eyes, looking hungrily at the food. Gautam smiled but the man looked away, embarrassed. Gautam beckoned him closer and when he came, hunched and creaking, Gautam divided his food into two piles and nudged the patra towards the man. The man was surprised but began eating quickly. He looked like a daily labourer with a crooked back, shoulders close to his ears, a thick white moustache, on his dark, stained face, wearing a simple banyan and a dhoti. He had a *jholi* around his waist and a *gamcha* wrapped like a turban on his head.

Gautam guessed that he worked in the chemical factories in the city. The man stopped eating for a second and looked up at Gautam.

"You're communist or revolutionary?"

Gautam laughed.

"Why do you think I'm either of them?"

"Only one of those would share food with a smile on his face."

"Well, I could be both."

"Then shhhhh!" the old man put his finger on his lips.

"Both kinds are in danger here," he said.

They ate in silence. After a few seconds, the old man spoke again.

"Are you really a revolutionary?"

Gautam thought for a moment and spoke.

"Dada, I want freedom."

The old man scoffed.

"You are sitting here, in Chakma, eating off a leaf on a dirty pavement. You probably sleep on the street, what difference will freedom make to you?"

"It's not just for me, freedom is for everybody."

"Aah! You're a communist then, not a revolutionary."

Then after a pause, the old man said vehemently,

"Both are bad."

Gautam laughed again.

"Why?"

"Both don't want to do any hard work. They want to run away from the real responsibility. You people will cause riots and not give a damn about your poor families. After the riots, you will escape to the hills where you will catch pigeons and eat them for the rest of your lives. Those left behind will all be caught and beaten and thrown in jails."

The man shook his head and began to eat again.

Gautam said emotionally, "Dada, one day we will be free and there will be justice and there will be prosperity and there will be no kings and rulers and no one man above the other. Your family will be just as free as my family or a '*gora saheb's*' family."

The old man looked sad. He spoke gravely.

"A man who spoke like you came to my village five years ago."

He spat on the side and with gritted teeth, he spoke after a moment.

"He was evil. All of you are."

Gautam smiled and said, "Because he tried to show you a new way to live?"

"No, because he brought death to the village. Almost all the men and young boys left for the revolution, a few weeks after he came. They left to get freedom."

The man scoffed.

"None of them ever came back. Not even for Diwali. Their mothers have stopped crying. There has been no harvest because there are no young men left in the village, and my s..."

He stopped.

"The sons of the village are gone; the village is dead. This is not just one village, hundreds of villages from here to Dhaka to Calcutta are all dying. I have been forced to come here and I will die here. That's that about your freedom and justice."

He spoke in a matter-of-fact manner.

"Who was this man? Who came to your village?"

Gautam asked softly.

"Who cares."

"What did he look like?"

The man finished his last bite and looked up.

"He was *Bangla*, tall, thin, and wore huge black framed spectacles."

"Suraj Roy?" Gautam recognized the description.

The old man gave no response to the name.

"Your son followed him?" Gautam asked kindly.

The man looked away at the mention of his son.

"I don't know, he left one night without telling anyone. That was many years ago. I heard he had joined the revolutionaries."

"Have you come here to search for him?"

"I gave up searching for him, a long time ago."

The old man said bitterly.

"I am here to work till I die."

"What if he's here?"

Gautam asked, rolling up his patra. He tossed it by the side of his bicycle. The man looked up.

"My son? In Chakma?"

His eyes lit up with hope.

"Could be."

"Then what?"

"They meet around here and talk to other people about the revolution," Gautam explained.

"This Suraj Roy? And his freedom soldiers?"

Gautam rummaged his bag and took out one of the pamphlets.

The man looked suddenly scared and grabbed his hand before Gautam could open the pamphlet.

"No no no, not here," he whispered in terror.

The two of them got up and walked into the empty lane behind the two storey house. They heard stray dogs and saw there was no one sleeping in the alley. Gautam spread open the pamphlet and looked at the man.

"Can you read?"

"A little, I can write alphabets and understand numbers."

"Keep this pamphlet with you. See this elaborate design on the border that looks like the border of a carpet?"

The old man looked confused. He didn't know what a carpet was.

"See the curves?

The old man nodded and said, "This is beautiful."

Gautam thought he would pass on the compliment to Dabir dada as he handed the pamphlet to the old man. "The next pamphlet comes out tomorrow. And another one will come out the day after. You will find both of them anywhere, on the streets, near marketplaces. The one that comes tomorrow will have the date of the next meeting, and one day after that will have the location of the meeting. The location will be somewhere here in Chakma. Look for the date and location hidden in the design, right here. Just keep checking the border of the design. You must come to the meeting. You might meet your son. Hundreds of men from all over the country will be there."

The old man took the pamphlet and began to fold it and put it in his jholi, looking around to see if anyone had seen them.

Then he asked softly, "Will the man who made this design be there too?"

Gautam smiled, "Yes, he will."

The old man looked Gautam in the eye and said, "His name is Dabir."

Gautam looked up at him in surprise, but before Gautam could answer, the old man had caught Gautam's head with his right hand, taken a knife from his jholi in his left hand, and slashed Gautam's throat. Blood spilled from down Gautam's shirt and he felt no pain, just a wet feeling on his chest. Blood, his blood.

He looked down surprised and found that he was unable to speak. As he tumbled to the ground, he watched the old man straighten up, the hunch was gone.

The old man, now stood upright, took off his gamcha and he began to wipe the blood off his knife. He watched silently for a long time, as Gautam's gurgled and choked on his own blood.

Davon, once again, looked around to see if anyone had seen him. The stray dog was sitting silently staring. Davon hunched his back, once again, looking like an old, destitute labourer as he walked away into the night.

CHAPTER 5

The Truth About The Truth

Far from the city, across the river, outside a lonely hut, and in the courtyard in the dark, Rewa sat with her Baba, in the light of an old glowing lantern.

They were sitting under the small awning, watching the rain fall intermittently. Rewa could hear the wolves in the forest. Amma, Tuku, and Kantha had gone to sleep.

They just sat in silence, which Rewa found comforting. She had spent the whole day being terrified. She rarely got to meet people, and to have Peelo come up to her and touch her and then getting 'the sight' again, had set up a trembling in Rewa which had lasted all day.

Finally, Baba spoke, "I am not a teacher Rewa, I am a revolutionary."

Rewa didn't tell him that somehow, she had known for a while.

"We belong to the New India Revolutionary Army. Peelo, I and, the others have sworn that we will free our country of tyrants and rulers. Gandhiji and the rest of them do not know the British like I do. These goras wield power and rule through fear. But soon, they will fear us because we will be the most powerful faction in the country. In a few days, thousands of young men and women will join us and fight with us. We have been working on recruiting them for the past three years. In one week, we will have an undefeatable army."

Dabir said, his eyes blazing with conviction.

"This army cannot fail. I can't fail this time. What you've told me today, about Peelo, has scared me."

Dabir's shoulders slumped suddenly, he looked defeated.

"Rewa, when you were growing up, everyone thought you had *mirgi*. I knew it was something else. When you started telling me about your visions, I was the only one who believed you. Your mother didn't understand what was happening to you. She wanted to keep you locked in a cage because you were violent and wild sometimes. She thought you were possessed, or a witch, or a demon, or a petni. Don't mind her, Rewa, she's an illiterate," he shook his head and continued.

"But I knew that you were something else. You were something that no one else on earth would understand, except me."

Rewa noted that he kept calling her 'something' instead of 'someone.' It bothered her.

Brushing the thought off, she listened to Dabir intently.

"So, I took you out of the cage and began to educate you. Look at you now." There was pride in his voice.

"Rewa, witnessing people die, is unnatural, I agree, but you possess the unique ability to see the future!"

His eyes were glittering.

"Don't you realize the wonder of it? You see something that is going to happen in the future, days before it actually happens. Only *you* know when and where it will happen. No one else but you know that. Now, we can use that power to make our army even more powerful."

Rewa had been holding her breath.

"How Baba?"

Dabir smiled.

"Rewa, you will be my secret weapon. You will tell me which one of our soldiers is going to die on which day, and which one will live to fight the next battle."

Rewa was silent.

A whole army of soldiers?

And she would have to touch them to know who was going to die?

"We will be invincible; they will never be able to harm us."

He leaned forward, and this time he touched her shoulder, she froze.

"But Rewa, we must be extremely careful. Once people know what you can do, they will not hesitate for a second to take you away, hurt you, or use you for their own purposes. You cannot trust anyone, not even Peelo. No one can know what you can do, and no one can guess.

Rewa, since you were six years old, I have been protecting you from the world. I kept you safe in the best way possible, considering how wild you used to be. This is why you were never allowed to meet people. This is why we moved from village to village every couple of years. This is why, you didn't go to school like Tuku. Tuku and Kantha are ordinary, you are not. Their life will be inconsequential, but not yours; You will help me change the world. But you *must* obey all my instructions. It will be hard on you, Rewa. Because no one will know that you have caused miracles. I will use your power to save our country, but no one will know. Our army *will* emerge victorious through every battle."

But what about the people who will die? Rewa thought.

What about Peelo?

Dabir was up and pacing in the courtyard, getting wet in the drizzle.

"Rewa, sometimes bravery means that no one will understand your power, and sometimes it means to stay silent. When you see the soldiers die in your visions, let them die. Their death is inevitable. But if their death can do good, if it can have meaning, then that is okay. Their death is their destiny. We must never attempt to save anyone. Sometimes bravery means being misunderstood. You must accept all of this, because..."

He stopped and looked at Rewa.

"...Tomorrow, I will take you to the city. You will meet the New India Revolutionary Army chief, Suraj Roy, and the next two in command—Peelo and me."

He was looking at her intently.

"It's just you and me, against the whole world, Rewa. I will always be there to save and protect you. Never tell anyone else about our plan, and *never* question what I ask you to do."

"It's just you and me, against the whole world, Rewa," he repeated emotionally.

CHAPTER 6

Daniel

After Eleanor had passed out on the floor of his study, Richard had carried Eleanor to her bedroom on the first floor. He sat next to her and watched her sleep as she moaned and tossed around before she settled down and began breathing heavily.

Richard glanced at the photo frame on the bedstand, which had a picture of them from seven years ago. A formal picture of the family with Richard standing behind a chair, had Eleanor in it. Richard was staring at the camera, his chin up, unsmiling, but Eleanor had the beginnings of a smile on her face. Though they all looked stiff and starched in the picture, it had been a happy time. He had been the youngest Mayor of any city in India. Back in England, they had been lauding him and here in Chittagong, he was respected and liked.

Then, Daniel had been born and both of them had been ecstatic. They had planned to live in India for another two years and then, move to England for Daniel's education. It had been Eleanor's idea that Daniel should be raised away from India, in England.

"A Mayor's son gets too much attention for nothing and it will go to his head."

So, they had agreed that Richard would wait a year and then, start looking at finding work in England.

Eleanor didn't look anything like the woman in the picture anymore. Her face was pale and clammy, her neck sagging, the skin around her closed eyes, darkened by sleepless nights, and discoloured by the alcohol. Her cheeks fell away from her pudgy face and her hair was straggled from batches of neglect and then, periods of overcompensation. Grief, trauma, and worry had added tinges and contours to a face, that make up was not an expert enough to hide. Richard looked at Daniel in the picture.

Daniel.

Their seven-month-old son, grinning toothlessly, the only one smiling in the picture. It seemed like he understood a joke that they didn't.

Daniel.

Richard remembered the day with a shudder. The sound of Eleanor shrieking, the unearthly wailing.

Daniel and the nurse had been on the grounds, on the picnic mat. The nurse Pushpa, had gotten up and was pacing on the grass, with Daniel in her arms, cooing and baby-talking. Daniel was grinning while Eleanor was on the verandah. She must have stepped inside for two minutes to ask for some lemon water and then, she had stepped back out.

The mat was there, but both the nurse and Daniel couldn't be seen anywhere. Eleanor felt her gut stir, but she kept looking around anyway. The grounds were huge. They must be walking around some trees. She called out for the nurse, and for Daniel. She walked up to the mat and looked around. She couldn't see them. She called out.

Daniel!

Pushpa!

No answer, no sound of Daniel crying or hiccupping.

The birds were chirping and somewhere inside the house in the kitchen, a steel plate fell loudly.

They must be behind that big banyan tree. She hurried.

No one was there.

Daniel! Pushpa! DANIEL! PUSHPA!

She was stumbling across the garden, screaming.

RICHARD!

He had been in his office, when the shrieking phone call came. He wanted to believe that Eleanor had merely panicked, but Eleanor never panicked.

It took him half an hour to get to the Mayor's Estate and by that time, Eleanor was insensible. Her dress was torn from her shoulder, her knee was bleeding and she was screaming incoherently in the garden, holding the picnic mat to her chest. When Richard ran to her, she wailed. It was a sound he would never forget.

Seven years had passed.

They had no clue about what happened to Daniel or Pushpa. The first few days went in waiting for a ransom phone call or a letter, but neither came. Richard and Eleanor spent torturous moments driving to the post office when a letter arrived with Richard's name but the wrong address on it. It was from Richard's old aunt in Cardiff. Richard ripped it away in frustration. Every time the phone rang, it would leave Eleanor a hysterical mess and if it was work-related for Richard, she would fly into a rage. There were only twenty-two phones in Chittagong, somehow the phone still managed to ring incessantly.

Daniel had been taken, and no one knew why? What did they want? The pointlessness of the kidnapping was heartbreaking.

The estate guards remembered a man, prowling outside the estate, a couple of days before the kidnapping, but they had caught him as he was trying to scale the wall. They assumed that he was just a daily wage labourer desperately looking for work, so they had let him go.

One of the guards telling this story had hesitated. He had felt that the daily wage labourer had sounded educated, but he hadn't spoken about it at that time. Pushpa must have been a contact for that man. And they might have planned it. The only way Pushpa would have escaped with Daniel was to have gone down the path to the river and that man must have whisked them away in a boat.

But where? And why?

Seven years. Richard and Eleanor had never left Chittagong. He went back to work in a week with renewed fury and budding hatred for Indians. All his obsessions focused on finding Daniel. Eleanor was left alone in the mansion, all that space filled with her anguish and fury.

Richard could never leave India now. Not till they found Daniel. Daniel was alive and somewhere out there. In England, the government showed a lot of compassion for one of their own and made every resource available to him but that made Richard angrier. He didn't care for sympathy or compassion, he wanted ruthlessness. He wanted someone who would be able to follow every clue, tail every man, and do it surreptitiously. Barging in with the British police in this vast overpopulated country would lead to nothing. He needed someone who could go deep undercover to find that man, Pushpa, and his son.

Eight days later, Davon had shown up. Highly recommended. Light eyes, icy calm. He had been working as a spy for the officer's mess in Calcutta, and he knew the area from Chittagong to Varanasi like the back of his hand.

For the first few days after he arrived, Richard met with the Police, the Army, and the local government workers. Davon listened in silently. The entire staff of the Mayor's estate had been stripped off their jobs and locked up in a facility near the Mayor's office. A new temporary staff had been hired with stringent background checks. The old staff was waiting to go back to their old jobs.

Davon proposed to Richard that they re-interview the staff, this time with him present in the room. The police had already interviewed each one of them extensively, but they came in obediently, one by one and submitted to yet another round of questioning. Richard initiated each interview, Davon stood behind him in the shadows, intervening only when necessary and typically at the end of Richard's questioning.

When Davon was satisfied, he would look at Richard and nod, and the person would walk out. The maids, cooks, butlers, security guards, and laundry men, all came in quietly and this time, Davon spoke to them in their native languages. Most of the staff was Bengali, but there were some Gujaratis and Biharis and Davon effortlessly switched to those languages when talking to them. The interviews extended into the evening of the second day, leaving Richard exhausted with worry and rage.

Ramu was talking. One of the servants, a Bihari boy. A nervous, short, and skinny twenty-five-year old. Davon was staring intently. Then, Davon walked up to Ramu, and stood square in front of him, watching his eyes. Suddenly, with his left hand, Davon slapped him hard across his face. Ramu, slammed to the ground and slid across the room. When he stood up on his knees, his tooth had broken and his mouth was full of blood. The sudden brutal assault had shocked Richard and the servant. Davon punched Ramu in the face again. He began to howl. Davon punched him again. The servant was on his knees and Davon was towering above him, holding him up by his hair and punching him. Ramu's face was bruised and bloody, there was blood on the floor and on Davon's knuckles. Davon's expression hadn't changed. Ramu was howling his truth.

"The prowler man had given me money to enter the Mayor's estate. I didn't know who that man was. I had never seen him before. He gave me twenty rupees *sahab*!"

He wailed.

"Forgive me Sahib, before the prowler could enter the grounds, one of the guards saw him and he ran away. I don't know anything about Pushpa."

He begged and pleaded and swore to that. Davon had continued to punch him, and Ramu's baying was heard all over the estate.

In seven years, that followed, Davon had exhibited no chink in his armour. He was obsessive, neurotic, cruel, and calm. Everyone was terrified of him. Sometimes even Richard feared what was going on in Davon's mind. Any clue that he could have followed, he had followed it to its last thread. He kept Richard informed in diligent and painstaking detail. If Richard set him a task, he never slept before giving Richard a report. Even if he got his information at 3 a.m., he wouldn't wait till morning and wouldn't care if Richard was asleep or not. He would arrive at Richard's study, slinking in from the window and would inform a servant. The servant would have to go and wake a grumpy, under slept Mayor.

And no servant would refuse Davon. Everyone knew what he had done with Ramu.

That is why Richard was still awake and watching Eleanor tonight. He knew that Davon would be back. Davon had never failed him.

Except for the task that he had been hired for.

Finding Daniel.

Seven years later, they were still searching for Daniel.

Davon had now become a part of Richard's team, unofficially, of course! He had unearthed more information and obliterated innumerable threats to the British Empire, but the disappearance of Daniel remained a gnawing mystery. Eleanor had never recovered and as per Dr. Martin, would never recover. Her body battered, bruised, and abused was joining her mind in giving up on the hope that Daniel would ever be found.

One brief trip to England had led to a nervous breakdown and in Chittagong, she had spent the last few years either wandering around the grounds, drunk and crazed, or in her bedroom, catatonic, staring at the ceiling for hours, moaning, groaning, and wailing at no one in particular.

Richard would keep rekindling her faith, like a fire dying in embers.

"We'll find Daniel, we will, my dear."

But she didn't believe it anymore and neither did he.

He had lost everything that night.

Seven years later, he was losing whatever remained of his family.

He sighed, pulled up her sheets to her chin, left the room and went down to his study.

Davon returned at 2 a.m. to the study, appearing freshly bathed. Richard groaned inwardly.

This always meant murder.

Davon had killed someone tonight, which meant Richard would have to 'steer' the investigation in another direction. Davon placed the pamphlet back on Richard's desk.

"They're here."

"Suraj Roy?"

"And from the looks of it, his Army heads."

"In Chittagong?"

"Yes, in Chakma. I'm not sure if they've planned anything other than a recruiting drive, but instead of doing it in villages, they've somehow managed to get the riff raff assembled here," Davon stated flatly.

"Why here?"

"I need to understand that. It's risky and can cause more problems. There has to be reason."

Richard asked grimly. "A riot? Mutiny?"

"Could be," Davon hesitated to confirm.

"Yes," Davon said finally.

"Should I alert the Army?" Richard asked.

"Yes, also the police. They're meeting at Chakma. The recruitment drive is happening there."

Richard picked up the phone.

"I'll send them now."

"No. Wait."

Davon moved closer to the desk. "I need to know more about what they are planning. If you tell the police now, and they start combing the area, the recruitment won't happen and Suraj Roy will disappear again. Let him get to the meeting, let me see what they're planning and then we get in the police. Let Suraj Roy and his team get inside Chakma, we will surround it and I will signal for the police to come in. If I have him, we don't have to worry about the rest of the crowd. You can arrest all of them or let them go."

Richard knew they would never be able to arrest thousand people in that slum. But if they caught Suraj Roy, that would be a master victory for the empire.

For years, the rumours had been circulating that Suraj Roy was working out of Calcutta, but his clandestine moves through villages and towns all over the east of India had made him hard to pin down. His notorious armoury raid, had given him the reputation of being a mafia gunslinger and an eloquent revolutionary speaker.

Two years ago, Suraj Roy and some of the New India Army 'soldiers' had raided two armouries near Dhaka, carried away a couple of guns, pistols, and ammunition into the mountains.

They had raised the Indian flag and cut the telegraph and telephone lines. The victory had been hollow, for they hadn't managed to capture the actual cache of arms, but since then, the victory had become an urban legend, and in the last two years, facts had been altered in all local discussions to create this amazing tale. Every small village whispered that hundreds of British soldiers had been killed, and enough ammunition had been stolen to destroy a city.

All lies, but now part of the folklore of Suraj Roy.

Suraj Roy had then issued an open challenge to the Queen of England. If they caught him tomorrow, it would be the end of The New India Revolutionary Army. The rest of the rabble would run back to their pathetic villages with their tails in between their legs. Richard was excited. He sat back and listened to Davon's plan.

***

Later that night, Rewa saw the dream.

The same dream she had seen many times before.

She was inside an old house, like a shack and she could see the door, an old wooden door, painted a gaudy bright green. Someone was fighting.

Two men.

One of them had a knife and was attacking Baba.

She was screaming as she lay on the floor. Baba was desperately fighting for his life, but somehow, she knew he was fighting for her. She couldn't see the other man. But he was screaming with anger as he flashed the knife and tried to cut and stab Baba. The two men fought like animals, falling, grabbing, with guttural shouts. Then somehow, Baba hit the man and his knife fell, as the man stumbled. Baba caught the knife and before the man could regain his balance, Baba had driven the knife in the man's chest with two hands. Someone else screamed in the room.

A woman.

Rewa woke up, her heart thudding.

For an hour after the dream, she couldn't sleep. She tossed and turned and stretched her arms.

"Peelo!"

She saw a strip of moonlight fall on her arms around the elbow. She lifted her hands to look at them.

Why is my skin different from everyone else's?

She wondered.

Why does 'touching someone' do this to me?

Two years ago, when they were traveling in the night, moving from one village to another, in the dawn, she had seen lepers crawling by the side of the road. She had caught sight of the sores and rashes on their arms. Their bodies, stiff like a dead tree, with skin peeling off in black like papery strips, were oozing pus and blood. Rewa had stared in fascination. They had looked back at her blankly.

How was her skin different from theirs?

If she did peel it off, would she lose this power?

Would she stop seeing death?

Would she be ordinary?

Baba's words, this evening, had scared her. More than anything else in her life, she wanted these *visions* to stop, so she could live free, like Tuku or Kantha.

But now Baba wanted her to do this all the time. *He wanted her to touch a whole army?*

They would soon know that she was a monster, a leper, like the ones she had seen on the side of the road,

Her skin attracted death.

She would never be like Tuku and Kantha, just a girl, just a sister. She would never be part of her family, and she wanted that so much.

She had not felt any remorse or guilt, watching Rattan topple from the tree and die.

Did that make her a monster? Was she worse than the British that Baba wanted to defeat?

And Peelo?

The ninth death that she had seen in her head.

Rewa shuddered.

And looked at her cursed skin again. Peelo wanted to be part of *this* family. With Dabir.

Rewa crept from her bed and sat in the middle of the room, looking at her family one by one, as they lay sleeping all around her in crooked poses. As the light from the window fell on the bodies, she reached out, but couldn't bring herself to touch them, and suddenly she started weeping silently.

Amma never touched her. She couldn't remember if Amma had ever touched her face with love, stroked her cheek, or brushed a stray strand of hair behind her ear. None of them had. She knew they were repulsed.

She scrambled back to her corner, lay on her mat, her elbow folded under her head, and stuffed her saree in her mouth and cried till her arm was wet.

Tuku peeped under the curtains and watched her silently.

Finally, long after she had stopped crying, she fell asleep.

CHAPTER 7

The City – Day 2

A cup of lemon tea stood steaming in the middle of the kitchen floor. Rewa stared in surprise.

Normally, Rewa always got up just before dawn, before anyone else did and, usually, she prepared her own tea. Today as she came back from the courtyard to the kitchen after washing and drying her own clothes, she saw that someone had lit the sticks under the stove and prepared her tea. This had never happened before.

Amma?

She squatted on the floor and sipped it. It was horrible.

"I guess it's quite bad," came the voice.

It was Tuku, speaking from the kitchen door.

"It is."

Rewa admitted and took another sip.

"But you've made it?" she asked.

Tuku nodded, walked in warily and squatted beside Rewa. She tried to shrink away.

"It's okay, I won't touch you," Tuku assured.

"I heard you and Baba talk last night."

Rewa held her breath.

Mostly Tuku and Kantha kept to themselves and treated her as if she didn't exist at all. They weren't mean to her anymore, well maybe Kantha was, she had thrown stones at Rewa last week, in the courtyard. Kantha made sure that Amma wasn't watching when she did that. Rewa still had a bruise at the back of her shoulder because of the stone. But Tuku had not behaved badly with her in years. Today, he was being kind and Rewa wasn't sure how to take it.

"You know about...what happens...to me?"

She asked hesitantly, not knowing how to frame the question.

"Yes." Tuku looked at her.

They were both silent after that.

"I'm not a freak, Tuku."

Tuku looked at her and said, "No, you're my sister."

Rewa remembered the years of yearning for any kindness from him, from Amma or Kantha. Instead, they had treated her like a diseased cat, when she was in the cage, and they had all protested when Baba had removed the cage.

In the last three years, every time they had moved to a new village, Tuku had blamed her. That Tuku, who felt anything other than indifference or active dislike where Rewa was concerned, was a surprise to her today.

Someone stirred in the bedroom.

Tuku got up to peek at who it was, leaving his teacup behind.

Rewa spat in his teacup, then regretted it instantly.

He came back, took his cup and disappeared into the courtyard, as Amma stumbled into the kitchen.

Rewa took her tea to her corner. Suddenly she smiled. She had woken up, feeling heavy and sad.

I am your sister Tuku.

She sat on her mat, feeling happy. She sipped her tea and nearly choked.

The tea was really horrible.

Rewa and Dabir were waiting by the river, and they hadn't seen a boat for the last fifteen minutes. There was no other way to get to Chittagong. You just went through the jungle till you reached a lane or a trail which you followed till you reached the river and yelled at a fisherman or a boatman, plying their boats towards the city.

It was a hot morning and Rewa was sweltering under her *burqa*. Amma had been silent and sulking when Baba had pulled the burqa out of his satchel. Amma had made no attempt to help Rewa, when she had struggled to wear it over her saree.

Then Baba had given Rewa black gloves. She had never seen gloves before. Fascinated, she had wondered why would gloves ever be needed by humans.

She hated them now. She was covered from head to toe and sweating profusely. It took a while because Baba wanted a private boat just for the two of them, but the boats they called out for, all had passengers seated already. No one would agree to take just two passengers across, when they could pack twenty on the same boat.

Finally, a fisherman passed by, who had only an old woman sitting at the stern. Rewa and Dabir got in. Rewa was terrified as she clutched the sides of the boat with both hands as she sat on the floor of the dinghy, petrified that they would capsize.

Ten minutes later, she was excited.

I'm going to the city with Baba.

I was never allowed to go to the village market and now I'm travelling to Chittagong.

I was in a cage and now I'm travelling to Chittagong.

With Baba.

Chittagong docks hit her like a punch in the stomach. The boat ride took an hour and the last twenty minutes were frightening. Theirs had been the lone boat on the river for a while. But as the city drew closer, many boats could be seen wrestling to reach the docks.

A hundred?

No, a thousand.

Wrestling with each other to reach the docks.

Everyone was shouting now. The boatmen, fishermen and passengers.

Over their noise, the sounds from the city grew louder, like a wave or a waterfall, steadily building from a distance until it finally splashed over Rewa.

Looking at the city, her heart sank, and her terror rose. Thousands of people on the docks, pouring in and out of boats. Jostling, pushing, shoving, *touching* each other. A mountain of people all the way from the water to the buildings behind, blending into one another and she couldn't believe that so many people were alive in this world.

A bare-chested young man, swam up to the boat and clambered in. He began to direct the boatman. Rewa, terrified at his sudden appearance, scrambled into a corner. The bare-chested man grinned at Rewa and jumped back into the water gracefully.

Baba spoke to the boatman. A few moments later, the sounds of the docks began to recede. She peeked over the boat and saw that they weren't docking there.

"Change of plans," said Baba as he sat next to her and looked out towards the docks.

"We'll go someplace where there are less people."

For another hour, the boat slid through the river into the city, and Dabir began one of his teaching lectures.

"The history is, Rewa, that Chittagong is one of the oldest ports in world. They say that Greeks, Romans and Chinese used to have Chittagong on their maps. They called it 'A sleeping beauty rising from mist and water'. Before the invaders started to come, they established a trading port in the ninth century, and then, when everyone became wealthy, the invaders came. The Portuguese and the Burmese, then the Muslim invaders and now the British. It's hard to know what the original Chittagong was like then. The roads, the buildings, the food, everything here has been tainted by its rulers. All of them treated us like stray dogs, took over our land, our culture, and our language. We no longer know who we are, we have been slaves for so long."

Rewa listened in silence as the boat slid past the crowded city, passing dirty slums, smoky factories and then lush gardens and beautifully clean huge sprawling buildings, beyond even her wildest imagination. This must be the British area.

"The revolution will change that," Dabir said.

"For the first time in seven hundred years, we will be our own kings."

The boat dropped them off at a woody and quiet area. Rewa was relieved that no one was around. Though they were still in the city, the stone promontory they landed on, was hidden by a thick bunch of trees.

Baba helped her get off the boat and then, the two walked on a stone wall which was covered in moss, towards the street. An ordinary couple, Baba in his Pathani kurta pyjama, and his burqa clad woman.

By the time they reached the Chakma market, Rewa was overwhelmed and exhausted.

She had never seen so many cars, or trucks, or buses up close. They were such ugly contraptions, noisy and scary and those buses, so high. Like elephants!

First, she prayed that Baba wouldn't make her get up on one of those. Then she prayed that he *would*, so she could get away from the crowd.

It was relentless.

Rewa was knocked over so many times, and whoever bumped up against her didn't even wait, they just moved on without even noticing, and every time someone brushed against her, her breath got caught in her throat. Rewa, who had never seen so many people in her life, let alone being elbowed or stamped on by so many, was scared, bruised and tired to the point of falling down after just ten minutes of the city.

Finally, they reached Chakma.

The slums of Chakma, in the heart of Chittagong, were another world all together. Millions lived in small huts built on top of each other like pebbles piled up. These houses were barely three or four rooms stacked up on top of each other in Higgledy- Piggledy fashion. These couldn't be called houses or homes. They were barely little rooms made of cardboard, brick, jute, and cloth. Each leaning on each other to stand. They were built so close together, that the door of one, opened into the other. It was like being part of a maze watching how a person had to find his way from the entrance of the house to his room, crawling and climbing through tiny rooms, sometimes without windows to what he called home. There were thousands of houses like this, growing in all shapes and sizes, like fungus.

They opened into tiny, slushy, crooked spaces which couldn't even be called lanes since these 'houses' could protrude or recede at the will of the owner and there was no road or pathway to speak of in front of them. The lanes were so narrow and cramped that two people couldn't walk side by side, or pass each other by, without their shoulders or arms touching. These pathways were sometimes so dark, even in broad daylight, because of how the houses had piled up to block the light, rain, and air. They were claustrophobic, dark wet places, made worse by the millions of humans who lived there, their bodies pouring out of these houses, unmindful of streets and boundaries of any kind.

Dabir led Rewa into these lanes. Rewa walking behind, lifting her burqa to jump over buckets, and plates and toddlers left on the street crawling around, bawling.

They stopped in front of a blue gate.

Dabir seemed surprised to see it locked. He fished out a key in his bag and unlocked the gate. They walked into a tiny courtyard and entered a small a two storey building. Dark with no windows. But there was a skylight. Rewa had never seen a skylight before.

It was the biggest house she had ever been in.

In the middle of the room, under the skylight, lay a big machine, massive and silent like a sleeping monster. The house seemed to be built around this machine. Rooms all around, on the first floor and the second floor.

Rewa took off her head scarf and stared. The room was strewn with crumpled papers and it smelt of sweat, dust, dirt and for some reason, walnuts.

"A printing press," Baba explained. "It's very old, and it malfunctions all the time, but it helps us print pamphlets about our revolution."

He picked up a paper and handed it to her.

"You made this baba?" Rewa asked.

Dabir nodded.

"I recognized your design," she said.

They heard the door open and Dabir quickly turned to her and whispered urgently.

"Don't talk, just listen, and don't touch anyone."

Rewa slunk into a corner. Peelo came rushing into the room, fell into Dabir's arms and began to weep.

"Dabir, it's Gautam!" she cried.

Dabir peeled her off and grabbed her shoulders.

"What happened to Gautam?"

With tears streaming down her face, Peelo said, "They found him; his throat had been..."

Dabir gasped. He held her away from him firmly by the shoulders and looked into her eyes piercingly. He was breathing hard.

"Who found him? The police?" Dabir interrupted.

"Yes." She sobbed.

"Did they kill him?"

"They're saying it was a robbery, his bag and his bicycle were taken."

"Do you believe them?"

Another voice from the door replied.

"Yes."

Peelo, Dabir, and Rewa turned.

There was a man at the door, a young man with long hair, wearing spectacles. He wore a crumpled white kurta pyjama. The young man was crying as he spoke.

"I believe that they don't care what happened because they're doing nothing."

Baba turned around and face the wall. The young man went up to Dabir and placed a hand on his shoulder,

"Dabir bhai, Gautam is gone. Last night some time before he reached this factory, he was..."

The young man couldn't continue. Dabir turned around and pulled him tight into his arms and Peelo too.

As the two of them clung to Dabir and wept on his shoulders, Dabir looked at Rewa.

The young man finally let Dabir go and wiped his eyes.

"I know what Gautam meant to you Dabir, you trained him for years, and he was our only family left."

The young man looked at Peelo and began to cry again.

"Now we're orphans again."

Dabir braced his shoulders and moved away from Peelo.

"We've lost another soldier, such a brave one, and the cruel part isn't that he's gone, but that he didn't die fighting for freedom, that he's gone without any glory, killed so pointlessly for a..."

He broke down.

Peelo blurted out, "Dabir, he was carrying the pamphlets, what if they've found out about our plan and that's why..."

The young man shook his head.

"Dabir's border design is such that they won't guess. Yesterday's pamphlet only had the date."

Then the young man noticed Rewa in the corner and stopped. Peelo recognized her, composing herself she turned to Dabir.

"Dabir? Your daughter?"

Baba made no move to bring Rewa closer to them.

"Yes, that's my eldest, but you're right Peelo, what if they've tortured Gautam and they know about the plan?"

The young man with long hair stared down at the floor. "If they suspected anything, they wouldn't have been so eager to get rid of his body. They just handed it to me, the first person who claimed it. It makes no difference to them and that's why I know that they know nothing of our plan."

Peelo collapsed in Dabir's arms again, and he held her tight.

Rewa was watching intently; this was the most physically expressive she had ever seen her Baba behave.

I don't think he's ever held Amma like that, ever.

"Later, we'll talk later," Peelo whispered.

The young man watched them for a moment, sighed and walked up to the big machine—the printing press and put his hands on it and leaned against it, with his head down. Dabir shuddered and straightened his back.

"I mourn the death of our soldier," Dabir said.

"But we don't have time, we must plan about tomorrow and about the mission," Dabir said and put his arm around Peelo. They went into one of the rooms and shut the door behind them.

Rewa was forgotten.

She stood there in the machine room with the young man.

Rewa realized he was just a boy. No more than eighteen years of age, he had a thick beard and moustache, long shiny black hair that fell to his shoulders and covered his face as he put his hands on the machine and leaned over, sobbing. A couple of minutes later, he lifted his head, composed and looked at Rewa.

"My name is Ajoy. I'm Peelo's brother." His voice was thick and heavier than she had expected.

He waited for her to respond. She didn't.

"...And your name is?"

"Rewa."

"Dabir dada doesn't mention his family or kids much. I'm his student. He's been teaching me Urdu for two years now. He teaches our whole family which has Peelo and there's my cousin Gautam, who..." Suddenly, he was silent.

"Dabir dada taught my cousin Gautam as well. Gautam was obsessed with Dabir dada, in fact, it was Gautam who was the first to join the revolution, and he would talk about it to us all the time."

"Peelo joined and then, me. We had to, Gautam wouldn't leave us alone. He would go on and on about the revolution." He smiled.

He sat down on the dirty floor, picking up a pamphlet from the floor beside him.

"Gautam helped Dabir dada design this. Can you read and write?" He asked suddenly, looking Rewa in her eyes.

"Yes," she spoke, hesitantly.

"What happened to Gautam?" she asked softly.

"He was killed last night; someone slashed his throat. Close by, just round the corner in a dirty alley. He had almost reached home. Another five minutes and he would have been here with us, safe."

He took a deep breath and said, "In a dirty alley. Some beggar saw his body this morning. A beggar!"

The door opened and Peelo came into the room. She saw Rewa and stopped as if she'd forgotten that Rewa was there. She reached out to hold Rewa's hands and Rewa froze before she realized that she was still wearing the black gloves.

"You must be hungry," Peelo said, her eyes still red and wet. She found her bag by the door and fished out a big tin box.

"Both of you, eat. We're going to be in there for a while." She said, handing the box to Ajoy, who took it without getting up and put it on the floor next to him.

"Is Suraj dada coming?" he enquired.

"No. Too many policemen in the city. Rewa, do you need anything?" Peelo asked kindly.

Rewa shook her head.

Peelo picked up a couple of papers and then, went back to the other room, closing the door behind.

Ajoy, pushed the box to her. "You eat, I'm not hungry."

"I'm not hungry too," Rewa replied.

Rewa sat down on the floor against the wall.

Ajoy kept staring at her.

"Has Dabir dada told you...anything?" he asked.

"About?"

"Us? What we do? What we're trying to do."

She hesitated and said, "Yes."

He leaned his head back and sighed.

"We've lost so many, and you're so young. He has brought you here means he wants you to join us."

Rewa didn't know if she was meant to respond. Ajoy closed his eyes and suddenly blurted out. "Go back home tonight and don't come back here, Rewa." He looked piercingly at her and continued, "Live your life, get married, have children. This is a dead end. We are all going to die, if not today, then next week, or next month. All of us know that."

He moved closer to her and sitting cross legged in front of her, he asked, "Who are we doing this for? Gautam is dead, all his dreams have died with him, Peelo and I and Dabir, all of us are going to die too. We'll never be able to free India, the British are too powerful, and we're nothing but bandits. What if we do drive out the British? Then what? Do you think the rest of us are ready to live in freedom after that? NO! Right now, we're angry at them, so we want to kill them. When they're gone, we'll just kill each other for nothing. For religion, for custom, for food or for land, for a bicycle and two annas like the beggar who killed Gautam. And do they care? Does anyone care?" His eyes welled up again.

After a moment Rewa spoke in a strong calm voice.

"And you think the person who is dying cares? In their last moments, what do you think their thoughts are? None of what matters to us, matters to them. All our joys and sorrows belong to this world. Not to the next."

Rewa was taken aback at her own words. And shocked at Ajoy's expression. Shocked at how suddenly the words popped out of her mouth. Death and the dying had been such a large part of her life and she had wondered for years:

What happens to the dreams of the dying?

What happens to the love in their hearts?

Does it die too?

Is it real enough to survive somewhere in this atmosphere? Does it change the world left behind at all?

Maybe they take a little bit of it wherever they go?

For the rest of the day, Baba and Ajoy worked in the relentless noise of the big, noisy printing press, making more pamphlets. The intimidating machine, a cacophony of clanks and whirs, terrified Rewa but she just sat quietly in various corners of the house, still covered in the burqa, and the gloves, but now without the headscarf. When she caught Ajoy's eye once, she smiled, Ajoy stared for a second and smiled back and then went back to working on the press.

Six times, some men came to the house during the day. Nobody took notice of Rewa and Baba didn't introduce her to anyone. They always entered stealthily and left the same way, first standing by the main door for a few moments and covering their faces before walking out, with pamphlets in their bags.

Rewa picked up one pamphlet and read it carefully. Ajoy came closer and she stiffened. He took a step back and picked up one pamphlet and showed her the intricate border design.

"Ingenious, isn't it? This looks like the border of a Persian carpet. This corner of the design looks like a door from an Arabian fairy tale castle. But if you look closely, you can see a number mentioned in Bengali and Urdu which indicates tomorrow's date. See?"

"But because your father designed it so beautifully, it looks like a border. This door is a sign of the New India Revolutionary Army. It's painted on walls, on streets, pavements, boats on the harbour, and everywhere in the city. People from all over the country have arrived at Chittagong over the last couple of weeks. They will follow that sign and come to the meeting tomorrow. Right there, hidden in plain sight, is the location and date of the meeting for all the revolutionaries, and the goras will never know or understand. Tomorrow we will have a thousand more revolutionaries in our army."

CHAPTER 8

The Club by The River

A small boat glided through the river, in the night. It had a small lantern at the stern and it drifted noiselessly through the city of Chittagong. Three people were in that boat; Dabir, Rewa, and the boatman.

Rewa was mesmerized by how large the city was. A thousand shapes and lights that she couldn't identify any more. She sat silently, her hand in the water, gazing at the city wafting by.

Baba took a deep breath and got up, looking at a distant building. He had a dreamy look on his face and his eyes glistened.

"The British Club," he said, pointing to a dark woody area dimly lit on the riverbank. Up the hill was a big building that seemed to be hidden by the trees. She heard something.

"What is that?" Rewa asked.

"Music," replied Baba

"That is music?"

"The music they listen to."

"Who?"

"The goras. They call it Zhazz."

"Baba?"

"Yes beta."

"What do they look like, these...goras?"

Baba looked at her and laughed suddenly.

"I didn't see a single one today," she explained, looking disappointed.

"You'll see them soon enough." He assured her. "You remember Rattan? The boy in the last village who had white patches on his skin and golden eyebrows, who couldn't look at the sun?"

She remembered clearly.

The seventh death, but the first one she had seen happening with her own eyes.

"Yes, I remember Rattan."

"Well, imagine someone with their entire skin being the colour of the white patches, red eyebrows and yellow hair and grey eyes."

Rewa tried to picture someone like that but she gave up, shaking her head.

"They're all there," said Baba, pointing into the darkness towards the building she could hear the sounds coming from.

"At that Club. Where the sign outside says, 'Dogs and Indians not allowed'."

"Dogs and Indians are not allowed," he repeated menacingly.

"Baba?"

"Yes."

"Peelo is nice."

She said as a statement, not a question. Baba was silent, still looking away in the water.

"Can't we save her? Just her, just this time. Just her. No one else. Please!" Rewa pleaded.

She couldn't see Baba in the dark, but she could feel his eyes boring into her. He was thinking hard.

He sat next to her.

"This is not your decision to make. And you forget that Peelo is a revolutionary. She knows what she has to do, and she knows what it entails, we all do. We made this decision years ago that our lives don't matter. I have taught you all the history of our country, you know how people have died, what all they have sacrificed."

"Baba, she loves you."

She knew she had crossed a line.

Baba was silent. All Rewa heard was the sound of the oars spelching in the water and the boatman's breathing.

"Don't talk like that again."

His voice was steel.

"My mission cannot be compromised. We have too much to do, to get caught up in...this. Always remember what I told you. It's just you and me against the whole world. Do not question me or my decisions."

She pictured Peelo, dying in the dark.

Ajoy!

How devastated he was going to be in seven days.

Her eyes welled up, but Baba couldn't see her face in the dark. She leaned back against the boat and closed her eyes.

Dabir spoke again. "We cannot lose, Rewa. Tomorrow, we put your powers to work."

His eyes were boring into her.

"I want to know if it is just Peelo who is going to die on the 24th."

"What?"

"Who else...Did you see anyone else?"

"I..."

"Is there anyone else with her, when she dies..."

"Baba..."

"Is there?"

"I can't see anyone..."

She took a deep breath and continued.

"I don't know but, in the vision, I saw her alone."

"Then tomorrow, we find out for sure."

Rewa felt her heart sinking to her stomach as Dabir continued, "Tomorrow, when I tell you, you must remove your gloves and touch the people I will ask you to touch."

Dabir looked determined.

"I must know who will survive and who won't. I must. I cannot afford to fail, and if I know some people are going to die, then our plans will be to succeed without them. And succeed we must, for us, for India. Tomorrow, you and I, we start making our future."

Rewa dreamt the same dream again.

The same dilapidated old shack, the old wooden gaudy green door. The two men fighting, one of them being Baba. The other man attacking Baba with a knife and some other woman in the room screaming. It was exactly the same as it had been for years. The same dream which always ended with Baba killing someone and a woman screaming.

This time something changed. The man lay dying at Baba's feet and Baba looked at Rewa with relief, sweat, and tears rolling down his face. Blood on his shirt. Rewa got up and walked towards Baba and looked down at the man who was dying at Baba's feet.

It was Ajoy.

18th September 1932

One more chance.
Please God,
Give me one more chance.
Not now, not like this.
It's not fair. I didn't have a chance.
What kind of life was this?
God.
You took Baba, you took Ma, and then Gautam...
Then...
NO!... Oh my god... How could you take him away?
Please forgive me, please, forgive me, I didn't mean to hurt you.
I didn't know what I was doing. He made me do it.
Forgive me for all my sins. Forgive him for what he made me do. Am I actually saying these words?
Haha...
Wasn't this the prayer we hated, Ajoy?
Ajoy, can you hear me?
Even at this moment I'm making jokes...
Ma was right... We are idiots.
I am an idiot.
These will be Peelo's last thoughts before she dies.

CHAPTER 9

The Recruitment Day – Day 3

At dawn, Tuku had once again made chai, but this time, he had been waiting outside, in the courtyard for Rewa, instead of the kitchen. Both the cups were kept on the floor next to where he squatted. Everyone was still asleep.

Rewa took a sip and grimaced again. “From tomorrow I will make the chai for both of us.”

Tuku grinned.

They sat quietly for a few moments, sipping the tea. Tuku went in and came back with some crumpled pieces of paper. Rewa saw them and went red with embarrassment. They were drawings that she had made, of their old house in the last village. Drawings of Baba, Tuku, Amma and Kantha, sometimes with coal, other times with a pencil.

“They were flying in the wind outside the house,” explained Tuku. “I think someone came to the door when you were making these and you rushed in to hide, they blew away, and I found them.”

Caught off guard, Rewa didn’t know what to say as Tuku spread the pictures on the floor. They were astonishingly good. In each picture, Rewa had captured a certain expression of either concentration or bliss. They weren’t looking at her in the pictures. They never looked at her really. Her family.

Tuku and Kantha were taught to never mention Rewa to strangers and if people asked if they had another sister at home, both were instructed to deny her existence. Rewa had half begun to believe that herself. She had never played with Tuku and Kantha due to the fear of touching them, she had never shared her meals with them.

Amma had long since ceased to interact with Rewa. Once Rewa had learnt to dress up on her own, Amma had ignored her, in fact, Amma had simply stopped paying attention and shrugged her off, almost like throwing away a cockroach that runs up your hand. She let Rewa be.

Dabir had never tried to get the family to bond with Rewa. Maybe he had realised that Amma would never understand what Rewa was and thought it better to keep them apart, to keep both the worlds apart. Dabir had become Rewa's only family. He was the one who educated her, sometimes he got treats from the city for her. He noticed when her clothes were becoming ragged and got new clothes for her.

He talked to her, asked for her opinion sometimes. When he ranted about things she didn't understand, it was the only time she felt like she existed, because no one else spoke to her at all.

Their last three homes had always been near the woods and *that* is where Rewa lived. In the forest, playing on her own, wandering about, singing her own songs, talking to herself, and when she found something beautiful, drawing it.

These pictures that Tuku had spread, were all made over the last year, but these pictures didn't show Rewa's envy or jealousy for Dabir, Tuku, Amma or Kantha. They were made with love that had never been reciprocated.

"They're beautiful, Didi."

Tuku had never called her didi before.

He neatly folded the papers again and placed them under the cup, so that they wouldn't fly away.

"When will I die?" he asked unexpectedly.

Rewa almost dropped the cup. Tuku was staring at her intently. "That night, you sat next to all of us. I guessed you wanted to know when we would die, then you went back to your bed and you cried...So, I thought I would ask, when will I die?"

Rewa was squirming but Tuku pressed on. "It's okay, you can tell me, Didi. I'm not afraid of dying. You don't have to tell me how but tell me when. I want to be ready."

"Tuku... Don't."

"I know Baba has told you not to talk to anyone about this. But I want to know. I want to do everything before my last day. I want to eat kulfi, I want to wear new clothes and wear shiny black shoes, which have that new shoe smell."

All the malice she had had against him, over the years, all the time she had suffered from his jibes, or the anger she had contained, just melted away.

Rewa looked at Tuku.

A twelve-year-old boy, small and skinny, with bright black eyes and unruly hair, loud and wild most of the time, but speaking so softly today, of things that mattered the most to him. In that moment, Rewa realised that she didn't really know Tuku at all. She knew that Tuku was always running away from the village school to play with the boys. That's how he spent most of the day, with other farmer boys in the fields. He was strong and agile and sharp and funny but also gentle with animals.

"Will we all die soon, Didi? All of us—me, Kantha, Baba, Amma? Can you see how *you* will die? Can you see your own death? What will you do after we all die?"

"Stop Tuku! Please..."

Rewa took a deep breath, placed her teacup on the floor and continued, "You all are going to be fine. I didn't see anything that night. I didn't touch ... anyways I got scared."

Tuku changed the topic instantly as twelve-year-olds do.

"Why is Baba taking you to the city? Why doesn't he take me too? He used to. I've gone with him a few times, but now he doesn't ask me to come with him." He was grinning now.

"Does he want to see how many city people will die next? What did you do yesterday, touch all the city people to see when they will die? Is that why Baba made you wear that burqa? So that no one can see who is touching them?"

Rewa felt her shoulders stiffen at that. Tuku relentlessly continued, "Kantha thought Baba was going to leave you there in the city forever. She asked Amma and Amma slapped her. Don't let him do that didi, you'll come back, won't you? Amma is very angry that he took you and that he's taking you again today."

"She shouldn't worry. Baba will take care of me."

"She's more worried about Baba than she is about you. She said that girl will be the death of me. That's funny didi, 'death of me!'"

Both of them began to laugh.

Then Tuku reached into his one and only pocket and brought out a piece of cloth tied up in a small bundle and placed it in front of her. Rewa picked it up and slowly opened it. Sugar and cardamom crushed together in a tight ball. It was obvious that Tuku had sneaked it out of the kitchen.

"I know you get dizzy when you get the '*sight*'. So, keep a little in your mouth, every time Baba makes you touch someone. You'll be fine."

Tuku gathered her drawings and his cup and went inside. Rewa sat there, clutching the bundle in her right hand and looking at Tuku as he went back inside.

Her body exhaled.

Even the tea began to taste better.

***

Somewhere down the lanes of Chakma were *bazaars.* The word 'bazaar' implies that people sold their wares there, but it was a lot more disorganised than it sounds. Carts, animals, children, women, gypsies, beggars, prostitutes and old people. Hundreds of people collected in that clearing of an area.

None of them were formally selling their wares; instead, all kinds of bargains were being shouted, and then accepted or rejected accordingly.

Bargains of anything and everything from food, clothes, sex, and mostly sex since most of the people had nothing else to sell.

There had been a series of famines in the last couple of years, along with that, a hundred years of the British ransacking Indian businesses, had finally made the entire population incapable of earning anything. Millions of people who had no food, land or resources in their villages had begun migrating to cities over the years to become beggars.

Dying of disease and desperation on their way there and then facing the harsh reality upon reaching the cities. The bazaars of the slums of Chakma had reeked of the stench of their resignation and acceptance for years.

The Tankir Bazaar in Chakma was one such slum bazaar but today it was going to become magically clean.

Three people walked into Tankir Bazaar at around 8 a.m.

A man, a young boy, and a girl in a burqa.

Dabir and Ajoy walked in the middle of the bazaar which, despite the early hour, had been fully functioning since 6:30 a.m. Ajoy spoke to some of the men. These men sprung to work and began running around whispering to the rest of the people in the bazaar. Within seconds, it grew into a louder buzz, and without any protest or delay, people began clearing the area.

Women picked their belongings and their children and men began cleaning and picking up whatever they were selling. Tents were quickly pulled down, mats were picked up, flimsy structures were dismantled immediately. A minute later, things were packed and hundreds of people were piling their wares on their heads or on their hips and moving without complaining.

Tankir bazaar became an empty space as large as a field. The people who had been selling things five minutes ago, were now trickling into the little dark lanes and soon they disappeared.

Dabir, Ajoy, and Rewa stood in the middle of the empty marketplace. Then, Ajoy ran into one of the narrow lanes. Baba grabbed Rewa by her arm and pulled her to a stained wall. The wall had a thousand *paan* spits and smelt of urine. Baba whispered urgently. "Sit down here and do not get up till I tell you to."

"Yes Baba."

"Rewa."

"Yes?"

"You remember what I told you?"

Rewa lowered her head.

"Suraj Roy will be here in a couple of minutes. I will point him out to you."

Rewa felt her breath quicken.

"You will take off your gloves and touch his feet. And whatever you see, you will carefully remember and tell me later. It's most important. If you see...a *vision*."

He stopped for a second and looked around to see if Ajoy was close by.

"I want to know. The when and the how."

Rewa nodded numbly.

She went near the wall and in one corner, found some shade and squatted. The heat and humidity were stifling. Rewa was itching and soaked with sweat. She could hardly breathe and the gloves were the most uncomfortable thing she had ever worn.

Ajoy came back with another boy. He was carrying a table, the boy carrying three chairs. They set them up next to the 'urine' wall.

Slowly, people began to trickle in from the various little lanes. Young men and women, some of them were not much older than Rewa, they weren't impatient or noisy. They were quiet and respectful and although all of them looked like peasants or manual labour, they carried themselves with a little more dignity. They didn't interact with each other and stood a distance from each other, eyeing each other. But as the place began to fill up, they began to speak politely to each other, still reserved.

Ajoy came and squatted a little distance from Rewa.

"The crowd is not sure if Suraj Roy will come today. It's very dangerous for him to be in Chittagong. There are spies everywhere. These people don't want to be caught."

"Spies?"

"The British—they have been sending people to many such meetings as spies, to catch us, the revolutionaries. Hundreds of comrades have been caught in meetings like this and killed. That is why your father came up with this idea of the secret messages about meetings. The British hate Suraj Roy. Suraj Roy has escaped at least three attempts to his life. So he lives in hiding pretty much. Sometimes even we don't know where he lives or hides or whether he is going to come to meetings or not."

The place was now packed.

The people, who had been squatting, were forced to stand up. While the first few people to fill the crowd were younger people, now it was a mixed crowd.

Rewa saw a woman, probably fifty years old who was wearing a crisp fresh red and white saree and hair in pigtails that had gone completely white, with a determined look on her face. Rewa thought she must be the oldest one here.

No.

The old man, a little behind her, at the other end of the crowd, hunched, a thick white moustache, on his dark, stained face wearing a simple *baniyan* and a dhoti looked older than her.

Near the stage, Rewa saw a young boy, who was dressed like a Buddhist monk—a maroon-coloured costume, and with him another boy, wearing the same clothes, but he had long hair.

She started. The boy. He seemed to be staring intently at her. Rewa checked herself. Her burqa covered her completely, yet the boy seemed to be looking straight into her eyes. She ignored him and began to look at the rest of the crowd. It seemed everyone had come here just to get a glimpse of Suraj Roy.

Something began to feel wrong.

It came as a sudden intense, hollow feeling in her abdomen and then, she felt it radiate all the way up her back.

A sudden shiver. Her forearms tingled.

At first, she felt like she was being lifted, but two seconds later, she felt a rage.

There was someone here.

He was somewhere in this crowd of hundreds. She felt his presence, like a jolt, like someone had gripped her by her shoulders. He was watching them. He was watching them like an animal watching his prey.

How was she able to feel his feelings?

She closed her eyes and tried to decipher.

What is he feeling?

What am I feeling? Anger? Fear?

No. It was both.

This person was angry, but he was also afraid.

Afraid of whom?

Afraid of Suraj Roy?

Yes, there was someone in the crowd.

She felt a shock in her gut. This man meant to kill someone. He was raging and he had murder on his mind. This was no ordinary fury. This was years of seething wrath.

She opened her eyes and began to search the crowd.

Baba, I must save baba.

I must get Baba away.

A moment later, a murmur in the crowd. From one of the lanes, a group of young men and women, all dressed in khaki shirts and pants burst through with purpose. Behind the men and the women, was Suraj Roy.

Tall, thin, dark, and fit—Suraj Roy was forty years old. He had a sharp nose and a chin with a cleft in it. He was wearing huge black framed spectacles, through which his eyes were absorbing everything. He was wearing a dark green army clothes. He looked grim, determined, and commanding. He had his hands folded as he walked through the crowd, towards the table and the chairs.

Dabir was looking at Rewa pointedly. Rewa caught her father's eye. She nodded. Suraj Roy came up to Baba and bowed with folded hands. The two of them hugged and turned to look at the huge expectant crowd that had collected here.

In secret, right under the nose of the British, over eight hundred young men and women had collected in the heart of Chittagong, in a slum, to enrol in the New India Revolutionary Army.

They had done the impossible. Suraj Roy seemed proud. *And Baba wants to know how he was going to die?*

Suraj sat down on the chair and Rewa felt her stomach stir again.

The man in the crowd!

She had to warn Baba and to get all of them out of here, safe. She looked at the all the entrances and exits in the marketplace and realised with a shock that they were all trapped. The narrow lanes were all crowded and impossible to get through.

Dabir was whispering something to Suraj. The two of them turned and looked towards Rewa. Dabir beckoned Rewa.

She removed her gloves.

She did not lift her veil.

She got up and walked towards the table.

Her heart was pounding.

As she approached them, Suraj Roy smiled at her, and folded his hands.

"So, this is the brave young woman who is joining the New India Revolutionary Army?" he said, his voice sounding deep and confident. Rewa bent down and touched his feet. A shudder went through her body. She lost her balance and Baba caught her just in time.

Suraj got up to help, but Dabir put out his left arm to signal that she was ok.

Suraj said, "I heard she's already been to the press. This is your eldest?

Suraj grinned. Rewa began to like him. He seemed warm, and commanding.

"I remember how I was in jail and Dabir, you had disappeared for years. No one knew where you were and then when I did find you in that small village, and called you, you told me that you now had a wife and daughter.

Suraj turned to Rewa, "Now he's got two more, not wives, children." He chuckled.

Rewa felt dizzy. "Baba?" She said weakly.

"Not now." he whispered in her ear. "Later."

Suraj Roy turned to Dabir and Rewa,

"Dabir, how old is she? Fourteen? And you're bringing her to join the revolution? You are an inspiration. I remember hearing that you've taught her yourself. That is wonderful. An educated woman educates the whole family. What is your name? Beta?"

"Rewa," she choked.

"Rewa, you must know how proud we are of you. God bless you."

Baba had his arm around her to keep her on her feet, she felt him trembling too. Suraj stood up and nodded at Dabir.

"Let's start," he said.

Baba led Rewa to the wall and as he made her sit on the floor, he whispered, "When?"

"Same day as Peelo. Same place."

Baba had a look of realisation on his face. He covered his face with his hands and took a deep breath. Then he suddenly moved back to the table.

Rewa was left alone by the wall.

"Baba" she called out to warn him about the man in the crowd, but he had already moved away.

She began looking into the crowd, scanning the hundreds of faces to see if she could figure out who the man was.

Asit dada stood in front of the table and began addressing the crowd. Ajoy came and squatted beside her.

The woman started the meeting and addressed the crowd calmly.

"Many of you have travelled far and wide to be here and to hear these two people speak. We, the New India Revolutionary Army are grateful that you are here. Your bravery is appreciated, but this is not enough. Hindustan needs more. For the sake of our motherland, you will have to sacrifice a lot. That is the only way we will have freedom. Please welcome a man who has sacrificed everything, his family, his future, his life all so that we can breathe as Free Hindustanis. Brothers and sisters, Shri Suraj Roy."

The applause was slow at the beginning but grew thunderous in a couple of seconds. The audience was in awe of Suraj Roy. She remembered what Baba had told her about the head of the New India Revolutionary Army—Suraj Roy.

He had been a schoolteacher in Calcutta some twenty years ago. Fair, patient and not entirely critical of the British rule. But then, in January 1915, when one of his best students Ravi had gone to the University in Calcutta and strayed into the area that was closed to Indians, the area meant for the Britishers, the constable had thrashed Ravi with a truncheon. Ravi had bled to death on the steps of the university, clutching his graduation documents in his blood-soaked hands.

Suraj, along with his students began protesting on the streets in Calcutta. In March the same year, The Defence of India Act made it possible for any protestor to be jailed, prosecuted, and sentenced without any evidence.

All that was needed was just the report of a British officer.

Hundreds of people were thrown in jail.

Along with them, Suraj Roy.

He was released two years later, in 1917. Now considered one of the leaders of the 'Chittagong Group of revolutionaries'. Suraj then recruited and trained passionate revolutionaries including his most trusted compatriot, Dabir.

Later the same year, Suraj Roy had been a huge part of the Non-Cooperation movement. Another jail sentence, but this time because he was a repeat offender, and because he had grown a reputation, he was tortured barbarically. Not just him, all his comrades as well. Half of the 'Chittagong group' of peaceful protestors died in jail, over the next two years.

Roy emerged from jail, militant and ready to avenge his friends. He began to show brilliant skill in organising raids with rebel forces of the New India Revolutionary Army - NIRA. Two years ago, his army and locals, in a series of fierce raids, had killed sixty British Soldiers and had lost thirty revolutionaries. The British Army enraged and vicious launched large-scale assaults on villages and towns looting, killing, imprisoning any one that they remotely considered supporters of the New India Revolutionary army.

Roy, Dabir, and other survivors dispersed in small groups to villages and towns and had been in hiding ever since, trying to recruit, train and relaunch the rebels.

Today was the biggest turn out of potential revolutionaries in eighteen months, and to have managed this in the heart of Chittagong, was a testament to the planning and execution of Suraj Roy's most trusted man Dabir.

Dabir had masterminded this whole operation in Chittagong over the last two years, keeping a low profile while planning and working tirelessly. No one knew where he lived and how Dabir managed all the work and then disappeared in the jungles of Chittagong across the river, lying dormant, until needed.

Suraj Roy stood up.

"My name is Suraj Roy, and I know that you have come because you have heard tales about me."

"Those tales are lies."

The crowd began to murmur and look at each other.

"You have heard that Suraj Roy killed thousands of British soldiers. That is a lie. You have heard that Suraj Roy destroyed cities. That is a lie. You have heard that Suraj Roy started an army. That is a lie.

"Suraj Roy did not do those things, a Hindustani did. A living breathing free Hindustani. Names do not matter. Neither mine nor yours. Our names will be forgotten. But what we do will not be forgotten.

"You must remember what we did, not who did it. I will die today or I will die tomorrow, then what good is this name. If all my name has done, is that it has made you see that the life you are living is not worth living, then it has served its purpose.

"Forget all names. Remember the one name that you need to have. Hindustani. That is what we are. Each one of us. And now Hindustan is calling for her children. Our land is bleeding and it is screaming—that we are free, and we will fight till our deaths to make these goras understand that we have had enough.

"Today you will all become Hindustanis.

"For the sake of your children, freedom.

"For the sake of your land, freedom.

"For the sake of your motherland, freedom. If you have a breath left in you, give it to the Hindustan!"

Rewa noticed the old man.

The one with the hunch and the thick white moustache. She had seen him earlier but hadn't paid attention. He stood up at the edge of the gathering at the other side of the crowd, right next to a bald-headed boy dressed as a monk.

The monk boy was still staring at her, but Rewa didn't pay any attention to him at all.

The old man. He was no longer hunching. He was standing tall.

Rewa felt him.

She *heard* his intensity in the air and knew instantly.

He's the one!

The man reached into his bag and pulled out a pistol. Rewa was too stunned to react.

He aimed the pistol.

Suraj and Dabir were in the direct line of fire.

CHAPTER 10

The Stampede

Rewa screamed loudly.

A shot rang out.

Rewa strained to see if Dabir or Suraj had been shot, but they had all ducked behind the table. It took a second for the stunned crowd to react, and then everyone began to scream, shriek and run at the same time.

Just thirteen years ago at Jallianwala Bagh in Punjab, British soldiers had openly fired on an innocent peaceful rally and massacred thousands of civilians, considered as the worst ever massacre in the British history. The fear was so strong that you could taste it. Everyone in the compound was a sitting duck.

People rushed towards the narrow lanes. They began to climb over whoever was in front of them, like ants, climbing over the houses and walls, braying hysterically, too petrified to realise that there had been just one shot.

Rewa found herself in the path of a stampede. Some of the people rushed towards the stained wall, towards Rewa. She stepped backwards and toppled to the floor and her back against the wall as a swarm of people, terrified and crazed, stormed in her direction. Rewa was going to be trampled over.

Suddenly someone yanked her arm hard. Ajoy was screamed at her to get up but she couldn't hear him over the noises. He pulled her to her feet and dragged her away from the wall, she stumbled and fell, but he didn't let go of her arm and dragged her before she found her feet and began running behind him.

A second later, the people reached where she had fallen. Two young men tripped and were instantly trampled over by the others, who crushed them, shrieking wildly and trying to get over the wall.

Ajoy dragged her away towards the nearest little lane, she began tugging against his hands to stop him. Rewa was still wearing the gloves and the burqa was stuck under her feet, so she was stumbling as she was being pushed and shoved by the crowd.

"Baba! Ajoy, we have to get Baba!"

But Ajoy held her wrist tight and kept running through narrow dark lanes. He looked like a mad man, his hair flying. Strangers pushed against Rewa, and she pushed them back as both of them tumbled through the lanes, away from the Tankir bazaar.

They came out into the sun and the main street.

They ran across the road unaware of the cars, rickshaws and carts that were plying about and finally turned a corner and stopped.

"Baba, what happened to him?" Rewa was gasping.

"He's fine."

Ajoy was bent over, breathing hard, his hands on his knees.

"I saw him and Suraj and they're are safe. The bullet missed them. You screamed and they turned...They're all okay."

Police vans trundled past the two of them and turned left and stopped. Police men jumped out of the van and ran inside the lanes.

"Ajoy, the man who shot at them," Rewa began.

"I saw him, the old man," said Ajoy.

"No, no, he's not old. He stood up and took the pistol out, I saw...the way he moved...he was disguised, and Ajoy."

"Yes?"

"He wasn't there to catch them; he was there to kill them. I heard him."

"You heard him? He said something? But I didn't hear anything."

Rewa didn't know how to explain that she had *heard* him. She was too shaken and she wanted Baba.

She darted back towards the lanes to the slums.

"I have to find Baba. I need to tell him."

Ajoy moved to block her.

"Rewa, we can't go back in there."

"Let me go Ajoy, Baba will be looking for me. He doesn't know what happened to me."

"Yes, I know that, but he won't be there anymore. They all must have gotten out of there. It's not safe. The police are here."

"You know where they went? Take me there Ajoy."

Ajoy looked scared and confused. His face fell.

"I don't know where their hideout is. We must hide ourselves."

Rewa was tired and dizzy and scared. This was only the second day of her being out in the normal world like this. She wanted to go back to the village. She barely knew Ajoy, and Chittagong was too loud, too big, too populated, and confusing. She had never been this scared before.

Ajoy was looking at her helplessly.

Suddenly, as if reading her mind, Ajoy looked at her and said, "Your village! Let me take you there. Dabir will find his way there. Come with me."

The two of them ran down the street, Ajoy ahead, his hair flying and Rewa in her burqa running behind.

Davon had stayed calm all throughout the stampede and the chaos. He knew he had missed his shot, because he had heard a girl scream just a second before he pulled the trigger. He was furious with himself for missing the target. He had seen him, clearly, for the first time in years, in Chittagong, not some village as he had been hiding, or so his sources had told him. And after having him so close, he missed the shot.

He shook his head, and placed his pistol back into the *jhola* as he made his way out stepping over a trampled bodies scattered clothes and shoes.

Davon knew that according to his instructions to the Mayor, the police would be here any minute. He touched his moustache to check whether it was in place, hunched his back, bent over, twisted his torso slightly and screwed his face, transforming into an old, hunched man again. No one would be able to guess how young he was as he hobbled out of the compound.

Suraj Roy had escaped.

Davon smiled to himself. Suraj Roy didn't know that many people in plain clothes, were milling around the entrances to the slum. His spies, who were now following Suraj Roy to whatever hideout he was heading towards. They had not escaped.

They had been allowed to escape.

This time he was going to follow them and get them all.

Rewa was following Ajoy thinking furiously.

Baba, she muttered to herself, *Please be safe.*

As she wandered around the streets of Chittagong, following a boy she had just met yesterday, someone she barely knew and was being forced to trust, she felt helpless and weak.

Come, find me Baba, she kept repeating. *Come, find me please. Tell me what's going on Baba? I need you.*

Ajoy kept turning around to see if she was okay and that she was following him. Rewa was muttering to herself.

Baba, who is that man with the pistol? Why did I 'feel' his anger?

What does he want?

He did not want to kill Suraj Roy, Baba. He wanted to kill you.

CHAPTER 11

The Man On The Boat

They walked for hours in the sun, and intermittent rain which made the heat and the humidity insufferable. Beneath the burqa, Rewa was sweating, but she couldn't take it off because she kept bumping into people. She tried to walk alongside Ajoy but the onslaught of pedestrians made it hard, so she finally walked a few steps behind, Ajoy constantly turning around to check if she was following him.

She bumped hard into an old man, who turned around and yelled at Ajoy.

"Control your woman, boy!" muttering away, he walked off.

When she finally heard the noise, of the docks, she stopped and looked at Ajoy as he turned around and told her.

"We'll go to the village and wait for Dabir and Suraj Roy there. If they don't come by evening then I'll know that the plan has changed for tomorrow."

"What plan?"

Ajoy turned away.

"Nothing. Come with me. We have to get a boat. Do you have any money? We'll have to pay the boatman."

Getting no reply from Rewa, Ajoy shook his head and walked on.

"My bag had some money," he said, "It fell somewhere in the stampede."

They turned a corner and reached a long-crowded road. Fish houses and dirty grey factories on each side of the road, and in the distance Rewa saw the river and the boats. She panicked. The smells of raw fish and the damp and the mud and the squelch were intense.

And the noise.

Like a thousand shrieking crows.

People talking at the top of their voices, the clatter and bang of tools from the shops, the rickshaws and their shrill rubber horns. The street was so crowded, she could only see heads and bodies jostling against each other. Everyone was rushing, pushing, talking and shouting without stopping.

Rewa stopped at the head of the road.

"I'm scared, Ajoy."

"He's fine. I'm telling you, I saw him." Ajoy misunderstood. Then he realised that she was looking at the road ahead, and he took a deep breath. He slipped his hand in her gloved hand kindly.

"I'm here."

Ajoy walked a step ahead of her with his arm outstretched, pushing people away so that she could walk next to him untouched. She tightened her grip as they dived into the crowd and slowly, the inched through the crowd, and they made it to the river in a matter of seconds. Rewa looked at him gratefully.

"Stay here," Ajoy said.

He left her standing by the river and began to talk to all the boatmen. Rewa could see that all of them were refusing to take them across, without any money. It was almost afternoon and siesta time. No one wanted to go and definitely not for free. Ajoy began running across the bank of the river calling out to the boatmen.

A little distance from where Rewa stood, there was a tiny dinghy with a man squatting in it. Rewa guessed that he must be around forty years old, but his gaunt face looked much older. Almost jet black from plying the boat in the sun all the time, he was sweaty and thin, and muscled. He was wearing just a dhoti and an old vest with holes in it. His head, covered by a cloth, tied like a turban. His eyes were yellow and blank and his face was tired. His boat was tied to the ramp and he was looking towards the river, lost in thought.

Rewa went up to him and said, "Dada, please can you help us? We need to go across to the village. We...don't have any money, but dada, I promise, I will get the money for you from the village."

This little speech terrified her. She had never spoken like this to a stranger before.

The man ignored her.

"Please help me, I lost my father and I need to go home, Please dada."

Still, the man paid no attention.

The sun was burning down on her.

Something strange happened. She felt it first in her spine and then she felt a tingle in her arms.

She heard it.

It wasn't quite like hearing, it was like *feeling*.

A combination of seeing pictures of things that had happened, a long time ago, far away, and hearing voices.

People in those pictures talking, crying, and begging. Rewa wasn't here anymore. She was with these new people, somewhere else. She had never been to this place that she was seeing, and she had never met any of these people, but she felt like she was there, right next to them.

Suddenly all the noise of the docks faded away. Her words spilled out on their own. She stared at the man in the boat and said urgently, "Dada, think of me as your *Mahua.*"

"What did you say?" his voice was gruff, and gravely, like he wasn't used to talking.

"Your Mahua, your daughter," Rewa said.

She was glued to the man's eyes and she was speaking low and fast, the visions playing in her head, as she continued to talk. "I know how you lost her, and your wife. I know how you have suffered dada. He works with the New India Revolutionary Army."

She grabbed Ajoy and pushed him forward.

"I know how much you cried for Mahua, dada. I know you have never forgiven yourself. I am like Mahua only. For her sake, please help us, we have to get across."

Ajoy was staring at her, mouth agape.

When Rewa finished what she was saying, the man got up, untied the dinghy and gestured to both of them to get in. They scrambled in. The man began to row silently.

Rewa sat facing him as he rowed. She took off her head scarf. The man was crying silently and rowing.

"I don't know," she said, addressing both of them. "I don't know what happened dada, but I saw, I *heard* you. I heard you call Mahua, like you called her the last time you saw her. I heard it from your heart. I don't know how, but I did."

The man continued to row silently.

"I'm sorry for what happened to her. Why did they take her and your wife?" Rewa asked softly.

"We lost our land," he said gruffly as if he didn't want to think about what had happened.

"We, my family and I, the land—all of it, belonged to the *Zamindar*, in Bihar, and he sold us all to the British, to pay his taxes. Mahua, my wife and I. Thousands like us in Bihar, twenty years ago. All taken and sold by our own people to the British and the Dutch as slaves and servants. All the young men and women, children sold for *paisas*. The foreigners took all of them away. Only the old people were left behind in those villages to die. We had been having famines and droughts for so many years, there was nothing to grow or to eat, so when they came to take us, we didn't even fight or care. I went to his house and begged the zamindar, to spare Mahua, I promised to be his slave for nothing, for the rest of my life, but he sold Mahua anyway, and he kept me back in his house to work for him. I didn't even know they had taken her and my wife. I never saw them again. When I found out that they were gone, I left the zamindar's house one night." His voice choked.

"She must have thought that her father didn't even care to come and see her before she was taken away."

Then he was silent for the rest of the journey.

Ajoy was staring hard at her. Rewa didn't want to meet his eye, in case he thought she was a witch or some sort of a freak.

"This has never happened before, Ajoy," she mumbled, still tingling from the experience. She thought of telling him about her 'powers' but stopped herself. *This was enough for one day*, she thought.

They reached the banks of the village, an hour later and as she stepped out of the boat and jumped onto the knee-deep water, she stopped and looked at the boatman.

He put his hand on her head.

Rewa stopped for a second and hesitated, then she turned around and began to run, through the water, and towards the jungle path to her house. She had seen the boatman's past earlier.

Just now, she had witnessed his death.

But she didn't tell him anything.

The man in the boat waited till she was out of sight, then he began to row. As his boat waded out, towards the center of the river, he saw another boat approaching.

CHAPTER 12

The Woods Are Alive

They ran through the woods, Rewa kept hesitating and looking around. Ajoy saw her stop and look around. He could see or hear no one.

"What is it?" he finally asked.

"I keep getting the feeling that someone is watching us," she said, stopping again.

"Who?" Ajoy asked.

"I don't know, but there is someone there."

Closing her eyes, Rewa lifted her head up, and stood in the middle of the path. She felt the same tingling in her arms, as she had felt with the man in the boat.

There was an eerie silence in the woods. No sounds of birds or rustling of the leaves. Everything was still.

Something had happened to her, this morning. Ever since she had 'heard' the man, the killer, felt his thoughts in the city, she had changed. Inside her head and her body, something had come alive. An energy, a light of some sort, which was spilling out of her now. She could feel it, even though she couldn't see it.

Shapes were changing.

She realized that earlier, when they had reached the docks, it wasn't the people who had scared her, it was how they were changing in front of her eyes. People were either blurring into each other or they were shining so strongly that she could see, she could *feel* their thoughts around their body.

Now, the forest knew she had changed, the trees, animals, insects, wet with rain, were adjusting to the new Rewa.

How could she explain any of this to Ajoy? She ran all the way till they came to the house.

As they burst into the courtyard, Rewa stopped. The courtyard was full of people. She quickly pulled back her veil. It was Suraj Roy and four of his soldiers, they were standing close together discussing something serious, when Rewa ran in. Peelo rushed from inside the house and enveloped Ajoy in a hug.

Rewa went into the hut.

The whole house was in a mess. Amma, tearful and angry, was packing clothes in bundles and tying them up. Baba was busy sorting out his books and packing a battered suitcase. Kantha sat on the floor looked indifferently at Rewa when she rushed in.

Baba looked upand said, "Pack your things," he commanded. "We're leaving now. Take only what you can carry on yourself. Leave the rest behind. Understand?"

Amma glared at Rewa and said accusingly, "Is this because of her?"

"No," Baba said and sighed.

Rewa quietly went to her corner of the room and packed her clothes in a bundle. Then she grabbed her precious diary and she was done.

She had a thought.

Where's Tuku?

She couldn't see Tuku anywhere. She was about to go and look for him in the courtyard when Peelo came in and stood next to Baba. Amma's eyes flared.

Baba didn't notice as he spoke to Amma. "You and Kantha are going to go with Asit dada and the rest of them. Don't worry, you both will be safe. Rewa is coming with me."

Rewa noticed that no one had asked her how she had managed to get here from the city.

"What about you?" Amma asked. "You're not coming with us?"

"Where is Tuku?" Rewa asked softly. No one answered. Baba was shaking his head. "No, I have some work in the city."

Amma's eyes widened as she said angrily, "In the city?! You'll go back to the city? They're all looking for you, you'll be killed. NO!"

Dabir opened his mouth and Amma shook her head firmly.

"Dabir, no! you're coming with us. I am not going anywhere without you. They just tried to shoot you; the police will be after you. NO!"

"Kako," Baba said patiently. "I'll be fine. Rewa, Peelo, and Ajoy will be with me."

This only made Amma angrier. She shook her head and pulled at Baba's arms. Baba shook himself free and grabbed Amma by her shoulders firmly and made her sit on the charpoi.

"Kako. Stop. Suraj and his man are taking you to Calcutta. I will meet you there in three days. I promise."

Rewa still couldn't see Tuku anywhere.

Amma was tried to get up from the charpoi and she was shaking her head violently. She wasn't calming down. Her sobs were growing louder. People from outside the courtyard began peeking in from the door.

"Where's Tuku?" Rewa asked again, to no one in particular.

Kantha spoke blankly, without looking up at Rewa.

"Tuku spoke to Baba and then he went out. He is in a dreaming."

Amma's wails were getting louder, Baba was getting more embarrassed and angry at her tantrum.

"What?" Rewa was puzzled.

"Tuku is in a dreaming," Kantha repeated.

"Kako!" Baba shouted and raised his right hand. He was about to slap Amma. Peelo grabbed his arm, Amma flew at her and ripped away her hand. Peelo staggered back and Ajoy caught her from falling. Suddenly, the room went silent.

Amma picked up her packed bundle, grabbed Kantha by her arm, dragged her up from the floor, and walked out the hut, without giving Baba, a second glance.

Baba and Peelo looked at each other for a few seconds. They were both breathing hard. Peelo went up to him, touched his cheek, and then stepped out, Ajoy followed. Rewa was left alone with Baba.

"Baba, where is Tuku?"

Baba was lost in thought, so he didn't speak for a few seconds. Then he looked up.

"He has work to do. Come."

Rewa picked up her bundle and followed him into the courtyard. Amma was standing in the courtyard, crying, holding Kantha's hand. She looked away from Dabir when he came to her. Suraj came up to Baba and hugged him tightly. He mumbled into Dabir's shoulder.

"Think about this, my brother, please. Come with us. Let it go this time."

"No dada." Dabir was firm. "It has to be now. Everything is ready. I've planned too long. I've waited too long. The recruits are all here. We must strike now. This cannot wait. You know it has to be now, or God knows, how long it will take to get everyone here. It took us three years. We can't stop now."

Suraj dropped his head sadly. "You're sacrificing too much for me for the revolution."

"I'm sacrificing nothing, dada. I'm only doing what is right. What needs to be done." Dabir assured him. "I promise I'll be safe. Nothing can happen to me."

Dabir was looking at Rewa when he said that.

"Now, go Suraj dada. We need you safe. We need you away from Chittagong right now. We will meet in three days now. God be with you."

Dabir and Suraj hugged each other tightly. When they separated, both of them had tears in their eyes as they looked at each other. Then they left, Amma walking away and taking one last look at Dabir, the four soldiers huddled around the group as they headed away from the hut, towards the mountains.

Left behind in the courtyard were Dabir, Peelo, Rewa, and Ajoy. Dabir went back into the hut to pick his bundle and lock it up. Rewa was puzzled.

What did Kantha mean?

Tuku was in a dreaming?

There was a tap on the door of the courtyard. Everyone froze. Rewa pulled back her veil to cover her face and straightened her burqa as she timidly went to the door and opened it gently.

'The Man from The Boat' stood there sweaty and breathless, he had his big wooden oar in his hand. He saw Rewa.

"They're coming."

***

"Six men have come from the city. They all have machetes, and knives and one of them, the leader, has a pistol. They are headed here, to the hut right now. They do not look like the police," said the man frantically.

Dabir sprang into action.

"They've followed us. Quick, let's go! We'll have to take the school path.'

Dabir, Peelo, Rewa, Ajoy and the man scrambled through the woods. They had planned to take the straight path through the woods to the river. That plan was quickly abandoned. Now, the plan was to take an alternative route to the river, from behind the temple, trick the six men as they reached the house.

This alternative route was a meandering path.

They would run up the hill, to the school building, then into the playground and from there, higher up the hill to the abandoned temple. Once they crossed the temple, they would run down a steep slope and end up next to a big banyan tree that was half submerged in the river during the monsoons.

The five of them were running towards the school building up the hill, when they heard a pistol shot. A piece of wood from a tree, just ahead of them, splintered off. It echoed in the forest. Dabir shouted, "Everyone down!"

They all tumbled into the waist high weeds and lay quietly on the grass.

There was silence, but they could hear the men approaching. Rewa heard them, slicing the weeds with their machetes.

The wall, that encircled the school building, was about five hundred yards up the hill. Dabir signalled to all of them to stay low and crawl.

Rewa began to crawl. The man was watching her as she crawled by him. He didn't move. Rewa looked at him questioningly, but he just shook his head. Then, oar in his hand, he stood up, and ran in the opposite direction. Rewa didn't call out to him.

"Now" shouted Dabir, and they all began to run. Rewa ahead of them all.

They four of them ran behind the wall and sprinted towards the school.

Behind them, a shout.

They had been spotted. There was another gun shot. Rewa's burqa was getting in her way. She knew which way to take. On many afternoons, when she was left on her own, she had wandered through these forests and paths. She knew every stone, every plant and every tree from here to the river. She decided to lead them into the school compound and to the empty classrooms.

She yelled at them to follow her.

But they didn't hear her.

Dabir was looking over his shoulder when he saw one of the men come up round the wall. They had clearly been seen now as they ran in the compound.

The school was two red brick buildings with two large empty classrooms each.

A small unkempt garden, in between the buildings, had some broken wooden swings. A little further ahead, there was a third building in the compound, which was used to store school supplies, of which were scanty. It was mostly an empty room with a few books but had a back door exit.

Rewa ran to one of the classrooms and heard Dabir shout.

"Here!"

By the time she stumbled into the classroom, she realised that Dabir had chosen to run towards the third building, ahead of the classrooms. Peelo was breathless, unable to run, and Ajoy was pulling her hand and coaxing her. The two of them followed Dabir through a door. All three of them ended up in the storeroom, while Rewa was alone in the classroom.

A man with a machete came running into the compound. He hadn't seen where all of them had run. Rewa ducked behind the window breathing hard. The man stood there in silence, his eyes darting right and left.

He began creeping slowly towards the school buildings. Rewa realised that her class would be the first one he would check and she had left the class door wide open. If he walked in, he would see Rewa right there, under the window.

There was nowhere to hide.

She saw him step slowly towards the class. He was looking all around for any sign of movement as he crept towards Rewa's door.

Then, behind him.

A figure appeared out of the shade of the trees—a small, thin, shirtless boy.

It was Tuku.

Tuku!

He was holding a spear in his right hand and staring fixedly at the man. His skin looked dark as if it had been painted, and his eyes were wide and cold. He began to creep stealthily, silently towards the man. The man had his back to Tuku.

Rewa couldn't believe her eyes.

Tuku stood still in the shadows of the trees, his spear held high in his right hand, and then, as soon as he left the trees, he crouched low in the grass, the spear now held tightly next to his ankle. Only Rewa could see him from the classroom window. The man had no clue that Tuku was right behind him. Rewa watched in horror as Tuku crept closer and closer, to the man who was now ten steps away from entering the classroom.

The man was going to turn around and see Tuku.

Tuku moved suddenly.

There was a sound of a thud, the man straightened up, his eyes wide and he made a sound like he was clearing his throat. The tip of the spear pierced him just above his navel.

Tuku had stabbed him so hard that the spear had gone through his body.

There was another sound, like a stone falling in a well, and the tip disappeared from the front of his body. Tuku pulled out the bloody spear, and blood splattered on Tuku's face. The man tumbled into the ground. Tuku stood behind him, holding the spear in his right hand, still crouching and his eyes wide and unblinking. He wiped off the blood from his eyes and mouth.

Rewa choked.

Tuku was standing, wide feet, his head leaning towards the right, as if trying to hear someone, his eyes were wide and unblinking. He looked wild and blood thirsty. Then, as if in a trance, Tuku turned around and sprinted out of the compound towards the old temple.

Rewa took five minutes to gather herself and crept out of the classroom. The man was lying on his stomach, in a pool of blood on the dusty floor. His eyes were open.

Rewa staggered out of the compound.

Tuku is a killer? My little brother!

She had to find Baba and tell him. She ran through the classrooms and then, to the storeroom. All were empty. In the forest ahead, she heard a distant pistol shot. It came from near the old temple. Rewa groaned as she ran up the slope, around the temple to the stone grounds. Peelo was screaming.

Ajoy was lying on the floor, rubbing his head, and looking dazed. Above him a man stood, twisting Peelo's arm as she screamed in pain. Attempting to reach a fallen machete, the man was trying to wrestle Peelo to the ground.

A moment later, Dabir charged roaring from the trees. He rammed into the man. The man tumbled over Ajoy and before he could recover, Dabir had kicked him hard in his face. The man lay still, one hand on his nose as blood spurted out.

Rewa was running towards them when she stopped.

The man with light eyes!

The man who had shot at Baba this morning!

He was here!

On the other side of the temple marketplace, he was walking towards Dabir, Peelo, and Ajoy. They hadn't noticed him, but the man was already raising his right hand with the pistol and aiming at Dabir.

"Baba!" Rewa shrieked.

The man with the light eyes shouted in frustration. They had seen him now. Dabir ducked and dragged Ajoy and Peelo in the trees behind him. Rewa ran after them into the trees. The man with light eyes shot on her trail.

They should take the river path!

But Dabir, Peelo, and Ajoy had disappeared. She couldn't see them in the forest and the man with light eyes was right behind her. She saw a big bush and ducked behind it, just in time. The man with light eyes appeared on top of the slope. He stood watching. Rewa controlled her breathing. He turned and walked away. She heard his footsteps crunching in the forest. They grew distant. For the next two minutes, she waited for any sound, holding her breath.

There was complete silence.

I'll go to the river and wait for everyone there.

She crept down the slope. Out of nowhere, another man came charging from the trees, towards her. Rewa screamed and froze. It was one of the men with machetes. She heard a loud sickening crunch and the man crashed to the ground as he was running towards her.

Behind the falling man, holding the big oar and looking triumphant was the 'man from the boat'. He smiled.

A loud shot rang out.

The man from the boat flew off the ground and landed on his face, a few feet down the path. He had been shot.

The man with light eyes again.

He was standing on the temple path, smoke coming the nozzle of his pistol. Rewa's mouth was open and she was gasping. She stumbled through the grass towards the man from the boat, lying crumpled in a heap. Rewa turned him over, and saw a big brown splatter on his chest, his eyes were open and unblinking. He was dead.

His face! It looked like he was about to smile.

The man with light eyes, was walking towards her pistol aimed in her direction. Then from the woods a man shouted,

"Davon, Here, I got them."

Remember the name, Rewa. His name is Davon.

Davon is the man with the light eyes.

At the bottom of the slope, emerging from the forest, a machete wielding man, led two captives.

Dabir and Peelo, oh god, no!

The man held a machete against Peelo's neck. Dabir walked ahead of them; his hands raised.

Where was Ajoy?

Davon ran down the slope and stopped mid-way to get a clear look. "Dabir. It's you, isn't it? I finally get to meet you." Davon trembled with anger, but he spoke smoothly, aiming his pistol at Dabir.

"I've been looking for you for seven years Dabir. You started this, and now I will finish it."

Dabir looked frantic, as he began to sputter.

Davon signalled his henchman to drag Peelo away from Dabir, as he kept the pistol aimed at Dabir. As the henchman dragged Peelo away, she began to struggle and shout. The man hit her on the face and she crashed to the floor. Dabir was shaking with fury.

Suddenly they heard a loud war cry, a child screeching. Everyone turned.

Tuku!

Tuku emerged from the shadows and darted out like a wild warrior. He charged up the hill with his spear held high and ran up to Dabir and stood in front of him to shield him.

Dabir held him there, a triumphant look on his face. Tuku had a crazy, wild look on his face. Rewa felt her heart sink.

Davon was going to shoot both Tuku and Dabir.

Rewa lifted her veil and shouted, "Tuku, No!"

Davon turned sharply to look at her, but his aim stayed steady. He wasn't going to be distracted this time. When he saw Rewa he looked bewildered. His mouth fell open. Taking a chance, Tuku charged towards him with his spear. Davon turned quickly. There was a loud bang and Tuku's chest exploded. He turned and crumpled to the ground next to Dabir. Davon had shot Tuku. The sound echoed in the forest for a few seconds. Davon looked surprised that the pistol had fired. A few seconds later, Rewa began to scream.

"Tuku! Tuku! Tuku!"

Rewa shrieked wildly and stumbled down the slope. Her veil slipped off her neck. No one else moved.

Davon stared at her as if he had seen a ghost. His mouth was still open, as he dropped the pistol next to his feet. Then Ajoy ran out from the woods behind Davon, roaring fiercely, an oar in his hands. Before Davon could react, Ajoy thwacked the back of his head. Davon fell flat on his face. Ajoy and Dabir turned towards the man holding Peelo and charged towards him.

By the time Rewa reached down the slope, Dabir had overpowered the man and Ajoy had come charging down the slope and slamming the oar on the man's chest.

Rewa reached Tuku first. Dabir stumbled towards her and held Rewa as she bent over where Tuku's lifeless body lay. No sound was coming out of her mouth.

Lying on his back, his arm outstretched with the spear still in his hands, was Tuku with his eyes wide open, and a big gaping wound on the left side of his bare chest. It looked like a big black skin burn, and there wasn't any blood spilling out.

He was dead.

Rewa was on her knees when Dabir covered her head with the veil first and then put a hand on her mouth.

"Shhh... they're still here, the rest of the men are still here in the forest."

Rewa was on her knees, swaying, her eyes wide open as if she couldn't believe what she was seeing. Tuku was dead. He was lying there on the slope in the forest.

Dabir kept his hand on her mouth as he knelt behind her, holding her tight in case she toppled over. He thought she was about to wail.

"Rewa, Rewa."

He kept whispering in a calm voice, Peelo was leaning on to Ajoy, her nose bleeding from the blow. Dabir shook Rewa slightly and whispered urgently in her ear.

"Shhh, we must go now, Rewa. There's nothing we can do. Let him be."

Dabir began dragging Rewa down the river path. He stopped to look up the slope at Davon, who lay there on his back. Dabir hesitated for a second and looked around. Any minute now the other men, who must have heard the gun shot would be here. They had to leave now. Ajoy ran back and retrieved the bloody oar.

They left Tuku there and disappeared into the forest. Rewa pushed Dabir's arm away and straightened up. They ran down from behind the temple and through the forest. Then, through the trees, they suddenly came up to the river.

They saw the little dinghy tied to the tree. Dabir hastily untied the rope, Ajoy shoved Peelo and Rewa aboard the boat.

Dabir looked back for a second to see if any of the men had followed them, before pushing the boat into the water and jumping in. Ajoy clambered in and began rowing furiously.

Rewa stood in the middle of the dinghy and stared back into the forest. She could barely see the dome of the temple, in between the trees. Suddenly all the crows flew away and she heard their caws.

Then, over the trees.

She saw a glint of light.

A whiff of something like smoke. It floated above the trees in the colours of a rainbow.

Rewa felt her heart lurch and suddenly, she was weeping piteously. She tumbled to the bottom of the dinghy and began to cry. No one spoke to her. She was crying for 'the man on the boat'.

A man she had met just three hours ago. A man who had agreed to help her for no reason whatsoever and had been killed for that. She was crying for the futility of his death. All that man had ever seen, was injustice, cruelty, and sorrow. He had lost everything, his land, his family, his dignity and now he was lying in the temple marketplace where he would lie forever, forgotten. Millions like him were gone. Generations were wiped out.

She was crying for Tuku.

This morning, she had been happy, for the first time, she had felt that they were actually a family. Tuku had spoken about how he wanted to eat kulfi before he died.

Tuku's dead!

She remembered how three nights ago, she had wanted to touch him and hadn't. Her loathsome skin, would have told her that this was how he was going to die.

She would have moved heaven and earth to save him today and would have happily faced the consequences. She didn't care about the 'laws of God' or 'Death is destiny' right now. Wrath of God? What would that be? The world would burn?

Let it.

At this moment she *wanted* the world to burn. Everything, everyone, everywhere needed to burn to hell for what had happened.

Mostly, she was crying with rage at the man with the light eyes.

Davon.

The man who had ruthlessly killed an innocent man and not wasted a second shooting a twelve-year-old boy. He was a monster and he was still alive and breathing when Tuku was dead.

Let the world burn to cinders. She would burn it herself if she could.

CHAPTER 13

Peelo And Ajoy

Chittagong, like most Indian cities, was a strange mixture of picturesque beauty and stark filth. Rewa had only seen the grimy, mucky polluted side of the city, but that evening, what she saw was pristine and green.

Wide tree shaded lanes, beautiful white coloured elaborately built mansions with massive wrought iron gates, long driveways and sprawling land scaped lawns. The gates, they passed, looked like they were protecting fortresses instead of houses. Like the palaces of kings that Baba had shown her once in a book about England.

But Rewa didn't care.

Seated in a *tonga,* Rewa watched numbly as they clip-clopped through Chittagong. Her body was aching, she was dirty and scratched and tired. This had been the longest day of her life and it still hadn't ended. The memory of the lemon tea she had had this morning with Tuku kept flashing before her eyes. And she spasmed. Dabir sat in front of the tonga with the driver, Peelo and Ajoy sat next to her. Dabir hadn't said a word since they had escaped on the boat and he hadn't cried. His eyes were bloodshot and his was body rigid as he sat in the front seat.

There were a few people on these streets, in comparison to the rabble that she had seen at the docks. A few Indian labourers stood under the trees smoking; a pillow maker carrying a huge tool on his shoulder which looked like a musical instrument passed by and a few women balancing baskets of fish on their heads, shouted their wares loudly as the tonga crossed them.

Not all houses on those streets were mansions, nestling into corners were small ugly brick houses with tiny lawns and brightly painted gates. They were still five times bigger than her own hut, but they paled in comparison to the villas and estates. They were built further away from the pavement, hidden in the trees, as if they were an embarrassment to the big houses.

The palaces needed the staff for them to function and these houses were where the staff lived, hidden from the beauty of the colonial world. They were needed close by for the *sahebs*. Indian servants, butlers, cooks, gardeners, carpenters all lived scattered in little ugly dwellings amongst the villas.

At the end of a lonely, quiet lane stood one such house with a bright blue gate. It was the only house on this lane. Thick trees hid the building, and there was a small courtyard, inside it, a tiny unkempt garden and behind it, the small house painted a strange peach and pink. A tiny veranda had old wicker chairs. Dabir helped the three of them down the tonga, opened the gate and led them in. Peelo walked up to the veranda, through the wicker chairs and unlocked the door. They all went in.

Ajoy began to cry for the first time since morning.

Peelo put her arms around him and caressed his hair and they both cried in each other's arms.

Rewa watched. No one consoled her.

Dabir retreated to one of the rooms in the house. It was a small, clean and airy home, with big wide windows, comfortable but bare. Old wooden furniture looked too ostentatious for the small house, because all furniture were discards from the big mansions.

Emerging after fifteen minutes in a fresh kurta pyjama, Dabir made to the door.

"Dabir, not tonight," said Peelo quietly.

He looked at her, and then without a word, left the house. Rewa was suddenly angry. Baba had just walked out leaving her alone with strangers. Questions buzzed in her head.

Why was she here? Why hadn't he sent her away with Amma and Kantha?

She wanted things back the way they were. She even wanted her cage back. This house was too clean, too big, too new, and she was uncomfortable with Peelo and Ajoy. The love and warmth between the sister and brother was making her skin crawl. She was furious at them for their comfort with each other.

Perhaps, Peelo sensed Rewa's feelings. She didn't speak much to her, but when she did, she was kind and patient. She set out new clothes for Rewa and then began to prepare dinner. She pointed to a door and told Rewa to clean up.

The bathrooms were inside the house?

A tap and running water?

A large mirror. She had never seen one before.

Peelo's clothes smelt like *rajanigandhas.* Rewa dressed and wore her gloves. If Ajoy and Peelo thought that was weird, they didn't mention it. They were getting used to the weirdness with Rewa around.

They ate at the dining table. Rewa had never sat on one before. She was used to squatting on the floor and eating with her hand. This table was too close to her face, and it made her eating awkward.

"Tuku loved the woods?" Peelo asked her gently.

"Yes," Rewa replied.

"He looked like a strong boy," Peelo said as her eyes were moist. Rewa had to ask, "Do you think there is a chance that we left him there and he would still be alive?"

Peelo looked at her sympathetically.

"No, he was gone," said Ajoy bitterly. "He's gone and Gautam is gone. He was our only family left. He practically raised us even though he was just five years elder than Peelo."

Ajoy was speaking tonelessly. The food lay untouched. "There was no one for us, when the British sent our father to *Kaala Paani.*"

Rewa shook her head.

Ajoy looked at her and continued, "Kaala Paani is an island in the ocean. It's nothing but a prison where the 'Enemies of the Empire' are sent to die. Thousands have been sent there since 1857. They're all kept like cockroaches and no one comes back alive. They say that our Baba lived, folded, in a prison cell smaller than a box for five weeks without food and water and drowned in his own..."

He stopped almost calmly and continued, "Gautam took us in, he was already working for the New India Revolutionary Army. He and Dabir helped Peelo complete her education and send me to school. Then Peelo joined Dabir and I quit college, a year and a half ago. I didn't want to learn what the British taught, what they 'allowed' us to learn."

Peelo piped in, "Ajoy writes so beautifully, he should be a poet. I wanted him to study further. I wanted him to go to Shantiniketan."

It was dark outside now. The food lay abandoned on the table, they were sitting in the light of the single lantern, a cool breeze coming in from the wide windows. It was going to rain tonight.

"I finished my education and became a school teacher." Peelo said, "But what am I supposed to teach the children? What good is education to them? What will they do? Become maids, servants, cooks? Will they be able to make anything of their lives as long as they are ruled?

She looked at Rewa with her eyes shining. "When I met Dabir, everything changed. Dabir looked at me and he saw my soul. When he talked to me, I felt like I could breathe. All of us feel like we're stooping when we are born. Under the open sky, bent, looking for hiding places under the British rule as if that is our natural state. Saying the *right* things to keep us alive."

Ajoy joined in.

"When Peelo took me to meet Dabir, he told me to find people who feel the same way. Millions of us are afraid to even think of freedom. Petrified that our thoughts will be visible on our faces. Is that life? Is this a living? Was the life of your grandfather a life?"

Rewa looked away.

Peelo asked hesitantly, "Do you know where Dabir is from?"

Rewa said nothing.

How could she explain to them that Dabir had been a completely different person to her till three days ago. She knew nothing about her Baba. She had thought that her Baba was a teacher in a school. He never spoke about where he was from. Not even a hint. The fact that he had been a revolutionary with a past, was unfathomable.

Now it was making sense, the secrecy, the lonely homes in lonely villages, the eight feet walls and the constant moving.

"Why has Dabir never told you anything?" Ajoy asked.

Rewa looked up, "It doesn't matter. I want to know now. Please tell me everything," Rewa responded, her voice sounding brittle.

Ajoy faced her. This fourteen-year-old girl, with big, fiery, black eyes, her determined chin and wide forehead, her small mouth now pressed together so tight, that her lips had almost disappeared.

He saw her for the first time out of her burqa, adorned in Peelo's old saree. She did not at all look like the scared girl he had seen yesterday, for the first time at the printing press. Peelo looked at him and nodded.

He took a deep breath and began his story.

Their story.

CHAPTER 14

The Truth About Dabir

"A hundred years ago, the British asked farmers in Bengal and Bihar to grow indigo. It's a plant that gives the colour blue to cloth, 'denim' as they call it. The humid climate and the monsoons are good for the plant. But it ruins the soil. If you grow that crop too many times, the soil dies and nothing grows there again for years, even with the rains. When the farmers found out, they wanted to stop growing those crops, but the British wanted the colour blue for the pants that they wear," Ajoy spat.

"The Nawabs of Bengal, under British rule, had no choice but to force the farmers to continue growing Indigo. Farmers had to take *dadons*—loans at such high interest that they were in debt their entire lives and after they died, the debt transferred to their families. Peasants would remain destitute and barely survive for decades with no possibility of anything changing for generations to come. The people who collected this money ruthlessly were called Tax Farmers. Do you understand debt?"

Rewa nodded. Baba had taught her accounts last year.

"The British passed 'The Permanent Settlement Act', where planters and zamindars could do whatever they wanted with the farmers, if they protested or tried to grow other crops or didn't pay interest. Murder, torture, rape, anything. The law was on their side because, according to them, 'the peasants were savages.'"

Peelo laughed bitterly as she spoke, "Your father is from one of the most highly educated families in the East. Generations of scholars, artists and land lovers from Bengal, now reduced to being peasants by the British. How long were they going to take it?"

Ajoy continued the story, "Some sixty years ago, a revolt started in Chaugacha, your grandfather's village. It spread to Burdwan, our ancestral town. Your grandfather's family were actively seeking to change the British laws against them, but they had no clue what the British were capable of. The British hired killers and dacoits to teach them a lesson. Thousands of farmers were killed all over Bengal, Bihar and around this area.

"Your great grandfather, his wife and three children were massacred. Your grandfather, just fifteen years old then, survived and ran away to Calcutta. He was beaten and bloody when he arrived, so all he could do to eat was beg around the city. A scholar and writer, begging!

"He lived on the streets for years before he finally got a job in a printing press because he was educated. He got married but your grandmother died at childbirth, so now it was just him and Dabir. Dabir began to work there from the age of seven. Your grandfather taught Dabir how to work the machines. Dabir learnt calligraphy and design. It was a British press, so the conditions were as terrible as ever, but at least they had a roof over their heads. They were fed but given little or no money.

"Your grandfather never let him forget that they were farmers, kings of their own land, now reduced to living like slaves."

Peelo got up to clear the table. The food uneaten.

Ajoy continued as Peelo took the dishes to the kitchen. "Our grandmother was from a village close to Chaugasa, where the revolt began. With her entire family gone, she escaped to Siliguri. There, in the tea gardens, a British lady hired our mother as an *aaya* for her children. Manoj, our Baba, was the same British lady's butler. It was a job of great prestige, an Indian man working as a butler in a British man's home. He actually managed the whole estate. He had worked as a servant with that lady since the age of twelve, working up to being a server, a butler, and then, a manager. He worked in that woman's house for nineteen years. Our baba was strict, severe, and loyal. But his loyalty made no difference to the lady. When he met our mother, and they fell in love, they told the British Lady that they wanted to get married. They imagined that it would be great, growing old together, secure, in service of the Lady."

Peelo came out of the kitchen and took over the story as Ajoy went to wash his hands. "Both of them were fired instantly and turned out of their living quarters. The Lady made sure they would not be hired by any other British family for their trespasses. "'Staff intermixing' was filthy," the British lady said. Nineteen years of service and my father was suddenly filthy.

"They left Siliguri and travelled to Calcutta. Baba got a job as a mechanic and a machine operator and that's when he met Dabir. The two became friends and began to attend Anti-British rallies. At that time, my Baba Manoj and Dabir preached *ahmisa* along with the thousands of people who followed Gandhiji. Ten years ago, Dabir quit his job at the printing press and moved to Asansol with your grandfather. My father and Dabir started a newspaper called *Chitto Jetha Bhoyshunno*—'where the mind is without fear'— a newspaper for Independent India. Your grandfather was scared of the consequences but Dabir convinced him to help. The British banned the paper, they called the writing false and incendiary. It was dangerous but they were determined to keep the paper going. Dabir wrote fiery articles and designed the paper, and Manoj would smuggle it into Calcutta. Suraj Roy was already famous for his radical pamphlets. He began contributing to Chitto Jetha Bhoyshunno."

Ajoy came back and joined them. He sat on the floor and spoke, "One day the police came and broke down the office and burnt the press. Your grandfather was at the office. They beat the old man mercilessly. By the time Dabir Dada reached the press, your grandfather was dead. That is when the three of them started the New India Revolutionary Army. It was supposed to be an organisation for protestors and new thinkers. When the British passed the Defence of India Act seven years ago, our baba was one of the loudest protestors. He was jailed so many times. They would beat him and jail him and he would come out stronger. Then they would arrest him again and be even more brutal.

"At one protest, the police fired on the peaceful protestors, killing a few of them. Those who didn't die were sent to Kaala Paani. My father survived for thirty-five days only."

Ajoy spoke calmly as if relating a casual anecdote.

"Suraj Roy escaped, Dabir was shot, everyone thought he was dead. No one knew where Dabir was for years.

Suraj dada came out of jail two years later and when he finally found him, Dabir was living somewhere in a village, with his family, with you. Suraj dada brought him back to Chittagong, and they've been planning their revenge. Revenge for what the British did to their village, their people, revenge for my father."

Ajoy shuddered, got up and went into the kitchen. Peelo followed. Rewa was left alone at the table. She spoke loudly, "What is happening on the 24th September?"

Heavy silence emanated from the kitchen. Then both Peelo and Ajoy emerged in the dining room. In the light of the lamp, her face in shadows, Rewa was staring at the two of them.

She suddenly realised that she had just put herself in danger.

CHAPTER 15

The New India Revolutionary Army

By the early 1900s, the British began to feel the pressure of Indian dissent. It wasn't merely in Hindustan, where the British officials had now lived with the natives for over a hundred and fifty years, Indians all over the world were uniting in their mission—freedom.

The Ghadar Movement, originated in the United States and Canada, when expatriate Indians united, and began to spread their message. The movement spread to Japan, Thailand, Mexico, Singapore, Philippines and even Africa, not just amongst the Indians living in those countries, but amongst local supporters as well. Over ten thousand Indians from Punjab entered USA and Canada between 1903 and 1913. Half of them had been foot soldiers in the British Military and were determined to use their knowledge. They operated from San Francisco and began smuggling arms and ammunition into mainland India. Copies of the banned newspaper, *The Ghadar* published in America, were found at various rallies all across the country, notably in Bengal, as a result the youth were enamoured, stirred and prepared.

The *natives* began to get bolder.

Calcutta became a hot bed for the violent faction of the revolutionaries who disagreed with the Congress's Non-violent agenda.

The 'Jugantar' group, which had started as a 'physical activity' group for young men in the 1920s, became a cultural force. It was initially made up of barristers, but now had over five hundred factions all over Bengal.

With support coming in from Berlin and Russia and USA, revolutionaries from India began to travel far and wide to receive training in strategy and in weaponry from the best underground revolutionary organisations in the world.

Suraj Roy travelled to Paris and learnt how to assemble bombs from exiled Russian revolutionaries. When he came back, his bomb factory near Calcutta became a hot bed for the Indian Independence excogitation. He joined hands with the Berlin Committee to get guns and ammunition.

The Berlin Committee in Germany had managed to steal ammunition during the First World War, with help of Indian Soldiers who had fought for the British Army in Europe. Those weapons began to be used in increasingly violent dacoities conducted from Calcutta all the way to Chittagong. The revolutionaries were looting banks, police stations and army camps, making away with whatever loot they could find. The mission was to fracture the British morale.

These revolutionaries were no longer natives who were a mere headache. These were organised, driven, violent, and fearless.

Today they had gone too far.

It was 4 p.m. and the day had been disastrous.

Richard Henley, the Mayor of Chittagong, was furious. Somehow eight hundred new recruits of the New Indian Revolutionary Army had managed to assemble under his very nose, in the heart of his own city.

None of his spies had guessed how the revolutionaries had managed to convey the location, date and time to these straggled peasants, who had arrived from all over country.

Then, there had been a shootout even before the police could get there, resulting in that stampede. A report, hastily typed and tossed on his desk, stated that six people had died. When the police did arrive, Suraj Roy and his New India Revolutionary Army had all managed to escape without a scratch. Davon and Richard had planned the entire operation, and not one single arrest had been made. There *was* no one to arrest. By the time the police had arrived at the site, it was deserted.

That was what was scary.

His spies had failed him, his police had failed him, but what he was most incensed about was that Davon had failed him.

Davon was standing in front of him, and for the first time in all the years that Richard had known him, he was looking dazed and unsettled.

"So, what went wrong?" Richard asked Davon.

"Who did that to you?"

He pointed to the bandage on Davon's forehead. Davon's jaw was clenched tight.

"A boy. One of those revolutionaries," he muttered.

"A boy?" Richard was incredulous.

"I was distracted."

"By?"

There was a pause. Richard asked bluntly. "What happened this morning at Chakma?

Davon replied. "I will find them...tonight. I have people looking for them."

"That's not what I asked. You were supposed to wait there in Chakma, as per our plan, but you weren't there. There was a shooting at the place, and you disappeared, I didn't know if you had gotten killed or if you had killed anyone, all I know is that instead of waiting there, instead of coming here and telling me about what happened, you went across the river."

Davon looked up surprised and said, "You had me followed?"

"Don't be stupid," Richard snapped. "You have your informants; the Mayor's office has their own informants. They saw you go across the river with some men. I assumed you had information on Suraj Roy, and that you were following him. Now you turn up, hours later, with your head in a cast. Was Suraj Roy there? Did you see him?"

"I *was* following him."

"So then, what went wrong?"

"Suraj and his men were in the forest, in a village across the river. He had a hideout there. We chased him till his people scattered in the forest and when I had one of his agents at gunpoint, just then, one of the kids came out of the woods and hit me. My men, instead of chasing them, began to tend to me. So, he got away."

"Davon, you're telling me, that you had one of his agents at gun point and then, some kid managed to distract you and hit you? YOU?"

After a pause, Richard blurted out, "I don't know what you're hiding from me, but you are."

Davon spoke in a clipped voice, "Three people got killed. One of ours, and a man of theirs."

"And?"

"A boy."

"How old?"

"Twelve, maybe thirteen. I shot him."

"God!"

Richard was aghast. Neither spoke for a minute.

Then Richard steeled himself and asked, "Can this be traced to us?"

"No, that will be taken care of."

"That was the distraction?"

"No. There's something else."

"What?"

"I don't want you to..." Davon was biting his lip. Finally, he looked up and Richard was surprised to see pain in Davon's face.

"I saw something...I think I saw someone and...I...I might have a lead about Daniel."

"What?

"But I don't want you to get your hopes up. I need a couple of days."

"Days?"

Richard's mind was racing.

Daniel!

He needed Davon to work on finding Suraj Roy. He leaned forward and placed his hands on his desk. Finally, he looked up.

"You don't have days. Davon, we don't have days! Something is happening now; they're planning something big and I need to know what it is. I... I don't know what to do."

Davon turned to go.

"Davon? Where are you going?"

"We don't have time. I'll find them both."

"Who?"

"Suraj Roy and Daniel."

Richard turned to the window. The city looked so calm. Seven years ago, he had considered this city his home. He had been living here for almost fifteen years then. Chittagong, home no more.

Richard had been born in Calcutta, and had been sent to England to be educated, and though he loved England, he always found India and Chittagong more *familiar*. He had met Eleanor in London and they fell in love. She had known that Richard was ambitious so she had followed him to Calcutta, a couple of years later, and their wedding had been an event in the social circle. Since then, Richard had steadily been working his way up the nobility, holding offices in Calcutta, Dhaka and then finally becoming the Mayor of Chittagong, almost a decade ago. He remembered his 'high flying' days. He remembered coming into the office, to this very window and staring out to the city. He had loved Chittagong then.

He had believed that the chaos of the city could be governed. He could organise the rabble, he had been sure.

It was, he realised, a grievous mistake.

Daniel had disappeared into this city, and Richard's love for the Chittagong, had been replaced by a seething, gritting, revulsion. He hated the heat which made his skin burn, he hated the rain that made the air so thick with humidity, it felt like you were breathing in something solid, like silk, through your nose. He hated the dust, that he found on his shoes when he walked into his office.

Today, if given a chance, he would set the whole city ablaze and watch with glee from this very window.

But he kept thinking, that somewhere, in some corner of this city, waiting to be found, was his Daniel.

Mostly, he felt betrayed.

Betrayed by the country he had loved, the natives he thought he had loved. They had destroyed his life, his family, his career. He had long since, lost any ambition to greater office. He just wanted to hold on to being the Mayor, because it gave him power to keep the search for Daniel alive.

So now India repelled him, Chittagong repelled him and his Indian "friends" repelled him. He reckoned that, in the last seven years, he had probably spent more time with Davon than with his own wife. Davon had shaken all his conceptions about being an Indian. Richard used to tell his English friends that he was practically Indian. Now, he doubted if a British subject could ever *be* Indian. The texture of being Indian had never permeated his skin, just like spending time with Davon had not made them friends at all.

Davon had remained almost impenetrable as a person, but that was not the reason for this chasm. Richard had realised that in reality, he would never be friends with Davon, just like he could never ever be friends with India, anymore. India would remain a costume he wore, he would never reveal its soul to Richard.

It could be because his formative years had been spent in Scotland. But truthfully, it was because the British had sought to create the same environs here in India. The same buildings, the clothes, The British Clubs, the ceremonies, the food and the staff, the 'Spirit of the Raj' were all replications of the things at home.

He would never be an Indian. He was an Englishman who lived in India. He knew the list of injustices heaped on this country by the British Raj would haunt them for centuries, and his personal absolution seemed petty and irrelevant. He may not have done anything cruel; he had been a fair and kind Mayor. But his mistake had been his lack of assimilation, not his lack of cruelty. He had mistakenly read his benevolence, to be the same thing as his acceptance of India.

It was the same for anyone who choose to leave their country for another. They would arrive, already hacked in half, split in two, trying to fill the half they left behind, with the new country.

Both halves bereft.

During his last visit to England, he had noticed the huge Indian community, at Harrow. The Indian men dressed as sahebs, the women as *memsahebs*, but the children were forced to dress in an Indian attire, to look like the boys and girls seen running around the streets here in Chittagong.

The sight of these kids gave the mothers some satisfaction of having kept home alive in a place, that would never be home. It had felt wrong, because he sensed that the Indians there were beginning to despise their 'nativeness', and crudity, in the face of the civilized English.

While here in India, the English had kept their smugness intact. They had never attempted to appreciate that 'nativeness'. The 'savages' had always been disparaged.

Now the savages were getting ready to slaughter them.

More than eight hundred of these vengeful, savage revolutionaries were all still *here* in Chittagong. The atmosphere in the city was boiling. He knew that he, and his wife were the primary targets. The most hated people in the city right now. The symbols of oppression and cruelty. Any incident would lead to them being the first causalities of this war.

An incident was all they were looking for.

It was going to be a British genocide.

CHAPTER 16

Tuku And The Dreaming

"Something was wrong with Tuku."

It was still dark and Rewa hadn't slept a wink. The mattress that Peelo had handed her, was too comfortable. The room she had been given was larger than her hut in the village. Bare, with wide open windows, with cream cotton curtains blowing in the wind, and strange white patterns on the floor, which resembled little coloured pebbles scattered on a white cold sheet. The floor was cool and smooth to touch, but too bright and distracting, so Rewa stepped out and sat in the dining room, facing the window and watching the rain.

Ajoy sat next to her, keeping a distance.

"It's late, Rewa."

Ignoring him, she repeated, "Something was wrong with Tuku."

"What do you mean?"

"He was strange, like an animal, like he was in a daze. When I was hiding in the school, I saw him. He was stalking one of the men like a hunter."

"Did he do that often?"

"No, never. He wasn't... like that. He was a happy boy, he liked to play and he liked kites, this was not like Tuku. He looked like...he wasn't in his senses."

She looked at Ajoy.

"He killed a man."

Ajoy sucked his breath in as Rewa continued. "At the school grounds. Tuku crept up to the man like a snake and speared him from behind. He was so ferocious that the spear went through the man's body. He killed him. I saw him."

"Did you tell Dabir that?"

"No."

"Why not?"

"It doesn't matter now. He must have...really wanted to save us."

Her eyes shining.

"That man, that Davon, killed him. He just shot him. Tuku was just trying to protect Baba and that Davon murdered him."

Two hours later. Rewa was still awake, Ajoy had eventually left her alone and slept in the kitchen. What Rewa hadn't told him was that she was terrified that something was wrong with her as well.

She was becoming more of a monster.

She had always been the one who's *chamra* sensed death, but today, stranger things had happened. She heard Davon. At the Chakmi grounds and later at the docks, Rewa couldn't understand what was happening. She *felt* Davon's hatred. It had floated above the crowd, found her and hit her in her chest. It wasn't touch, they had not touched, Davon had never even walked close to her, but she had heard his thoughts, his voice, his sound.

Later, near the old temple, just before he shot Tuku, Davon had spoken and Rewa instantly recognized the voice. Was she going crazy? Was she becoming a demon? She had hated her skin. She was used to scratching her arms with soap till her skin was raw, but now was this a monster was inside, growing? Rewa realised that she was trembling, even as the night was warm and the rain water that splattered on the window sill felt cool against her face.

Rewa covered her mouth with her arm and bit into it so hard that it bled, as she wept silently.

Just before dawn, Dabir crept back to Peelo's house. The monsoon rain lashed through the open windows. Rewa was still sitting alone in a corner of the living room, in the dark.

Peelo came out of her room and took Dabir in her arms. They had no idea of Rewa sitting in the corner and watching them. Dabir stood there in Peelo's embrace.

Rewa watched in silence.

Another aspect of life that Rewa would never experience. The comfort of someone holding you. Dabir, her father was in another woman's arms. It was obvious that the two of them cared deeply for each other.

Where did Amma fit into all this?

She didn't want to think about that. Her life was hurtling forward in directions she would never be able guess or cope with.

A couple of months ago, one sunny afternoon at the village, she had been standing alone at the top of the hill behind the old temple.

The same temple where Tuku's body lay alone in the dark right now.

She had stretched out her arms and dashed down the slope. Halfway through she had realized that she was going to fall and tumble down the path, but she continued to gallop down the slope. It was a strange exhilarating sensation in the pit of her stomach. She had the same sensation right now.

Tuku was dead. She would never, ever see him again. Amma and Kantha were gone, and Baba was with Peelo.

Life, as she knew it, was over.

Peelo took his hand and led Dabir to the bedroom.

With a shudder Rewa realized that...

Dabir knew that Peelo would be dead in two days.

Dabir was the reason she was going to die and, he wasn't going to do anything to stop it.

Peelo made breakfast the next morning, Dabir had left early. She was sanguine today as she buzzed around in the kitchen, with Ajoy helping her. They ate and then Peelo brought out a pair of scissors and sat in a chair, Ajoy sat cross-legged in between her legs and Peelo began to cut his hair. Peelo was tender. "Your hair is such a mess, why did you grow it dada? You think you look very good? Not one girl has liked you since you grew your hair and now that beard. Uff, my brother doesn't look civilized at all."

"I am a revolutionary."

"Oh, ho! Revolutionary? Suraj Dada looks dirty and messy, is it? Or Dabir? What? They look clean and washed. Ever since you moved in with Gautam you became like this. Both of you with your stupid ideas. For a whole month, I didn't see you when I had exams and you were at the press. You've lost so much weight. Three months of living away from me and this is what happens. No one there to feed you? When all this is over, you come back and live here and I'll feed you again."

Rewa felt a lump in her throat. She wanted to yell at Peelo that it was never going to happen. Peelo and Ajoy should just pack up right now and run away from Chittagong. Get as far away as they could. Today. This very moment.

In three days, Peelo wasn't going to be alive. She would never feed Ajoy, and they would never live together again.

Rewa choked and turned it into a cough.

I should tell them right now.

No, they will call you a demon, Rewa.

Like Amma.

Ajoy will think you're a witch.

'Death is Destiny. Death is destiny,' she kept repeating.

"I made *mocher jhol* for Dabir the other day, and I missed you both so much." Peelo continued, as she snipped away at his tresses.

"Remember how mother used to walk down to the other tea garden markets when we lived in Siliguri? Sometimes she would come back with fish and make Mocher jhol. Hey, do you remember once when we ran down the road and hid on the tree and when mother came by, we said, *'Machh diye ja'* in a booming voice?"

Both of them were laughing now.

"How she screamed *'Mecho bhoot'* and ran up to the house. Did we get a beating for that?" Ajoy asked, looking up at Peelo

"Na!" Peelo said.

"She knew it was us, she was just playing along."

Peelo looked at Rewa and said,

"I remember our mother. Her smell, her skin, and how her finger curved when she was drinking a cup of tea. I remember her looking at Ajoy when he was learning how to read. She was so proud of him."

Peelo put down the scissors and pulled Ajoy's chin. "I remember how she used to stand by the door of our small shack when it rained, she loved getting wet, and she would sing. Do you remember Aju?" Peelo went back to cutting Ajoy's hair.

"I miss her so much," he said after a moment.

Peelo put her arms around him and rested her head on his shoulder. Rewa watched them from the corner of the room back near the window where she had sat the entire night.

'This is what they call a family?'

Something Rewa had never known, and never would know. Nothing about her life was normal.

Then she laughed to herself at the thought of Peelo and Ajoy being normal. Both of them were the New India Revolutionary Army. They were about to lead a bloody revolt against the British empire

Normal?

And what *was* normal?

Was it normal, how her Baba had not cared to console her? Was this normal? How these two were consoling each other in their own way?

Was her loss bigger? Because she had lost her brother?

The very same brother, who had ignored her most of his life till two days ago, when some misplaced sense of sympathy had made him notice Rewa as a person for the first time, and not the weird human pet who lurked around in the house.

Ajoy and Peelo, were risking their 'normalcy' for what? An impossible dream which would only bring more pain and destruction? When love like this existed, nothing should be more important and satisfying than this kind of love. How *abnormal* that these two souls would be willing to destroy all that they had, for 'a cause'.

To do that seemed cruel and ungrateful to her, compared to all the years of seclusion and loneliness that she had experienced herself.

"Hey, look at me," Ajoy called her.

His hair was now completely different, shorn, you could see his scalp and he had shaved. He was handsome. Rewa found herself staring. He smiled and she noticed the dimple on his cheek.

Ajoy looked younger, more like a friend her age, that she would have had, under other circumstances.

She couldn't look away.

Now anyone who had seen Ajoy at Chakma, or in Rewa's village would never be able to recognize him.

CHAPTER 17

The New Plan – Day 4

In the dark of the night, Dabir sneaked from the shadows into Peelo's house, trailed by five men, entering one by one, carefully watching to see if anyone had followed them here. All of them were in disguise, like some tradesmen. They were wearing turbans and had covered their faces. Ajoy knew all of them. Jaidev, Siddharth, Ashok, and Harshal.

Peelo shut the windows quickly and they all gathered around the dining table. Rewa stood by the window and Ajoy squatted next to her. There was a single lamp at the centre of the table, lighting up the room. They could barely make out the faces of the people at the table and with the windows shut the room became hot and stuffy. The last person to walk into the house was Suraj Roy. He went to Dabir, looked him in the eye and then they hugged. Dabir broke away and wiped his eyes.

"How is she?" he asked.

Suraj shook his head. "How can a mother deal with something like this?"

She would be devastated, Rewa thought.

Amma was besotted by Tuku. Her son was all that she lived for. She would be inconsolable. Dabir squared his shoulders and said, "I've found him."

"The man who killed Tuku," Suraj said flatly.

"He's at the Mayor's house. His bodyguard, hitman, henchman. Davon."

"You know him?"

"No."

Rewa looked up.

Was Baba lying?

Davon knew Baba. He had said so. Davon had said that he had been looking for Dabir for seven years. He had recognized Baba.

"Was this personal?"

"It is now."

"Dabir."

Suraj looked pained.

Dabir did not meet his eyes. He said, "Just before he shot my son, that he was going to finish what I had started. He was wrong. I will finish it. Tomorrow night, Ashok, Harshal, Jaidev, Siddharth and I, will enter the Mayor's estate and kill that man. Davon has his own house at the estate. It's approximately a ten-minute walk from the Mayor's house to his house, it's across the garden and closer to the river. He lives alone. It's also far away from the rest of the servant's quarters, so no one will hear."

Suraj Roy was patient with Dabir.

"Dabir Dada, the Mayor's estate is heavily guarded. There are at least ten armed guards outside the main gate, another ten that patrol the road from outside and the five who patrol the path inside. We know this. We've researched this before. It's impossible to enter. You'll be shot the moment you're even seen close to the road going towards the Mayor's house."

"We won't use the road. We'll use the river."

"You can't. When his son got kidnapped, Henley fenced it up."

"There is the boat house."

"Which is locked from inside."

"Not locked, bolted. When it is dark, a boat will take us mid river and we will swim from there, enter the boathouse underwater. Rewa will unbolt the door."

Rewa was startled.

Dabir outlined his plan. "Rewa, at the perimeter of the estate, there is a gate, which is only small enough for the guard dogs. But a child your size can enter. I have seen and measured it. They have four dogs that are only allowed to run free around the estate after nine p.m.. Till then they are tied up. The five guards that patrol the inside of the estate, change at 6 p.m. A new crew comes, but they only resume patrol by around 6:20 p.m..

For about twenty minutes, there is no one on the path inside the estate. It's absolutely deserted. That's when you will enter from the small gate. You will go left on to the path till you reach the river, you will see a small hut—the boathouse. It's built on the river. Unlock the bolt from outside and come right back up the path. Leave through the dog gate, before the guards come. It should take you no more than five minutes. Ajoy will wait for you outside. We will wait till it's dark, enter from the boat house, go up to Davon's house. I'll be silent, but...I'll try to make it as painful as possible before I kill him."

"Dabir..."

"No Suraj. Don't say anything to me. I need to do this."

"No Dabir. You don't," Suraj said sternly. "Everyone here in this room has gone through what you've gone through. Didn't we just lose Gautam? Haven't Peelo and Ajoy lost their father? - all of us have lost our entire families. Have you forgotten what they did to my father and my wife? Your grief is bigger?"

Dabir was in no mood to listen.

"Dada, I don't care about anything else right now. He shot my son in cold blood. He's not even a gora. He's worse. He's a traitor. He works for them. He killed Tuku for them? How many such traitors have we killed till now? I have to do this."

"What if you get caught? Or killed. You would risk all that we've worked for? For revenge? Two more days. Give it two more days. After 24th, do what you want."

"No! Not a moment more. I will not wait a moment more. My son is lying there in the forest. Wild animals have probably taken his body. I couldn't even..." Dabir had his hands held in front of him, helplessly, as if holding Tuku in his arms.

Suraj was pleading now. "Dabir, you *must* wait for two days. We have hundreds of people in the city waiting. This plan was set in motion *years* ago. The Lieutenant Governor is arriving on 24th. He's at The British Club on the 24th night. What if something happens and they change his plan? Everything we've worked for will be useless. Years of traveling, talking, getting people to come to Chittagong. All gone. Please just wait. Have you forgotten 'Purna Swaraj'? Do you remember what we swore, when we began to work for the New India Army? Friends and Family all mean nothing. We live to fulfil the dream of a free India."

"I didn't call you here for your permission, Suraj dada."

There was silence. Suraj Roy looked angry.

"This is not like you Dabir."

Dabir looked coldly around the room.

"All of you are welcome to leave if you don't want to be part of this. Rewa and I will do this on our own."

Rewa shivered.

No one moved. Suraj looked at the four men. The four of them stared back. They would not leave Dabir alone at a time like this. They were devoted to him.

Suraj went up to Dabir. "Then why did you call me here Dabir?"

"So, you can let Kako know that Tuku will be avenged."

Suraj turned to leave. Dabir spoke calmly.

"Suraj dada? Believe me, I will not die tomorrow." Dabir was looking at Rewa. She knew what he meant. Dabir continued to stare into Rewa's eyes while he spoke.

"The mission on the 24th will proceed as planned. Trust me, nothing I do will stop that. I will not let you down."

As soon as the door shut behind Suraj, Peelo spoke up, "Dabir, why?"

She came around to face him. Dabir looked away. Peelo knelt down and looked up at him.

"She's just a child, Dabir. You told Ajoy to stay away, but you're taking her to the Mayor's house?"

"Peelo, I know what I am doing."

"Well then tell me what you're doing, because I don't understand. Why did you bring her to the press? Why is she not with the rest of her family, safe? You trained Ajoy for four years, till you brought him in for the first meeting."

"Are you jealous?"

Peelo looked hurt.

"No Dabir, I care for her. Like I care for you. I care for your family, like they are my own. In fact, they are my own. Did you not know that? I wish things were different in our world and we didn't have to sacrifice children to our cause. She's just lost a brother and you're not giving her a moment to breathe."

"Hindustan doesn't have time to wait."

"She is not Hindustan, and neither am I. We are people who love you and would do anything for you. Can you spare a moment and think of us, instead of *Inquilab Zindabad*?"

Half an hour later, Dabir and his men were gone.

Later in the night, Ajoy, Peelo, and Rewa were sitting silently in the living room. No one was talking to each other. The coming days weighed heavy on every one's mind.

Rewa asked, "This new plan is for tomorrow, what is happening on the 24th September? Now can you both tell me."

Peelo didn't say anything at first. Then, she looked up at Ajoy and nodded. Ajoy spoke.

"There is a club, a place where the British officers go to drink and play and eat. It's a huge place on the river in the city."

Rewa remembered the building by the river with the jazz music.

"It has a sign outside—'Dogs and Indians not allowed'. We are going to attack The British Club and burn that sign."

Peelo spoke up, her voice hard.

"The British Club will be attacked when the Lieutenant Governor and the Mayor are all attending a dinner there on the 24th. We won't just burn the sign. We will burn down the whole Club, and everyone in it. The British can either quit India or burn in it. The British Club will be a spark. If the British try to resist us, they will be slaughtered. This city is full of their victims. All those hundreds who have travelled to be part of the New India Revolutionary Army, will rise. Chittagong will begin the uprising in history. India's independence will start here."

Rewa's heart was beating so fast.

The British Club!

That was the place.

There.

Everything was going to happen there.

Peelo was going to die there, protecting her Baba.

And.

Suraj Roy was going to die there too!

21st September 1932

You're crying. Dabir, why?

It's not over yet.

Never give up, my dear Dabir.

Never let go of the fire.

I'm okay, letting it go.

I am, honestly.

Don't look so sad Dabir, It's okay.

Yes, I wanted so much from life. I had so many dreams.

Why do we see these dreams? If none of them are to come true? I wish I hadn't seen any of those dreams.

I wish I hadn't learnt how to hope and pray and believe.

I wish I hadn't learnt how to wish.

Maybe they all had it right.

The millions who came before us, those who didn't dream.

They never dreamt about wonderful things that they would accomplish.

They never had dreams about a perfect love that they would experience.

They never desired for magnificent sights to see.

If they did dream, they let those dreams stay buried

They hid the dreams from the world and from themselves, somewhere in their own body, under their intestines and their guts, never letting them awake.

When dreams rise up from the gut, they move up to the heart, then they become your breath.

They become real.

But not real enough to come true.

That is when desolation happens. Defeat.

Everyone feels that because they believed so hard, their dreams must come true for them.

I did it too. What a fool!

But I wouldn't want to change anything even if I could, Dabir. This was the only way.

So don't cry. I understand.

This is how Suraj Roy will feel in his last moments.

CHAPTER 18

The Woman With Paper Like Skin – Day 5

Rewa thought she heard someone stepping on a twig, and she grabbed Ajoy's arm, but they heard nothing for the next four minutes and then, started moving again.

It began to rain as soon as they stepped out of Peelo's home, and soon, it turned into a thunderstorm. By the time they reached the bottom of the hill that led up to the Mayor's estate, both Ajoy and Rewa were drenched. The estate was surrounded by a mangrove, a dense tangle of trees, bushes and roots. The leaves kept hitting Rewa in the face, and the brambles kept tripping her burqa. Her back was soaked.

It was five thirty p.m. and it was dark, they could not light a torch or they would be seen. Dusk had come sooner than expected, and the rain clouds had made the atmosphere oppressive and humid. But they were almost at their destination.

The Mayor's Estate—the home of the most important official of the British Empire in Chittagong.

It was built on a hill. The only building there.

The estate inside had manicured lawns, beautiful gazebos and pathways surrounding a white manor which looked like a gothic castle on the top of a mountain. Especially now in this tropical downpour. From the top of this magnificent stone Victorian building, you could see the whole city and the river running through the city, snaking its way from the mountains and flowing next to the Mayor's grounds.

But right now, Ajoy and Rewa could barely see anything in the storm. They first huddled on the side of the road and made their way to the main entrance of the Estate, where guards were stationed.

They saw the massive entrance gate. Ten foot high and spears on the top, welded together. Ten armed guards stationed there.

Now as per Dabir's directions,

Walk one mile to the left of the main gate.

Stay hidden from the road.

Rewa hadn't said a word last night, when Dabir had repeated his plans over and over.

She didn't ask what would happen if something went wrong, she didn't ask what would happen if she got caught, or if something happened to Dabir and he couldn't escape from the estate. She just stood there numb, memorizing the map that Dabir drew.

She had slept a dreamless, deep sleep and had woken up this morning, steeled and ready.

Now stumbling through the forest with the huge castle like mansion seen above the trees in the darkness, she was determined to not think about things that could go wrong.

She stopped ducked and pulled Ajoy down with her.

There, towards the left, a guard.

A rifle slung on his shoulder, rain lashing against his hat, walking casually, humming a song. Behind him another guard, about ten feet away. They had almost spotted Ajoy and Rewa. The two of them squatted behind a bush and watched the guards stroll by. They would be back in fifteen minutes.

Ajoy grabbed Rewa's gloved hand and ran across the road. They reached the small gate with a rubber flap on it.

Dabir had been right.

Even Peelo would have been too large to twist through. Rewa would barely fit. "All my years in a small cage will help," Rewa mumbled. Ajoy turned sharply.

"Good luck," he said, then took of his spectacles to rub off the pelting rain.

Ajay had not approved of Rewa agreeing to put her life in such danger for Dabir. But it had not been his place to speak, so he had been silent all this while. He gave his instructions stoically.

"It's 6:00 p.m. Get inside that gate. Find a bush to hide under, or a tree to climb, but stay out of sight. You have twenty minutes to run down, unbolt the boathouse, and come running back here. It's dark, this dog gate is small and probably can't be seen clearly in the hedges, so find some landmark near it to know you've reached the gate on your way back from the boathouse. Do not miss the gate, be as silent as you can. I'll be waiting right here. I won't leave."

Rewa squatted and lay down.

"Rewa, be careful."

Wearing a burqa and gloves and squeezing through a tiny opening in a wooden gate with the rain pelting down on you, was hard and uncomfortable. The floor was muddy, and the rain kept falling into her eyes and mouth. Her gloves, now wet and stuck to her skin, wouldn't allow her to grip the wooden frame and haul herself in. She had gotten halfway through, when she got stuck.

Her left hip was scraping against the frame. Rewa squawked in pain. She began to puff as she writhed in the muck and tried to pull herself through the opening. She moved two inches and stopped, groaning.

"Hurry!" Ajoy said, leaning in.

Rewa wanted to kick his face. She felt his hands on her legs, she yelped in shock, Ajoy was pushing her in.

"Shhhhh!" he said, and he heaved. Rewa got some satisfaction when her foot hit his chin, and she heard a muffled groan. There was a tearing sound, her burqa ripped from her hip, but Rewa slid in. She was inside the compound. She scrambled to her feet and looked around.

The path was empty. She needed a place to hide. In the middle of the lawn, away from the path, was a clump of palm trees, she ran towards those, breathing hard.

No one had seen her yet.

She leaned against one of the trees and slumped to the ground. She was off the path and hidden. She was completely in the dark here, and safe.

Everything was still.

The sound of rain, the drip drop, the pat pat sound of drops on big leaves. Not a moon or a star was visible. A couple of minutes passed. Rewa got up and began running towards the river, the wet and muddy burqa stuck to her legs and made a spelching sound as she ran. She was terrified that she was making too much noise. As she stumbled down the path, she saw a small hut. Half of it was on stilts, stretching out into the river like a pier with a roof on top.

The boathouse.

A barbed wire fence was in the river, about five feet away from the bank. It stretched on both sides into the river and was attached to outer walls of the hut.

The only way to get in from the river to the estate was through the boathouse. Or someone could swim up to the boathouse and then, find the door unbolted and enter the estate.

With fumbling wet hands, Rewa unbolted the door and cringed at the loud squeaky sound it made, till the bolt was free. Then she turned around and ran back up the path towards the small flap gate where Ajoy was waiting. She was worried that she was going to miss the gate in the dark. So as soon as she thought she was close, she tumbled down behind a bush and held her breath to see if she had been spotted. The guards would be back on the rounds soon.

Someone was walking in her direction.

Who was that? A guard? She turned around, but it was so dark around the trees that she couldn't see anyone. Only parts of the path were lit up. All around her, the lawns, were all pitch dark.

But someone was closer.

There!

That sound again!

Someone heavy was trying to walk stealthily. Slowly coming closer, walking up to her. She heard a muffled thud, close, just behind her!

Rewa slumped against the tree, not daring to look up. She could feel them standing close by. Almost above her head, a foot, an inch away from her hand.

She heard a raspy heavy breath. This was not her imagination. They were standing right next to her.

They were looking at her.

Waiting for her to move.

Rewa couldn't move, she was so frightened. Her eyes tightly shut; she wanted to call out for Ajoy, but her voice failed her.

Then wafting towards her—the smell. A damp, musty smell of decay and dankness and wet clothes.

What kind of creature was this?

She began to count and pray. She counted to one and then said,

"Narasimha Kavacham Vakshye, Prahladenoditam Pura." (I shall now recite the Narasimha Kavach, recited by King Prahalad. It will vanquish all impediments and protect me from harm.)

She counted to two and repeated the verse.

Before she could reach the third verse, she heard a rustle.

It was moving. Towards her?

She leapt up on to her feet and whipped around to face her assailant.

There was no one there.

It was walking away from her through the lawns. Rewa could barely make out a shape. She stood up and began to walk towards the sound.

That raspy breath again.

Towards the right, a little distance away.

She stretched out her arms and followed the sound. The rain was coming down in wooshes. A flash of lightening made her stop.

What am I doing? Where am I going?

Ajoy!

She should get out of here. She stood in the dark thinking furiously. She heard the thud and a slide, and a raspy breath. She ran after the sound. Soon she saw a dim light ahead in between the trees. She must be somewhere near the Mayor's mansion.

Suddenly the rain stopped.

She walked up to a huge mansion, its massive windows lit from inside.

I've gone in the opposite direction. This is the Mayor's bungalow.

She was standing on the steps of a veranda. There was a door leading inside the house. The door was wide open. The floor was so white, and glistening. Rewa took off her muddy shoes. She entered a massive room. It was brilliantly lit.

White and beige couches and big wooden tables dominated the grand room. There were huge mirrors on the wall. She saw ceiling fans ten times the size of the wheel of a bullock cart. They were whirring and creaking as they moved slowly across the ceiling, a massive chandelier in the middle of the ceiling was swaying. It looked like a bunch of lotus flowers, with glass petals that glowed.

The floor is so soft.

She marvelled at the maroon and blue carpets as she stepped on them. It was like walking on someone's skin. She had never seen opulence like this.

She caught her reflection in one of the mirrors. Torn muddy, ragged clothes. Mud-streaked face. Her braids opening up at the bottom. She felt cheap and dirty. Any minute now, someone was going to come in see her, and they would raise an alarm.

No one came.

Then she felt it again. The tingling in her arms and the rush up her spine. Like she had felt at the rally just yesterday morning. Like with 'the man in the boat' near the docks yesterday afternoon. Like someone was lifting her up from under her shoulders and carrying her in the air.

That floating feeling.

A series of flashes almost blinded her, the flashes were happening in her mind.

She felt her eyes well up. The sadness.

Oh my god, the sadness.

She 'heard' the torment piercing through her. This was pain, and sorrow, and despondency.

This 'pain' was breaking her heart, she found herself sinking to the floor, she tried to grab her head, but her arms felt too heavy. She felt a tug. She was being pulled towards *it.*

She left the big room.

On her left were stairs. She climbed up the marble white staircase. At the landing on the top, towards her right was another corridor, brightly lit with smaller glass lotus lights on the ceiling. There was a door on the left and a door on the right.

She took the left door and entered.

It was a large bedroom, dimly lit. A four-poster bed and a *macchardani* net all around the bed, stood in the middle of the room. Behind the bed, a large window was open and the curtains were blowing in the wind.

It had started to rain again.

The dark room had candles on the dresser and an old-fashioned lamp was hung above the window. Only the bed could be seen, in the light of the lamp.

Someone on the bed moaned and moved.

Rewa waited a moment, then she padded across the cold wooden floor and reached the bed. She lifted the net. On the bed, was a woman. Her skin reminded her of the boy Rattan.

Goras!

Pale, like paper, this woman's entire face looked like she was made of powder. Her stringy hair, the colour of kite thread, strewn on the pillow. She smelt unbathed. This woman smelt unhappy. She was asleep but she was crying at the same time.

She stood transfixed. Rewa had never seen a white woman or blond hair before.

Suddenly Rewa knew what she had to do. She knew why she had been 'called' here from the lawn. She stripped off her glove, reached out and placed her hand on the lady's arm. The surge of energy was instant and her temples singed with energy.

"Eleanor."

The name came to her, like a sigh from within.

"Eleanor, you're so sad, and sick."

Then as the words started forming on their own, she began to see more things in her mind. Pictures—a baby boy, in a white night gown, laughing and crawling on the floor, a white handsome man, laughing, on the bed, next to the white woman, watching the boy crawl.

A garden and the three of them having a picnic.

A spacious, room, in the mansion that she had entered last night. In daylight the room looked spacious, bright and airy with white curtains flowing in window. The three of them were laughing, really happy.

Rewa felt the floor dissolve and slide away from beneath her feet. She felt her feet sink deeper into something soft, like she was walking on marshy land, next to the pond in her village.

She was sinking into the images that she was seeing. At first, she was floating above that room where the Mayor and his family were, and then drifting closer and closer to them. Closer to Lady Henley. She felt herself pour into where they were at that moment. She was now in her, at that moment. She was feeling Lady Henley's feelings. She was her.

And then, the pain hit her in the centre of her chest, and she began to speak.

"I miss him so much. Oh my god," Rewa began to weep, loudly. Her voice rang out in the room.

"I'm dying without him. Where is he? God, please bring him back to me. My baby, I'm so sorry I let you go. Take me God. I'm done. I don't want this life. Why have you punished me? Where is my Daniel?"

She was speaking flawless English. Her voice had changed completely. She didn't sound like Rewa at all. *She sounded like Eleanor.*

Then, the memories changed.

Now there was a dark room, and a dirty bed and the man was staring down at the woman as she thrashed about in her sheets. The cot by the side was empty and there were broken bottles on the floor. Then, the scene morphed and the woman was in the river the water engulfing her, the man was pulling her out of the river and both of them were weeping.

Then she saw her death.

The woman, would be lying alone on the bed, in the same room, the man would be by her side, and someone else. Rewa tried to see, but the woman's grief was so intense that she felt giddy. Rewa snapped open her eyes and clutched the bed for support. She looked up puzzled and unsteady on her feet.

Eleanor going to die, the same night as Peelo and Suraj?

What just happened to me?

I didn't just see her death.

Then, from the corner of the room, in the dark, behind the bed and the net, Rewa heard someone gasp. Terror surged through her body and she dropped the woman's hand. Instinctively she put on her glove.

The creature from the garden was here!

In the room, waiting in the dark. *Waiting for her.*

Across the mosquito net, on the other side of the bed, a voice—cold, creaky and raspy, "So, what did you see?"

Rewa dropped the macchardani and backed away from the bed.

A thud, a step, and then a slide across the wooden floor. The sound of a lifeless limb being dragged across the floor.

It was moving.

The creature was walking around the bed. Slowly coming into the light and creeping up towards her.

It slid into her view. Rewa tried to scream but couldn't.

Stooped, twisted, and bent, like an old tree, this figure was holding a staff and was dragging one lifeless leg behind it. A red saree wrapped around and covering its face.

The raspy voice asked again, "What did you see? Who are you?" Then, from outside the window, across the lawn. Shots rang out. The sounds of men shouting.

Dabir and his men must have found Davon.

The creature began to limp towards her. Rewa looked around the bare room in desperation. Next to her on the right, on the dresser, a photo frame made of wood. Rewa grabbed it and tossed it towards the creature in the sari. It hit her on her head and the staff dropped from her hand. As the creature tottered on one withered leg, Rewa ran out of the bedroom, down the stairs towards, through the brightly lit hall room, into the veranda and towards the garden path. The cold rain hit her face.

It shook her to the core. She was still unsteady from her encounter with Eleanor. She ran into the garden away from the mansion and then stopped in the dark.

She didn't know which direction to run in. She didn't know where the path was and how she was going to get to the flap door where Ajoy was waiting.

On her right, in the dark, she could hear shots still ringing. She debated if she should run towards the shots. Then she had an idea. She would run to the boathouse and swim into the river. She stood and tried to figure out where the river path would be, and then pelted towards it. Two minutes later, she saw the lamps that lit the path and she felt a wave of relief. Now all she had to do was follow the path towards the boathouse.

She saw a flash of light to her right. Another shot, she could hear men were shouting. The rain was lashing too loud for her to hear what was being said. From behind her, she heard the sound of shoes, people running towards the boat house. The path curved and whoever was running couldn't see her as she turned a bend. In front of her the boat house loomed and she saw that the door was ajar. She ran in and tumbled to the floor.

It was a small boat house. Clean and orderly. A kerosene lamp gave dim light from the wall. There were three boats all tied up in a row. One of them looked so narrow that it wouldn't hold more than one person. She ran to the second boat, which looked like it could hold seven to eight people. The third one was the same shape and size as the second one. The river water was lashing against both of the boats. Rewa ran to untie the second one, then she saw that it had no oars in it. She looked around the room in panic. The shouts of the men were coming closer. They would be storming in any minute now. She suddenly saw oars standing up behind the door, she hadn't seen them when she had rushed in. Right next to them was an axe. Rewa stopped.

Three minutes later, Jaidev ran in. He screamed when he saw Rewa, quickly lifted his rifle to shoot. Rewa screamed and whipped open her burqa.

"It's me, Rewa!! Don't."

She cowered down with her head in her hands.

Jaidev began to shout!

"They knew we were coming; they were hiding inside that bastard's house. Three of them, Dabir's been shot."

Rewa gasped.

A moment later, Ashok and Siddharth stumbled into the boat house, carrying Dabir between them. They each had Dabir's arm around them. He didn't seem awake. His feet were dragging on the floor. Behind them Harshal came inside shut the door and bolted it. He broke one of the windows with his rifle and aimed it out towards the Mayor's mansion, and began shooting. He got return fire. Jaidev picked his rifle and broke another window and shot out into the dark. Both men were screaming

Ashok and Siddharth laid Dabir on the floor. Rewa ran to them and squatted next to Dabir. His left arm was completely covered in blood. He was moaning, but his eyes were shut. Siddharth ripped open Dabir's shirt from the shoulder.

"Left shoulder!" he shouted to the others. The men from outside were shooting back. A window smashed next to Harshal, the sound of a bullet passing through.

Harshal shouted back.

"He can't swim. What do we do?"

Rewa stood up and shouted.

"The boat," she said and pointed to the second boat. She had put the oars in it.

In two minutes, while Jaidev and Harshal kept firing at the soldiers, Dabir had been placed at the bottom of the boat. Rewa grabbed the kerosene lamp and tossed it at a set of ropes lying in the corner. The ropes caught fire, instantly, as Rewa clambered into the boat and sat next to Dabir. Jaidev and Harshal jumped in next, took up the oars and began drawing out into the raging river. The two men were strong but the moment it drew out of the boat house, the current swooped the boat and they were swept into the middle of the river.

"The other boat," Ashok shouted over the rush of the river. "They'll come after us."

"They can't," screamed back Rewa and held up the axe. "Both the boats have holes in them. I chopped them."

She turned around and looked back at the boat house which had now caught fire and the flames had risen to the side of the small building.

As she watched. A man stepped out from the darkness of the boat house, and stared grimly at Rewa. He held a pistol in his hand. She saw his face in the flicker of the flames.

Davon. The man with the light eyes.

CHAPTER 19

The Boys With White Eyes

Tuku, her son was dead. And she was still breathing and living and eating and shitting and pissing. It was as if her body had no idea what her heart was going through. Didn't the heart live in the same body? Didn't her agony translate through her blood and her veins to every organ?

Tuku was dead and she hadn't died with him. Her breath inhaled and exhaled as if nothing had happened. She had tried to will herself to stop breathing, and tried to will her heart to stop beating. But her own body was proving treacherous, overlooking her grief, callously.

Tuku was lying somewhere in the jungle unclaimed, probably attacked by wild animals and she, Kakoli, his mother had spent the last two days crying, and being consoled by strangers.

When she had her first bite of food after two days, it tasted of accusation. When her whimpers subsided, she knew that the accusations were true, because Kakoli, his mother, had not died with him. How cruel was she. She would pay for *this* cruelty and *that* cruelty.

Twelve years was all the time, that she had had with Tuku, and now for the rest of her life and for eternity, she was going to live, breathe, eat, drink, wear clothes, speak words, clean, drape, cook and cry.

Without Tuku.

If that wasn't punishment enough for all the evil she had done, then she didn't know what was.

Kantha was her daughter too, and thank God, that she was alive and well and with her mother, but Kakoli also knew that Kantha was always going to be a poor substitute.

No matter what Kantha did and no matter what Kakoli did as a mother, Tuku was going to be as alive as ever, living like a wall of grief between the mother and the daughter for the rest of their lives.

Kantha was never going to be enough. Remorse and atonement were never going to be enough. Kakoli would have happily died right this moment, not caring that she had Kantha to take care of. God knows Kantha's father Dabir didn't care at all.

But she still had other tasks to accomplish.

She was going to find Tuku and cremate him.

She was going to atone for all the evil she had done.

***

Baba cannot die.

This cannot be happening.

I saw it, I saw it so clearly. He doesn't die now.

Then how is this happening?

Rewa was raging and confused. She was crying under her dirty, muddy, drenched burqa and head scarf.

Has something happened to me?

Did I see something wrong?

There were supposed to be no deaths tonight.

I did not see this when I touched Baba last night.

She sat at the bottom of the boat next to Dabir. Harshal sat next to them. The boat swayed dangerously, but stayed afloat. All four men were silent as they used the oars just to keep them steady, the current of the river did the rest, as it swept them past the wet, miserable, dark city. They were aware that this last mission had almost cost them their lives. They were plain lucky that they had all survived. Davon and his men had known they were coming. His men had been hiding inside and around his house, by the time they had drawn close to the house and those men had started shooting.

Before the shooting, Dabir had been the first to notice that something was amiss and had stopped Jaidev from entering the house. That one moment had saved Jaidev's life. He looked down at Dabir and at Rewa.

"God was with us today," he said. "He saved us."

Harshal was examining Dabir's shoulder. He looked up and smiled at Rewa.

"He'll be fine. The bullet passed through. He'll be up and about in no time." He looked up and shouted to Jaidev.

"We'll need to go a market in the city tomorrow to get something for this. We can't take him to a hospital. We'll need to buy supplies."

Harshall looked at Rewa and then at the rest of them,

"We will have to take her to the camp."

The rest of them nodded silently.

Rewa almost laughed hysterically.

Dabir was fine as she had known he would be.

But what about the white woman with the skin like paper? She looked up at the sky and began to count the deaths she had seen in her short life:

Thakurma,

Shah Jahan,

The old beggar in the forest,

A gypsy woman,

Shanta's baby,

Shanta,

Rattan,

Tukul.

The deaths that had already occurred, and now

Peelo,

Suraj, and Eleanor, deaths that were all going to happen the same night.

What was the difference between those visions and what had just happened with Eleanor? With the earlier deaths, they were things she saw in her head, but tonight, she had abandoned her own head, her own body, and gotten swept away in another reality, feeling Eleanor's woe as if it was birthed inside her. With Eleanor's vision, she had seen her entire life swim by and she had submerged in it, as if Rewa was now Eleanor.

This time she hadn't just seen her death. She had seen her life and her soul.

But how had she ended up in Eleanor's room? Something or someone had sent her up there. Rewa had been in the garden and yet she had been called to the room on the first floor. Who?

The answer came instantly and shocked her.

Eleanor's soul.

Eleanor's soul had called her.

Eleanor's soul had called Rewa to show her, when Eleanor was going to die.

***

They were in a crowded market place. Looking for a shop to buy some medicines for Dabir.

Rewa groaned inwardly when she saw the huge crowd. Ajoy walked beside her and kept looking at Rewa as if he wanted to say something.

There was a vegetable vendor sitting on their side. Rewa moved towards him and suddenly almost got swept in the bustling crowd.

She was glad that she was wearing her gloves and glad that promptly, Ajoy was at her side. He kept so close to her that none of the women or men in the marketplace managed to touch Rewa. The two of them began to wander around, looking for a *vaid*.

Ahead, she saw a building.

Like something from Arabian nights, the book with pictures that Baba had shown her once. Tightly squeezed into this marketplace, it looked as if it was shrugging its shoulders while being crushed at the waist. From outside, the distinctiveness of the building was lost in the marketplace. Bleached white in colour, four stories high and had a string of massive windows which looked like black square eyes and big blue door set in the centre like a mouth to the face. All windows were shut. It looked like a tomb.

She stopped a hundred yards away from the entrance. At first Rewa thought that it was the massive crowd on the streets that had discombobulated her.

It was happening to her again!

All her senses were firing and her body was heating up inside the burqa. She looked around, trying to figure out the source of this feeling. It was building.

No, it was coming from the building.

She felt her shoulders square up and then lift. The floating sensation overcame her. The noise of the marketplace receded.

There was complete silence.

Everyone was still around; the thousands of people, but they were silent and frozen. They walked slowly like ghosts, like boats sliding in the water. The building ahead of her was radiating a strange light.

Slowly, a window opened.

A head appeared. A young boy. Bald. He stretched his neck out of the window. His face was familiar.

His eyes!

Rewa felt her terror rise.

There was no iris in his eyes. The entire eye was a milky white. Yet he seemed to staring through the crowd.

He was mumbling something. His lips were moving and his head swayed slightly. Rewa froze. Another window opened and another head emerged. All the windows of the tomb were opening and heads began to appear on each one of the windows.

Boys, hundreds of them. All of them had white milky eyes.

All of them had spotted her. In the middle of this congested, overpopulated street, they were looking straight at Rewa. They were all chanting. She could hear them. All the other sounds were gone, but she could hear the chants. This was not a language she knew.

The first head disappeared back into the window.

Then the rest of the heads began to disappear inside. The main door of the house began to open slowly. The boy stepped out of the house. He was wearing a maroon pant suit.

She couldn't talk. No voice came out of her mouth.

Ajoy was standing next to her, frozen. *Ajoy! Oh god.*

He seemed to be in another world. He wasn't moving and she began to shriek his name and shake his arm, but he was looking away as if staring, at something else on the floor.

Wake up Ajoy! They're coming for me.

No sound came from her mouth.

The bald boy was standing on the door step of the tomb. Behind him, one more boy appeared. Then one more, then ten, then twenty, thirty, fifty. A hundred boys. All grotesque with white milky eyes.

The boy took a step towards her. Rewa dropped Ajoy's arm and began to run back towards the tonga. The boy began to follow her. The rest of the boys stepped into the crowd behind the first boy. They began to fan through the crowd. Rewa turned away from them and ran pell mell through the silent, stationary horde. They were coming closer. The chanting was getting louder. Rewa began to wail, but no noise came from her mouth.

Then, footsteps rang close to her and a hand grabbed her shoulder.

Rewa screamed and turned.

It was Amma.

Amma? Here?

The world switched back to normal.

The sound of the crowd was loud again. People turned around to look at who had screamed. Ajoy was in the crowd looking for her and as he saw her, he grinned and began to shove through the people towards her and Amma.

Kakoli said urgently, "Rewa, listen to me, come alone and see me. Nothing is what you think it is. Trust no one, I will be here waiting for you. You must come tomorrow."

She pointed to the white building.

Rewa stared. The door and windows were shut, there was no one at the door step. There was no sign of any of the boys. All of them had disappeared.

CHAPTER 20

The Camp – Day 6

Rewa woke up with a start.

She was breathing hard. Dabir was moaning. He was on a charpoi, his arm in bandage. Rewa had been sleeping next to him on the floor. They were in a large tattered tent. The flaps were open and Rewa could see that it was now morning and 'The Camp' was up and awake. They were in the jungle, somewhere on the outskirts of the city. It wasn't raining anymore and the sun was gaining heat.

She shook away the memory of her strange dream. Amma and those boys with the milky eyes. Rewa shuddered and sat up. She was still dressed in last night's torn and muddly clothes. The burqa was stale, smelly, damp and her scarf strewn on the thin *chattai* where she lay. Her gloves, miraculously, had survived the night with no damage and were still on hands. She began to examine her torn clothes and wondered how she was going to get fresh ones.

"I got some for you," A voice came from the opening of the tent.

Rewa looked up at Peelo. Looking bright, clean, and happy. She stepped in with a bag and went up to the charpoi where Dabir was sleeping.

"Clean clothes for him. New ones for you. Your burqa is badly torn," She said and sat next to Dabir, not looking at Rewa.

She shook her head playfully.

"He worries about you all the time, but one would think that he would notice when his daughter might need new clothes." She ran her hand against his forehead and rested it on his cheek.

It was strangely intimate.

"No fever. Now he just needs to rest. Come with me."

They walked out of the tent.

In the middle of the forest to the west of Chittagong, somewhere between Rewa's village and the city, the New India Revolutionary Army had set up the camp.

The camp was a small settlement of ten tents, all put up in a square with a place to build a fire right in the center of the area. There were a lot of people milling around. There was a shed under a thick clump of trees and Rewa could see that it had sacks of food grains. All around the shed wet clothes had been put to dry, rifles and pistols hung on old ropes, like curtains. The whole camp was buzzing with men in various stages of undress. A big black pot hung above the camp fire and something bubbled inside which did not smell good. Near the shed, some men were exercising. Some men were lying in the tents, sleeping.

Rewa noticed that there were no women around, and nobody spoke loudly. They either whispered or spoke in signals. Anyone a hundred meters away would not be realize how near they were to the New India Revolutionary Army. Suraj and some men were in one tent having a deep discussion. Peelo waved to him.

Jaidev, the man who had been in the boat with Rewa last night, smoking a beedi, by the fire, turned when he saw Rewa step out of the tent. He smiled and nodded and gestured towards Dabir.

Peelo answered, “Sleeping.”

A very tall dark man stepped out of the tent.

“What about the mission? Will he be able to...?”

Peelo stopped.

“I don’t know Aswanii, depends on how he feels tonight. I’ll decide tomorrow morning.”

“What does Suraj dada say?” He looked at Suraj’s tent.

Peelo lifted her chin.

“It’s my mission, not his.”

Peelo walked away, and Rewa followed. Aswanii was staring at them. As Rewa turned back to look at him, he smiled.

Peelo led Rewa through the thick forest, till they arrived at a stream. It was shallow and but clean, there were fish in the water.

“That’s Aswanii, he’s from Kerala. He’s Suraj Roy’s favourite,” she said. “They all have a problem with a woman leading a mission.” She pointed to the stream.

“Here are your new clothes.”

She hung the bag of clothes on a tree next to the stream.

“I also got you a pair of new gloves. And soap. It’s a British one.” She held out a bar of green soap.

The soap was the most luxurious thing that had ever touched against her skin. She smelt glorious. The new clothes fitted her better than Peelo’s clothes, but they didn’t smell as good. When she returned to the tent, Dabir was still asleep. Peelo was sponging his face and chest. His shirt was open. Rewa sat on the floor and watched them. Peelo looked up from her task, smiled at Rewa and continued with her task.

“Peelo?”

"Yes."

"Don't you ever think of my Amma and his family?" Rewa added, "Us."

Peelo was silent.

Then she put down the sponge, walked to the tent flap and looked out.

"That tall man, Aswanii? He is a Mappila. Twelve years ago, his father was one of the people who rebelled against the British in Mysore. They put many of these rebels in a train to Podanur jail in Tamil Nadu. One of the carriages had no windows, and a hundred of these prisoners were put in it. His father was amongst them, and they didn't open the carriage for nine days."

Peelo turned and looked at Rewa. She said, "They couldn't even recognise the rotting body. They just chose one of the bodies as their own for burial. Dabir found him outside the city of Mysore living under a railway track."

Peelo turned away again. Jaidev was sitting near the shed, praying.

"Jaidev, who went with you last night, is only twenty years old. He's just two years older than Ajoy. When he was about seven years old, the Bombay flu happened. A ship carrying British troops from the great war came to Mumbai, and they carried the flu. The British didn't want to quarantine the men who had come from war, because they were in celebration mode. They gave full medical care only to their own. Six million Indians died. They did nothing, except give out quinine tablets, while two hundred people died every week, week after week, after week. They prevented wood for cremation to get to the cities. They needed the trains for their own trade purposes. By the end of it, people just threw the bodies in the harbour. Everyone in Jaidev's family died in his home. The boy was seven. Ashok and Siddharth found him in a big empty abandoned bungalow, living along fifteen dead bodies. He had been locked in with them for three months. They brought him to Dabir, many years ago."

She turned to Rewa and smiled.

"When Dabir and Gautam found me and Ajoy, after father died, we had been begging on the streets for seven months. We were sleeping in Chakma. On the street in a slum. We couldn't even afford a room."

"We are all Dabir's people. Each one of us, saved by him. He has collected us and put us together here. We are his family. He belongs to us, as much as he belongs to you and your Amma. We were nothing before he chose us."

She came back to the charpoi and sat next to Dabir.

"Rewa, his ambition is big enough to include my little life and my simple dreams. You and your Amma have nothing to fear from me. I pose no threat. Don't you see? I do not want him to be mine, he can't be. He's everybody's, especially your Amma's and yours. In fact, you must believe that I belong to you too, through him."

***

After Peelo left the camp, Rewa spent the whole day with Dabir. She thought it was the most wonderful day of her life. Around midday, he suddenly woke up, breathing hard, and gasped in panic. Rewa ran to his side. He focused on her, grabbed her hand, then he relaxed and smiled. His eyes shut again and he went back to sleep.

"Rewa!" he mumbled.

Rewa felt tears slip down her cheeks. She took off her gloves and stared at his sleeping face for a moment. Then, she rested her head on his chest.

Throughout the day people kept coming to check on Dabir, while Rewa would sit in the corner, the burqa and gloves intact. Nobody noticed. Suraj Roy came around mid-afternoon and sat by his side for a half an hour, just looking at him.

"You know," he said, "I didn't want him to go after that Davon, but I have learnt over the years that Dabir is a strange beast. We've worked together for so long, but he doesn't work with me, he works alongside me. Do you understand?"

Rewa didn't.

"I am older perhaps, but Dabir is the older soul. He has his reasons for everything, and he never shares. He understands people so well, sometimes it's scary how much he can read your mind. Once he is inside your head, you cannot hide anything from him. I just wish he would let me in his head, like he has let me in his heart."

The rest of the New India Revolutionary Army came in one by one. Some would come and sit on the floor, while some sat outside the tent, cross legged, as if they were watching a saint. Ashok sat there amongst them, tears streaming down his face. Later, when the rest of them had gone, he crept in and touched Dabir's feet and ran out. Siddharth came in, bruised and limping, from last night, Harshal followed him in the tent. They were tall strapping north Indian men, who were obviously devoted to Dabir. When she told them about how he had woken up for a bit, they almost whooped with joy. The whole day, the two of them and Ashok kept wandering close to the tent aimlessly, just to catch a glimpse of him, hoping to see him awake. They would look at Rewa and she would shake her head. Without him, they seemed lost and helpless.

When the sun went down, all three of them were in Dabir's tent, lazing around talking, no longer noticing Rewa in the corner. A kerosene lamp hung at the entrance flap, attracting flies. The three of them discussed how a scottish pilot Jim Mollison had just flown across the Atlantic Ocean.

"He only had a compass, and a watch," Ashok said, "And there was fog, so for all he knew, he could have been flying over Germany before he landed."

"Yeah, like you, when it comes to directions," Siddharth said and laughed. "Remember near Shanti Niketan, he kept going in circles, when we could see the camp down the hill."

"Bastards, let me do it for hours. Till Dabir dada came up from the camp." Suddenly they were all sober.

"How are we going to do this without him tomorrow?" Harshal asked, hesitatingly.

"We will have to."

Suraj dada was standing outside the tent, in the light of the lamp.

"Come to my tent, let's discuss the plan again. Peelo isn't here, but we have consider doing this without Dabir."

Rewa shuddered.

Tomorrow. 24th September. The night of the slaughter.

The three of them trooped out of the tent, leaving Rewa alone with Dabir.

***

At first, she thought, it was Dabir's moaning that had woken her up, but he was sleeping quietly.

Maybe it was a sound from the camp. Rewa got up and walked to the entrance of the tent. The camp was quiet. One lamp hung from the make shift weapons shed. It was lit. Every other tent was in complete darkness, the campfire was barely smoking. No clouds or rain today, so a clear moon shown in the sky.

It was too quiet.

Rewa remembered her dream from last night. Her heart began to beat. The woods were in complete silence. No animal sounds, no crickets, no breeze on the leaves. Dark and silence.

Rewa felt uneasy. She should wake Dabir. Something didn't feel right. Shouldn't there be someone awake and guarding the camp? Someone was watching them from the woods.

Someone was watching her.

She ran back to Dabir. "Baba, wake up, there's someone outside," she said and shook his arm.

"Baba," she whispered urgently.

Dabir stirred but didn't wake up. She gave up and ran out of the tent. She had to wake someone else. She stood at the entrance and tried to remember which tent was Suraj's. It was one of the tents on the other side of the campfire, closer to the stream she had bathed in this morning. She began to walk uncertainly in the dark towards what she thought was Suraj's tent.

She stopped suddenly.

Someone was close by, a shadow just across the camp fire. From the corner of her eye. She could see a figure.

Standing there silently, watching.

She turned towards it slowly.

The figure did not move.

They were now facing each other across the campfire. It was too dark, but Rewa could clearly see it. A figure standing in between two tents, distant from the embers of the fire, so that the face could not be seen.

What is that?

Rewa turned and began to run. She was stumbling towards Suraj's tent. The figure hadn't moved. Rewa was gasping. Another twenty steps and she would reach the tent. She wasn't thinking clearly. A chant rose in her mind:

Suraj dada! Suraj dada! Suraj dada!

She stopped in her tracks.

Oh no!

The figure was now standing in front of Suraj dada's tent. Rewa wanted to scream.

It began to sway.

Then it moved away. Slowly. The head didn't turn, it was facing her, but the figure began to melt through the camp towards the forest. If it was walking, it's feet made no sound as it began blend into the darkness.

The bushes and plants began to tilt out of the figure's way as it glided through the forest.

It would be gone in a moment.

It stopped.

Rewa's feet began to move.

She followed the figure. There was something soft, something inviting about it. Her panic rose, but she couldn't control herself as her feet lifted in the figure's direction. She wanted to turn back and look at the camp. She couldn't. They were now in complete darkness and complete silence in the forest. The only sound was from Rewa's feet on the dry forest ground.

Her last thought before she lost sight of the camp was, "Baba, help."

How long can the feeling of terror last? A minute? Five minutes? How can you cope with a feeling of horror that just won't abate? She was following a ghost into a thick forest, away from everyone, and help herself. She couldn't stop and she couldn't call out for help.

Ahead, a clearing in the forest.

The figure standing at the edge.

Standing? It was floating a few inches of the ground.

Rewa stepped into the clearing. The moon lit up the space. And a sliver of light fell on the figure.

A woman.

Rewa peered a little closer and almost gagged.

Tukul?

The young girl who had drowned? The only girl who had been nice to Rewa? Beautiful, kind Tukul. Her friend for a moment.

But Tukul is dead!

The figure nodded.

It was reading her thoughts!

After a long, terrifying moment of silence, Rewa spoke.

"You're not Tukul?"

Tukul smiled and shook her head.

"No."

Her voice was silky. It sounded like Tukul's, yet it was not Tukul's voice at all.

"Then who are you?" Rewa asked.

"Doesn't matter yet, you'll find out my name soon enough."

"Are you a ghost?"

"If I am, then why don't you recognise that?"

"What?"

Tukul giggled. It was a scary sound.

"I'm not a ghost," she said, tittering.

"Is this a dream?" Rewa spoke just to stop that sound.

"You've been having a lot of them lately, haven't you?"

"What do you want?" Rewa asked.

Tukul considered the question.

"Tell me why did you call Tukul to you?" she asked, her voice soft and probing. Rewa was flabbergasted.

"I .... I did not call Tukul at all, she came to see me, on her own."

"Aah! seventy-three children in the whole village and Tukul wanted to meet the one child that was hiding?"

The figure was suddenly looking at her icily.

"And one day after she met you, she died," she said coldly. "And you never wondered why?" She giggled again.

Rewa shook her head.

"But I had nothing to do with that, I just..."

"Saw her die, like all the other deaths that you've been seeing," Tukul finished the sentence.

She knows?

"Yes, I do."

She grinned. It was ugly.

"And they know too."

"Who?"

"The ones who are looking for you. They're close now. Very close."

There was a silence.

Rewa pleaded and said, "I don't understand what you're saying at all."

"Then maybe, it's time you stopped running and hiding."

There was challenge in her voice. Her face was changing. It was losing its colour. Rewa was terrified.

"Are you going to kill me?"

Tukul laughed out loud. It sounded like a bad cough.

"No. That would be...dull."

Then she was silent for a long time before she spoke.

"Hmm! Not yet. There is time. You have a lot of growing into to do."

She said growing into. What does that mean?

Now the mirth was gone. The voice was hard, grotesque and terrifying. It sounded like wet cloth being slapped against a rock.

"I had heard about you."

Tukul began to walk around Rewa.

Not walk, float.

"That was a long time ago, then I forgot about you. I sensed you, suddenly, three days ago. That's why I'm here. But now that I've seen you, you're nothing like the legend.

Legend?

"You're nothing. You're no match yet. You're a waste of time. You're so naïve, trusting, and full of love. Only when you grow out of that..."

Then she smiled.

"And now is a good time to start doing that. Don't you think?"

Rewa was shaking.

"When I'm gone, Rewa, I want you to remember this night, the night we first met. Because it starts here..."

Her skin was turning black and peeling off now. Rewa was cringing. Tukul sensed it and smiled again.

"W..what starts?" Rewa murmured.

"Us."

"Us?"

Tukul's eyes were boring into Rewa.

"What did your Amma say to you?

"My Amma?"

Tukul's face was jet black, as if her skin had been burnt like paper. Her eyes and lips were red.

"Yes. She said—nothing is what it seems."

Tukul disappeared.

Rewa was completely alone in the middle of the forest.

CHAPTER 21

The Green Door

Through the trees.

There was a light.

When her heartbeat had steadied, Rewa began to walk towards the light. Whoever or whatever Tukul was, it was gone. She was alone in the dark, with only that light in the distance guiding her through the forest.

A hut. It looked abandoned and run down, then how did it have a lantern at the door? Rewa stood a distance away from the hut and called out.

"Hello? Is anyone there? I need some help?"

No answer. Nothing stirred or moved. The hut was completely empty.

Rewa pushed open the wooden door. It opened easily. The inside was musty, stale and dirty. It looked like no one had entered this place for a long time. There was another lamp lit and hanging on the wall opposite the door.

Why does it look familiar?

There were two charpois placed against each of the walls. The walls were mud, unpainted, and flaking. There was a smelly mattress on one of the charpoi and some broken dishes strewn around on the floor.

She stepped in and the door closed behind her. She looked around for ... She didn't know what she was looking for. It was bare. There was an old dirty shirt that hung on a nail on one of the walls, above the charpoi. She removed it. Under the shirt, hanging on the same nail, a satchel. An old worn-out jute bag, colourless and shapeless.

It was stained. *Blood?*

There was something inside it. She pulled a sheaf of papers. Drawings, and some letters. She walked closer to the lamp and spread them on the floor.

Drawings, hand sketches. There were about twenty of them. Some writing on some sheets. Rewa's mouth fell open.

She recognized Baba's handwriting. These were his papers.

Here? In this hut?

The designs were the kind of designs that he had put on the New India Revolutionary Pamphlets. But these looked old, and amateurish compared to how beautiful he had made them last week. These looked like doodles. But she was now sure that these were Dabir's drawings. The other pictures took her breath away.

They were pictures of her.

Beautiful pictures of Rewa. A young toddler Rewa. Maybe four years old, with short hair, and smiling gorgeously. Rewa stared at the pictures dumbfounded. She had never seen any of these before.

Baba made these?

There were more pictures. Sketched perfectly, Rewa at six years of age. Longer hair, brighter eyes, laughing. Rewa at eight years of age. Suddenly short hair, almost like a boy.

Rewa stopped.

She had never cut her hair. Was this someone else?

No, it was unmistakably Rewa. Her eyes, nose, her chin.

The next few pictures had her hair in different cuts. Sometimes short, sometimes long, but she looked happy and smiling in all her pictures. She couldn't remember if she had ever laughed in Dabir's presence. Her heart melted.

Oh Baba. Is this how you see me?

He was strict and demanding and tough, but Dabir loved his Rewa. She picked up the pictures and crushed them to her chest. She began to put them in the satchel to take them with her. But then she noticed something else. She took them out again and spread them again, put the other pictures with the border next to these ones.

She examined them carefully.

The pictures were not made by Baba!

They were by a different artist. The designs were Baba's but not Rewa's pictures. All Rewa's pictures were done by someone with a less steady hand than Dabir's. There were no more pictures of her older than around eight years of age. Had the artist stopped sketching Rewa after she had turned eight? Why? What had happened?

She gathered the pictures and put them in the satchel and stood up. She grabbed the lantern and turned to leave. She staggered when she saw the door.

The inside of the door was a bright neon green.

The green door!

It all came swimming back. Rewa stood there staring. *This was the shack of her dreams.* That is why it looked familiar. She had seen this place hundreds of times. The same room, the walls. She opened the door and stepped back into the shack.

Yes, the silhouette of the monster would be standing right there at that door. This was how the dream started each time. Then, the monster would enter the hut.

There would be a scream, another wail, and then, Baba and the other man would fight.

She twirled around the room, remembering the sequence of the brawl between the men.

There, in the corner, a woman was screaming. She was bleeding and crying. Right next to her, someone else was wailing, but Rewa couldn't picture who.

The other man was shouting savagely while Dabir and he scrambled on the floor with the knife. Then she remembered how Dabir had overturned the man and plunged the knife in his chest. Then he had looked at Rewa.

She had told Dabir about this dream so many times. Why had he not said anything to her? About this place. About the fact that it had really happened.

Dabir had let her think it hadn't been a real incident. Why?

This had never been a dream.

This was a memory.

CHAPTER 22

The Day of The Gala

Dr Martin shook his head. "A couple of days, a week at most sir," he said.

Richard stared at him. He felt nothing. Eleanor, his wife, mother of his lost child, the love of his life, was going to die, and he was blank.

Last night, her health had taken a turn for the worse. He had come home to find her in such intense pain in her abdomen that her howls had sounded like they came from the depths of her soul.

Four days ago, she had been barely aware of anything except her pain. She had almost overdosed with pain killers and sleeping pills downed with a vodka once, and Dr Martin had been called on an emergency. Since then, it had been pills with gin, or whisky, and blessed slumber had kept her placid, till the next bout of bone piercing pain had begun.

She would awake only when the pain sliced through her unconsciousness, to bring her back to her ailing, deserting, destroyed body.

These awakenings had become more and more frequent in the last couple of days, and she needed the pills two or three times a night. She never slept anymore, she only passed out.

She was done, he was done.

No matter how hard Richard had tried, for years, to bring her to some semblance of normal life, she had found ways to disappoint and destroy his plans. The litany of servants and maids and nurses all had been corrupted by her, either through money, threats or sympathy to keep providing her with any kind of alcohol.

So even though the Mayor's estate was supposed to be alcohol free, by Richard's strict orders, there were always bottles of whisky, vodka, and gin hidden away in various hiding places for her to find and down. Richard was used to finding bottles on the terrace, in the garden, underneath the potted plants, and once, hidden on the kayak in the boat house.

How had Eleanor, who on most days couldn't manage to get up from her bed and come down for breakfast, managed to walk the entire length of the lawns to the boat house by the river, was a mystery that stumped Richard.

But those walking days were over. Her body was finally giving up. Her bereavement had finally blunted Eleanor's existence. Now all they could do was wait. Richard should have been devastated.

All he felt today, was an irritation, that Dr Martin chose this day to give him this news. 'Not the day I have the Lieutenant Governor visit,' he mumbled. Then he felt something inside him break at his own callousness.

Edward Bayley's visit was an official and an important one. Richard was not going to let this visit end in his disgrace. That would mean that India had defeated him. This country had taken Richard Henley, chomped on him and spit out the remains of Richard, sans family, sans child, sans prospects. He wasn't going to let that happen.

When he *did* leave India, it would be on his own terms.

"Thank you, Dr Martin," he said officiously "I would like you to arrange for a medical staff to be here permanently till..." He stopped.

To his discretion, Dr Martin acted like he hadn't noticed what Richard was about to say. He nodded, and went downstairs to the telephone to make some calls, leaving Richard alone in the room with Eleanor.

Richard looked down at Eleanor, lying motionless in bed, moaning in pain. He was dressed in full official gear, the red coat and the badges on his lapel. He was supposed to meet Edward Bayley in half an hour and spend the day with him. There were going to be official visits, a meeting with the Chittagong Business council and then a dinner at The British Club with Richard's entire staff and Edward.

Richard turned around and left abruptly.

At the foot of the staircase, Davon stood beside Dr Martin, and when Richard descended, Davon matched Richard's pace, heading out towards the door where Richard's chauffer and car were waiting.

"How many people will be present at dinner tonight?" Richard asked Davon as he strode.

"Forty, including the Governor's entourage."

"Food and drinks?"

"All taken care of, also the band from Calcutta are ready."

"Good, I'll leave for The British Club at around 6:30 p.m.. You can go home."

Davon understood that the Governor and his team wouldn't expect to see 'natives' at The British Club. Except maybe the waiters. Richard grimaced at the thought. He wanted this dinner to end quickly so he could come home.

"Do you think I'll be able to slip out early?" he asked.

Davon nodded.

"The Governor is also tired after the journey, it seems. He will want an early night as well, but he did mention to his bodyguard that he really wanted to drink tonight."

"God!" cursed Richard. "Tonight, is going to be so dull."

***

"Tonight, is going to be a sensational," said Ben Hardgrave.

'The event of the year' was going to be a big party at world famous, The British Club in Chittagong, when the Mayor and the Lieutenant governor would join the rest of the British Business Council Chittagong, for dinner and festivities. Tonight.

Now at 9 a.m., eleven hours earlier, The British Club was buzzing with activity and anticipation.

The event had been booked months ago and Ben Hardgrave, the manager, a trim bald man of about fifty, who looked much younger, and wore suits as if he was born in them, had spared no effort in to make it the biggest night of the year. He was wearing a dark royal navy-blue suit, and he looked every inch the man in charge.

Ben had arrived early this morning, all dressed and prepared to stay at The British Club the whole day, to make sure that everything was ready for the night. Food, décor, china, lighting and the bar, all had to be checked on.

The jazz band had been brought in from Trinkas Park Street Calcutta. They band was ready to play *Gershwin and Louis Armstrong*, even though Ben was sure that neither the Governor nor the Mayor knew who either of these musicians were.

Dinner was going to be a four-course affair. The menu was:

Blinis Demidoff with Caviar and cream,
Quail in puff pastry with foie gras and truffle sauce,
Savarin au rhum avec des figues,
And coffee with bourbon.

That is, if the Mayor stayed long enough for coffee. Rumour had it that his wife was very sick and wouldn't survive the week, so he would be in a rush to head home. The price of the ingredients, some of them imported from France, had almost given Ben a heart attack.

Alexis Soyer, one of the finest Chefs from Calcutta, had been paid astronomically to come here and supervise the meal tonight. He was a tyrant, but if everything had to be impeccable, he was just the man to do it. Alexis had personally checked and hired the kitchen staff, only for tonight.

Alexis's only criteria had been that the staff and waitresses be English speaking without an Indian accent, and that they should be presentable. The British Club didn't allow women in its premises, so this was going to be a really special occasion. The women had better be worth the effort.

A hundred women, that had auditioned, had been pruned to thirteen. Ben and the Mayor's office had checked into their histories of their employment. All references were filed and kept in triplicate with The British Club and with the Mayor. The waitresses had been whetted and trained, by Alexis himself. Alexis only wanted waitresses on the dining room floor, and one male bartender. Ben had given up on the argument. He was concentrating on the linen and the china.

The linen had been bleached and starched within an inch of its life. The tableware was bone china and expensive, white and blue with gold borders. It was fake gold, but only Ben Hardgrave knew that and he would never admit it to a soul. It looked frightfully expensive and terrifyingly delicate.

Maybe it was better that they had waitresses on the job tonight. They tended to be careful. Alexis wanted the waitresses to wear pants. Ben had finally put his foot down.

Most certainly not!

They would be wearing white starched shirts with flared collars, tight fashionable red skirts that covered the knees, a red coat with three buttons, and flat black shoes with block heels so that they wouldn't be tottering around the dining room.

All the thirteen young girls were trying out their costumes and shoes and parading in front of Alexis and Ben. Some of them were finding the heels uncomfortable. Alexis advised them to wear the shoes all day long, even if the leather cut into their skin. Today was not going to be about their comfort. Ben looked at one of the girls, who was walking confidently towards him. She gave him a flirtatious smile as she passed him by. Ben was amused. Indian girls never had such cheek before. She was pretty, and the best part, her hair was tied up in a tight bun, which pulled her eyes back and gave her a slightly oriental look.

"You?"

The girl turned.

"Can you run in those shoes?"

She grinned and promptly darted across the room.

"Good, now pick up a tray, from that counter next to the kitchen door."

The girl walked confidently and picked up a large wooden tray.

"Now hold it up on the palm of your hand, flat. And walk briskly towards me."

Ben could see that she didn't bounce at all. He was relieved, drinks wouldn't spill when she carried them.

"Good," he said and beckoned her over.

"I'm going to put you in charge of the champagne at the start of the meal and coffee at the end of the meal. You will serve the Mayor's table. Do you understand?" he said loudly.

"Yes sir, of course!"

Peelo smiled and curtseyed as she headed back towards the kitchen.

Step one clear.

She was in.

***

Dabir woke up with a start. Sun was streaming through the flaps of the tent. The tent was empty. The first thing he realised was that he had a throbbing headache and his arm was hurting. He looked at his left shoulder and the bandage, and then swung that arm around. It hurt a bit, but it was better.

There was a buzz outside the tent. People were milling around. He spotted a young revolutionary, walking by, towards the weapon's shed.

"Azim!" Dabir called out as he stumbled on his feet. Azim didn't hear him, as he brushed past the tent flap.

Jaidev was sitting by the camp fire, polishing his rifle. He spotted Dabir come out of the tent and whooped with joy, slowly the entire camp began cheering and clapping. Dabir looked wildly around at the faces. He saw Harshal and nodded at him then he limped up to Jaidev and caught his arm in a vice grip.

"Ashok, Siddharth?" Dabir's eyes were blood shot.

Jaidev grabbed his hand reassuringly.

"We're all okay. Nobody was hurt."

Dabir spotted Suraj outside his tent, clapping and smiling. Dabir went up to him, and pulled Suraj, into his own tent.

"How are you feeling?" Suraj asked.

"I'm fine. I'm .... Nothing. I'm fine. What day is it?"

Suraj's smile faded.

"It's the day of the gala. Go, eat something first, then we'll talk."

"So, are we ready for tonight?" Dabir asked heavily.

"We are. But you are not going."

"The hell I'm not!"

"Dabir, you've been shot, you lost a lot of blood. You were out yesterday. Had it not been for Rewa..."

"What?" Dabir was stunned. "Rewa was here?"

"Yes, she came back in the boat with you and the rest."

"Where is she?"

"I sent her back to Peelo's house this morning with Ajoy. Once we leave for the city, I wanted her safe."

Dabir rubbed his hands over his face. Suraj put his hand on Dabir's shoulder.

"She was frantic about you. She didn't want to leave. She kept insisting that she had to speak to you, but I told her there'd be no one at the camp once we left."

Suraj looked at Dabir.

"And god knows, which one of us will return."

Suraj picked up a chair, the only chair in his tent and made Dabir sit in it. He leaned over him, with his hand on Dabir's shoulder.

"Are you sure you can come with us today? We leave in four hours. I would try to stop you, but I know that it would be impossible to do that if you've made up your mind." Suraj grinned.

"Where's Peelo?" Dabir looked up.

"At The British Club already. We made a plan without you and Azim was supposed to lead your team."

A voice came from the entrance of the tent.

"But now that Dabir dada is fine. I'm happy to follow." Azim, a fair, handsome Kashmiri revolutionary was standing at the entrance of the tent.

Both Azim and Suraj looked at Dabir, who nodded as he stood up.

"I'll get something to eat and then, get ready."

Dabir squared his shoulders and said loudly.

"We go back to the first plan. The Revolution will begin tonight."

He walked back into his tent and looked around. He needed a bath, a shave, and something to eat. There was some *roti* on the small stool next to the mattress on the floor. As he went to pick it up, he noticed the satchel next to the mattress. It looked familiar. It was old, colourless and stained. He picked it up and stared at it. He rummaged inside. It was completely empty.

Suddenly, he gasped and dropped it.

He had recognised the blood stains and the bag.

He remembered where he had last seen the bag.

He sat down on the floor heavily and groaned, suddenly frightened.

"They're here."

CHAPTER 23

Ekaki

The boy had been standing by the river, alone.

He was so tiny, Rewa didn't see him.

Rewa and Ajoy were in a boat, gliding back towards Chittagong. They had left the camp, half an hour ago. Their meeting had been awkward. Ajoy had come from the city to pick Rewa up, and Rewa had protested that she didn't want to go. She had been determined to stay back and nurse Dabir. After listening to her for a minute, Suraj had quietly ordered Rewa to pack up and leave.

When they got in the boat and left the camp, Ajoy asked Rewa, "Why didn't you want to come back? Dabir will be fine." Ajoy reassured her. "And he will be fine tonight as well. Nothing will happen to him."

"It's not that," she said and shook her head. "I wanted to ask him about... I just...wanted to talk to him before I left. Now I won't see him till after..." she said guiltily.

She already knew that Dabir was going to return safe and healthy back from The British Club tonight. Whereas poor Ajoy was going to lose the only family member he had left and here Ajoy was comforting Rewa.

Rewa looked away as Ajoy continued, "You don't know how scared I was when you didn't come back from the Mayor's house." Ajoy looked down at his feet, shyly.

"I nearly died. At one time, I heard gun shots and I tried to get in through the flap door. Look."

He showed her bruises around his neck and shoulder and cuts on his hands.

"I was trying to dig my way in. But couldn't."

Rewa wanted to touch the cuts on his hand.

"Only after I went back home in the morning, and Peelo told me that you had managed to get out with Dabir dada on his boat, did I breathe easy." He stopped and bit his lip.

"Are you alright?"

Rewa nodded.

It was a calm and clear day, and the sun burnt over miles of green thick forests and hills and the brown river, snaking through to Chittagong, brimming with the monsoon flow. Over the impenetrable thickness of the forest, she suddenly saw a steeple. And recognised the temple close to her village. They were passing by the unnamed village on their way to the city.

Her village. Home. Her last home. This village was where she had seen Amma, Kantha, Tuku last—before her family, her world had splintered in a second.

Tuku. Was his body still lying somewhere near the temple?

Suddenly she stared.

The boy.

He was standing at the edge of the forest.

He was wearing a maroon pant suit. Like a monk's costume. A tiny boy. Facing the river and staring at the boat. His eyes. They were blue. The brightest blue she had ever seen.

He was looking at the boat straight at Rewa. Their eyes locked.

You're here.

She heard him.

He turned around and walked into the forest.

Rewa began to shout at Ajoy to stop the boat.

A minute later, the boatman had landed the boat near the bank and Rewa got off and ran in the direction of where she had seen the boy disappear into the forest. Ajoy was left behind. By the time he told the boatman to wait for them, Rewa had disappeared into the forest.

Rewa instantly recognised the path. On the left was the huge banyan tree, and up ahead was the slope, covered with thick vegetation. There was the dirt trail that only the natives of the village knew, which led them up to the massive stone courtyard, that had been a market place for the abandoned terracotta temple.

In that courtyard, the body of her slain younger brother Tuku must be there.

Rewa ran up the trial. She could hear Ajoy calling out for her. She didn't stop and she didn't even think of asking Ajoy if he had actually seen the blue-eyed boy like she had. She was dodging branches, twigs and bent trees as she bolted up the hill. Halfway up the slope she stopped to catch a breath, and looked around.

This was the spot. She almost called out for him.

Tuku.

There on top of the hill was where she had been standing. Dabir and Peelo had been standing right here. Facing them with his back to the top of the slope had been the man with the light eyes.

Davon.

She felt sick in her mouth at the thought of him. This is where Davon had shot Tuku. He should be lying right here.

Wild animals must have taken him. She squatted down and began to sob.

"He's been cremated," a tiny voice said, and made her gasp.

On top of the slope, the boy.

He looked about seven years old. Small and fair and beautiful, and those big bright sky-blue eyes. He had light brown hair cut very short.

"We prayed for him, two days ago, before we cremated him. Was that his name? Tuku? He was your brother, wasn't he?"

The sun was behind him. Rewa was blinded for a second.

"We wanted to wait for you, but Oma said it needed to be done."

He turned and walked away and Rewa couldn't see him at the top of the hill anymore. She got up and raced behind him, up the slope, and stumbled through the courtyard towards the temple.

Rewa sprinted towards the temple and stopped in shock.

In front of the old temple. Stood the boys. Rewa couldn't count how many. All dressed in maroon pant suits.

Like in her dream.

They stood silently, staring at Rewa. Slowly, they began to move towards Rewa. She froze in horror. They surrounded her. Rewa found herself in the middle of over a hundred boys. She stretched out her hands to keep them away, but they didn't come any closer. From behind the group, there was a movement and the boys separated. Two boys came forward.

The boys from her nightmare!

One of them was bald, and one of them had long hair.

Rewa shrank back, but she was surrounded. As they walked up to her, the small boy with blue eyes appeared in between the two.

Their eyes began to turn milky white.

Rewa began to sob in fear.

Then, the three boys folded their hands in a namaste. All the boys went down on their knees and lay on the floor.

They were praying. To her, like she was a goddess.

From inside the temple, she heard a sound that wreaked horror in her heart. She remembered when she had heard it last. At the Mayor's house. The sound of a wooden staff on a stone floor, a step, and a leg being dragged behind. A figure was limping towards them. A figure in a bright red saree. She saw her face.

It was the oldest woman she had ever seen in her entire life. Old, bent, gnarled, she was leaning on to her staff and as she walked towards Rewa. She stretched out her hands towards Rewa.

The last thing Rewa remembered thinking before she collapsed on the floor was, Ajoy.

***

There was a sliver of light falling on her face when she awoke. She was inside a massive high ceiling room, it was an indoor garden, overgrown and wild. Trees bloomed from inside the cracks and crevices of the mud walls, and wrestled their way through other overgrown plants that stretched from one side of the dome to the other. The roof had caved in a bit and the sun trickled through to light a patch on the floor. Sparrows flitted around the ceiling and their twittering echoed through the room. Here and there, placed in between the crevices on the walls, there were small clay lamps—*diyas* flickering. It took her a few seconds to realise that she was inside the old terracotta temple.

She sat up suddenly. Sitting next to her was the old woman in the red saree. Rewa shrank away in fear.

The woman was swaying, with her hands to her chest, as if in ecstasy.

"Oh! My dear child! Look at you."

Her voice was raspy and weathered and deep, comforting and disconcerting at the same time. Acid poured over velvet.

"Look at how you've grown."

She began to weep.

"I held you in these hands when you were a child. I said to you that I can die in peace now that I've held you, and you know what you said? You said, not now Oma, you will live another hundred years. I told you I am already ninety-six years old and you called me an old hag."

She cackled.

Rewa felt her fear fade.

"You *held* me?"

"Yes, my dear child."

"Who are you?" Rewa asked.

"I am Oma, your *Daimaa*. I was sent to care for you."

She wiped her face with her saree, her eyes still wet.

"I failed at that, my Queen, forgive me, but look at what I've done when you were gone." She pointed towards the door of the temple.

Rewa saw the boys. All of them seated patiently on the floor, cross legged, hands to their chest, praying. It was then that she noticed that there were a few girls as well. But mostly boys. All peering into the temple, at Rewa as if she were an apparition. They were dark, fair, brown, Indian, Nepalese, Burmese, Bangla children. Some of them looked

Caucasian as well. The three boys were sitting right in front of them. Their eyes were not milky anymore.

"The eyes..." Rewa gasped. Oma grinned.

"They were 'sending' you. That's when their eyes do that," The old lady croaked.

"Sending?"

"Yes, my Queen."

"Why are you calling me...?"

"My Queen?"

Oma looked at her sympathetically.

"You have forgotten, my child." She shook her head sadly. She grabbed her staff and began to stand. The boys outside began to chant. Their lips began to move. Rewa realised that they weren't speaking out loud, but *she could hear them in her head.*

Oma stood in front of her and bowed her head.

"You are Jhara, our queen. Ekaki, the whisperer of souls. I am Oma, your Daimaa. We are your Anthsena. Your last army."

Rewa thought she was going mad.

"My name is Rewa."

"That is not your name. You have forgotten who you are."

Rewa looked at the entrance with the boys, and for a second thought of making a run for it. The little boy with blue eyes stood up, as if ready to block her.

Can he read my mind? Rewa thought.

She didn't notice that all three boys had nodded their heads as an answer to her thought as she turned to Oma,

"You are mistaken. This is...Please let me go."

Oma looked hurt.

"You think we've captured you? No, Jhara, we're just happy to see you safe and sound. You're free to go."

"I am not Jhara."

Oma cackled.

"But my child, of course you are, I recognised you and so did they. Three days ago," she pointed at the three boys.

"Did you not see them at Chakma? When they saw you, they were so happy. They started sending you right there and then. Did you not feel them?"

She looked at the three boys and slowly a face appeared in her memory, she remembered seeing the bald boy in the crowd and how he had stared at her. The boy nodded and bowed.

"My name is Aleya," he said softly.

He was Burmese and tall, the most handsome young boy she had ever seen in her life. Right next to him the other boy with long hair, was now smiling wryly as he sat cross legged, his right leg shaking.

"I'm Kanan. I was there too."

Rewa remembered and nodded.

The blue-eyed boy spoke up next.

"I am Fahim, but they didn't take me to Chakma that day. I was sending from here. I knew you were coming down the river."

All this was sounding absurd.

"I am so sorry," Rewa spoke plaintively. "I am Rewa, and I am no queen. I just happened to be there at Chakma. All of what you're saying isn't..."

Oma looked at her intensely, Rewa stopped speaking.

"If you are not Jhara, then tell me—all your life, have you not seen people's deaths, if they touch you?

Rewa's mouth fell open.

She knew? They knew about her?

Oma continued calmly.

"They touch you or you touch them and you see their deaths, don't you? Isn't that true?

Rewa was suddenly breathless.

"Have you wondered why? Why you have been chosen to see that?"

Rewa dropped her head to her chest. Oma continued.

"Then, three days ago, after Aleya and Kanan began to send you, did you not start to feel different? At the Mayor's house, the very next day, how did you come up to that woman's bedroom? Did someone bring you there? I was there. I saw you. How did you know where to go?"

Rewa remembered Eleanor. She spoke hesitatingly.

"I just knew. She...I can't explain, but I was downstairs and I heard her, I heard her *feelings*. They led me to her."

"And then when you touched her, did you see her death? Or something more this time."

"I saw...But it was different...I took in her sadness. I have never felt sadness such as hers. She's broken, she doesn't care to live anymore." Tears began to fill in Rewa's eyes. "She made me want to die," she said quietly. Oma looked at her sadly.

"Don't despair, my Queen. This was destined. You have the gift to see a soul's journey."

She turned to the monks outside the temple and proclaimed loudly, "She's here. Our Ekaki. The angel."

Rewa cringed.

"Please stop," she said loudly.

Oma sat down next to her. The look of reverence on her face made Rewa uncomfortable.

"You're calling this a gift?" she blurted. "It's a curse. It's a horrible curse."

Rewa felt blood rush to her temples. Years of anger and fear and revulsion poured out as she began to shout.

"I go through everyone's death. It used to scare me, but now it hurts so much. All I feel is fear and pain and sadness. All the time. I see it and I can't stop. I just want to die, just to make it stop. You don't understand, you'll never understand!!" Rewa sobbed. Oma tried to put her hand on Rewa's head. She lifted her hand awkwardly and then let it fall.

"Yes, you're right, I will never understand," Oma said solemnly, "I can't. I am merely your Daimaa. It is your burden to bear, my child. But trust me, it will end suffering and bring peace."

Rewa had had enough.

"I don't understand what you're saying and I don't know how you know all these things. Please, let me go, I need to find ...Ajoy."

Oma moved aside, and the boys outside got up and parted. No one was stopping her. Oma said softly, "You are free to go wherever you want. These boys will take you where you want to go. But don't you want to finish what you came here to do?"

The three boys stepped inside the temple. They were carrying a copper pot. It was covered with a red cloth.

Aleya, the bald-headed boy said quietly, "This is Tuku. He did the last rites as a father, but he said that you would right person to spread his ashes."

Rewa's eyes were frozen on the copper pot, and she almost didn't hear Aleya.

"Who did the last rites?" she finally asked.

Aleya pointed to man who was coming from the courtyard and walking towards the temple. He was wearing a dark blue safari suit. He had light eyes. He was smiling.

Davon.

CHAPTER 24

The Protector

He walked between the boys. He took off his shoes as he stepped into the temple. He bowed to Rewa and then laid down on the ground, face down as he prayed to Rewa. Rewa almost dropped the copper pot.

Davon.

The man who had killed Tuku, had also performed his last rights? The man, who had tried on so many occasions to murder her family, was bowing to her?

Rewa felt her head and heart would explode. She was frozen with anger and fear and confusion.

He straightened up but remained on his knees, kneeling in front of Rewa.

"I am Davon, sworn protector and servant of Jhara, the queen of the Dushonus. My family has been waiting to serve you. For two hundred years, we have waited for you to come and I consider myself blessed that you are here with us."

"You killed Tuku," Rewa said slowly.

His smile faded, he placed his hands on his thighs and looked down.

"Yes," he said, dispiritedly.

"He was a boy, just a boy," she began, raising her voice. "He was twelve years old and you killed him. You killed my brother," Rewa said and cried.

"I am sorry," The man said morosely.

She hadn't expected an apology.

"I had no choice," Davon said.

"What? Of course! You had a choice."

"No, I didn't. If I hadn't shot the boy, he would have speared me. It was an impulse. I reacted..." Davon put his head down.

Rewa didn't believe him at all.

"No, that is not true. You were going to kill us all. I heard you say that you were going to finish it. You had already tried to shoot my father. I heard you. I heard you at Chakma. You wanted Dabir dead."

Davon was staring at the ground in front of him, silently, waiting.

"That man," he said quietly.

"Dabir is not your father, that is not your family, that boy" he pointed towards the copper pot in her hands, "Was not your brother. You are not related to them at all. What you have known your entire life is a lie."

CHAPTER 25

Jhara

"Dabir is not your father."

Davon was studying Rewa. "Tuku was not your brother. You are not related to them at all, and if to protect you, I have to kill them all? Then I will, with no hesitation... for you."

Davon looked like a child, kneeling in front of Rewa.

"That is my life's purpose. No harm will come to you as long as I am alive. I will destroy anyone or anything that tries to hurt you. I was born to serve you; protect you, help you. *We* were born to do that. And that is what I was doing."

The cold-blooded murderer was on his knees, looking at her with such reverence. This didn't make any sense.

He moved to get up and Rewa shrank from him. He looked pained.

"Please do not be afraid of me. I am only your servant."

He bowed his head and settled on his knees on the floor. Rewa looked at him, incredulously.

"Why do you want to kill them, my family and my Baba?"

"HE IS NOT YOUR BABA!"

His anger was palpable.

"My Queen," he continued, calmly.

"Don't call me that. Please," Rewa begged.

He bowed his head and waited for a moment, then he continued.

"You are not his daughter. He is no one to you. You do not remember, for you were just a child. This is a terrible story and I'm so sorry to be the one to tell you."

He looked at Oma and she nodded sadly. Davon stayed on his knees his hands resting on his thighs.

"Almost ten years ago, Dabir kidnapped you. He took you away from your family, from your people, and raised you as an ordinary peasant."

What was this man talking about? Rewa's head was in agony. She wanted to put her fingers in her ears to keep her from listening.

"Tell me honestly, haven't you been kept captive, hidden like a dirty secret, running from village to village? Raised like a leper?" he asked angrily.

Rewa suddenly thought of the cage that had been her home for years.

Davon's voice began to rise.

"And, whenever your powers were discovered by someone in the village, your family would run away. They would bundle you up, hide you at the back of a cart, like a hostage and escape from there."

Rewa's eyes showed that he had guessed right.

"How do I know?" he answered. "Because we have been searching for you for years. We have followed every trail and reached every village where he hid you. So many times, we got to the village just a day late, or we would have rescued you years ago," he said angrily.

"We saw your house, two days ago. You were kept in a corner, shunned from the rest of your 'so called' family. Tell me if all of this isn't true?"

"That was to protect me, He loved me, he cared for me, he taught me..."

"He taught you just enough to use your powers for himself. I don't know what he had planned for you but he doesn't care for you at all. You are his weapon, his tool. That's all you mean to him."

His eyes were wide and he was pleading.

"My Queen, your purpose is far greater than anything *that* man could teach you. What did he tell you about who you are, where do you come from? Why do you see the souls?"

Now Davon's voice had steel.

"He lied. He told you he was your father? What kind of a father is he? That boy Tuku was his son, but he left the boy there, dead, and he ran away. I came back and claimed his body and performed his last rites. Dabir ran away to save his skin. He cares for no one. You, his wife, his son are all tools to be *used* by him."

Rewa suddenly saw tears in Davon's eyes. He covered his face with his hands.

"Lord knows, I will regret what happened two days ago for the rest of my life. I didn't want to kill a child. I had no plans to hurt him. My Queen, you appeared so suddenly at the top of the hill and I couldn't believe my eyes, I recognised you instantly. And then when I turned, Tuku was charging at me with the spear. I ...it happened. I fired the pistol. If I hadn't done that. He would have stabbed me."

Rewa wasn't ready to believe him at all.

"Tuku was just a boy. He was just standing there and you shot him."

"No, he was stalking all of us, he had been stalking us, ever since you and that boy Ajoy landed in the jungle. He was stalking you when you reached the house and he was stalking us, when we entered the jungle. I felt it. Didn't you feel it too?

She *had* felt it.

"He was just a boy, a harmless boy," Rewa was muttering,

"Nobody around Dabir is harmless," Davon answered. "Everyone around him is controlled by him. Manipulated and hypnotized to do anything he bids them to do, even kill anyone. Especially anyone who comes close to you."

"Hypnotized?"

"You saw Tuku before I shot him. Didn't you see? Wasn't the boy acting strange? He didn't know what he was being made to do. He wasn't a child at that time. He was an assassin and he was getting ready to kill."

Tuku *had* killed a man. Stalked him like a hunter and then speared him without remorse. She remembered the sound Tuku had made when he had charged at Davon. A wild cry, like an animal, not human. She remembered what Kantha had said cryptically, that Tuku *"was in a dreaming"*.

Kantha had said that Baba had spoken to Tuku. That was the last time anyone had seen Tuku before he appeared in the jungle like a wild animal.

Baba had hypnotized Tuku? She shook her head vehemently.

"You all are wrong. Please listen to me. You are all mistaken. Baba is not like that at all, He is a freedom fighter, a poet and an artist. He didn't kidnap me, he loves me. Look!"

She ran to her cloth bag and pulled out the drawings she had discovered in the shack last night. The beautiful pencil drawings of Rewa. She had carried them with her to take back to Peelo's house. They were beautiful drawings of Rewa.

"He made these. See? Don't you see that you're wrong about him?"

Oma dropped her staff with a loud noise and limped forward to grab the drawings with surprising agility.

"Where did you find these?"

"Last night, in the woods. In an old shack," Rewa said and stopped.

Oma had a mysterious smile on her face.

"Didn't you recognise that shack my child? It was your home for the first four years of your life. And I made these pictures, not Dabir. After you were taken away, I lived in the shack for three years and made hundreds of these pictures so that even after I'm gone, someone would recognise you. I imagined what you would look like when you were grown so that all of us would instantly know that you were Jhara."

Davon stood up and came up behind Oma. He said, "That is how I recognised you outside this temple. I had been searching for you all over Hindustan and there you were, right in front of me. But then Tuku got shot and that boy hit me over the head, and I thought I had lost you again. Once again that man, Dabir had stolen you."

"Stolen me?" Rewa asked and almost instantly dreaded hearing the answer. Her voice quivered.

"Then what happened to my real family..."

Oma looked at her sadly.

"Your mother and father were simple peasants. She made wicker baskets to sell and he was an iron monger in the city. You were only three years old, when you told them about your visions. They were simple but good people, so they called a very famous astrologer from Calcutta to meet you. He had heard of your legend, and he went back to the city telling everyone that Jhara, The Ekaki was born. As soon as I heard about you, I rushed from Varanasi, met your parents and begged them to let me be your Daimaa. It was my destiny. Your story was spreading, and people started to come to take your blessings."

Oma was shivering as she continued her tale. Rewa began to tremble too.

"One stormy night, that man arrived at the shack. I sensed something was wrong and I pleaded your mother not to open the door, but she was a kind woman, who never turned away anyone who came to seek your blessings. She opened the door."

The monster outside the door in the silhouette. Please don't let him in.

"He stood outside the door crying and saying that he needed to see the Ekaki, because he was going to die and he wanted to know what could be done to help his family. He said he had a wife and a young son. Your mother let him in.

The monster is inside the house.

"The moment she took a glass of water to him, he took out a knife and stabbed her. She screamed and began to run towards you."

The woman is screaming.

"I tried to run past him with you in my arms, but I was an old woman, and he stabbed my right knee and wrestled you away from my arms. I was wailing."

Another voice is wailing.

"Your poor father who had been asleep, woke up and the two men began to fight."

The other man? My father?

"I lay helpless trying to stop your mother bleeding, while the two men fought viciously. Your father was a strong man, but he had just woken up and the shock was too much for him. Dabir suddenly stabbed him. I will never forget the look he gave you when he plunged the knife in your father's chest."

Baba is looking at me as he drives the knife in the other man's...my father's chest.

"He saw I was awake and I was holding you tight, so he crushed my injured leg with his foot as I begged and wailed. I don't know why he didn't kill me, because he was looking at me when he picked you up and ran away in the night."

CHAPTER 26

The Family Reunion

As the sun was right above Chittagong, a couple of miles away, at the foot of the Korpos Mohol hills, fifteen soldiers from the New Indian Revolutionary Army stood in the forest next to the river, listening to Suraj Roy. He was inspired.

"God be with us tonight.

"The journey has been tough and long. It has taken us three years to get here. All of us have sacrificed much. And tonight, we may have to sacrifice our lives as well. Do not fear the moment. Be brave and fill yourself with love.

"For three years, we travelled across this country, in disguise, hunted by the British police and Army. Almost everywhere we went, we had to escape or flee, moments before we were caught. Dabir and I, spent those years looking for people to join us in our fight for liberty. We needed people who knew in their hearts that we are fighting a war where *we* will never reap the benefits of victory. The life of freedom is not for us. We will pave the way and we will light up the path. But we *will* fall by the side.

"Others will follow.

"They will run up the same path and when they see us lying by the side, they will pluck the torches, from our dead bodies, and they will walk into a free India holding the torches and their heads high.

"Believe it!

"Believe that we will never be forgotten. Every year on the 24th September, believe that we will be in the prayers of millions, for the rest of history.

"That will be the only taste of victory that I can promise you tonight. For us just the blood and the glory. This country has long been treated as a whore by the bandits who came from far and wide, only to plunder. Some came disguised as rulers and some as tradesmen, but they were all nothing but dacoits. It's time for all of them to die by the sword. Do not hesitate when the moment comes, for they are not deserving of your sympathy. They have had none for us for over a hundred and fifty years. If we are savages to them, then tonight we must show them how savage we can be.

"Do not let any one of them be spared. Remember we didn't ask them to come here, they came here and pillaged us, at their own will. But have we not asked them to leave?

"Have we not told them time and again that their time is up?

"Have we not shown them that we will not go quietly in the night?

"Have we not shown them that you can torture us, jail us, starve us, kill us, but we will not rest till they leave us in peace?

"They deny us liberty, we will deny them their life. We will wipe out every gora who stays on our land and profits off it. They are parasites who have to be crushed. Then, when every last one is gone, will there be a new dawn for Hindustan. Where we all live in freedom. Where there shall be no ruler and no subject. Where everyone lives in harmony and no man is lesser than the other. You may not see that dawn, my friends, but you shall set the spark tonight. Tonight, we will burn down the sign outside The British Club that says, 'Dogs and Indians not allowed.' Then we will burn down The British Club. We will burn down every gora that's in The British Club. Those flames will be seen and felt all over Hindustan. Every Hindustani will come out to light their own fire from that spark.

"God be with you till the end."

They got into three boats and shared a grim look with each other before each boat dispersed in different directions towards Chittagong.

The mission had begun. The New India Revolutionary Army was going to take The British Club by surprise.

Team one, Dabir's team, with Azim, Siddharth, Ashok, and Harshal in one boat, would jump over the wall and hide in the lawns. They would attack The British Club from the servant's road.

Once they heard the signal they were to storm the building. At 7:30 p.m.

Team two, Suraj Roy's team, with Aswanii and three others in the second boat would approach The British Club house from the river, and then swim up to the boat house. From the boat house they would crawl up the stone paved path and wait.

Once they heard the signal they would storm The British Club from the river side. At 7:30 p.m.

Two teams attacking from two different sides would catch everyone inside, off guard. An alarm would be raised and security from the main gate would run inside to aid and rescue.

That's when the team three, Jaidev's team would jump into action. Jaidev and four other soldiers would be waiting somewhere down the main road, half a mile away from the main gate. They would be carrying the heaviest arsenal of weapons—pistols, revolvers, and handmade bombs to reinforce and aid the two teams already inside. Once the alarm was raised, the security at the gate would rush in and the four people from team three would lay a siege from behind, trapping everyone inside The British Club building.

One of them would stay at the entrance and burn the offensive sign 'Dogs and Indians Not Allowed.' Jaidev, had asked to be the one who would set the sign on fire.

This was a suicide mission.

Whoever set the sign on fire would face the full fire power of the security forces and Jaidev was ready. He was praying and chanting as his boat was pushed into the water, and before it got midstream, Jaidev began to sing his favourite patriotic song, loudly

"Aye Vattan, Aye Vattan. Tumko meri kasam."

Fifteen men, in the three boats, now separating in the middle of the river, joined in the song with tears of grim determination streaming down their faces. Their voices echoed, till they were too far away from each other.

Then they all fell silent.

They began to pray.

***

The boatman said he would only wait for five minutes and if they didn't return, he would leave for Chittagong. Ajoy tried to convince him to stay, the man told him, there will be other boats, but he wouldn't wait. Ajoy gave up and ran into the forest behind Rewa.

In less than a minute, he was lost.

"Rewa!" he began to shout. But he heard nothing but the sounds of the forest in response. A branch scratched him on his cheek. He had been in these forests two days ago, but nothing looked familiar. Of course, that day, he had stumbled behind Dabir, Peelo, and Rewa who knew the forest like the back of their hands. Ajoy was completely disoriented.

"Was it the right trail that led to the house? Or was it the left trail?" He was mumbling to himself. And where was Rewa heading? The last thing she had screamed at him was,

"The boy!" And then she had disappeared.

The sun was high up and the heat and humidity was suffocating. He was drenched with sweat and the flies that buzzed around were relentless. He kept swatting and screaming out her name. He fell a couple of times and kept stumbling deeper into the forest.

He arrived at a clearing and to the left, far away, above the trees, the steeple of the temple. But the underbrush was so thick that the moment he went around the bushes to proceed in the direction of the temple, he lost sight of the steeple and was lost again.

Ahead to the right, he saw a wall. A brick and mud wall, at least eight feet high. He whooped with relief. He tripped through the twigs and ran towards the wall, and through the wooden door. It was Dabir's house. Empty.

The house was pristine and orderly. Everything was clean, scrubbed and spick and span. He looked into the bedroom and stared.

There was an area in the bedroom, which looked like a separate area from the rest of the house. The rectangular area had a fresh coat of paint, and in its centre was a burning candle, almost finished. The area looked like a holy space. Rewa was nowhere to be found. Ajoy was in tears now. He stood alone in the courtyard, frantic with worry.

There was a sound at the door. He gasped and turned around.

A woman stood, her head was shaved. She looked about thirty years old. She was wearing a maroon pant suit, like a monk.

"Ajoy?"

He nodded, tiredly.

"Come with me," she said and disappeared from the door of the house.

***

Rewa was too exhausted to understand what was going on. The entire last week flashed before her eyes and she felt her head swim.

"What is happening," she asked herself. A week ago, she had been playing right here in forest near this temple, and now her home, her life, her family was gone and from what she was hearing, her father wasn't her father too.

And she didn't know what to believe. Dabir, a murderer? The man who had raised her, fed her, taken care of her.

He kept me in a cage.

Davon, the man she hated with a vengeance was bowing to her like she was a goddess. They were saying things to her that made no sense. They had to be mistaken. Everything she had known was capsizing.

Nothing is what it seems.

She needed to breathe. She stepped out from the temple and stared across to the forest. The temple shaded the courtyard and the breeze was cool. The boys and girls sat cross-legged staring at her, they were making her awkward. Davon and Oma followed her out of the temple, but stood behind her, respectfully. This only made her angrier.

"Look." Rewa pleaded. "I'm sure this is just a mistake. If you just speak to Baba and clarify, this will be solved. He is not that kind of a person. He loves his children. He's a family man."

Davon looked at her.

"Maybe you won't believe us, but you will believe his family."

He pointed behind her. Coming up the slope was a young man and a woman.

Ajoy was the first to react.

"Rewa!" he shouted, hysterical and rushed towards her. He stumbled. He was about to embrace her; Rewa froze and he stopped. His clothes were crumpled and he looked almost frail. The scratch on his cheek was bleeding.

"You're alright," he said, brushing himself, embarrassed. "You're alright, I was so worried sick. You're alright."

He looked around and noticed all the people around Rewa. The man with the light eyes, the old woman and all these monks.

"Who?"

Rewa stared at the woman, who was with Ajoy and staggered. Instantly Davon was at her side, holding her up. Ajoy noticed, but he followed Rewa's gaze to his companion.

Finally, Rewa found her voice.

"Amma."

It was Kakoli. Dressed like the other monks and her hair had been shaved.

"Amma, why are you dressed like that? What happened?" Rewa was bewildered.

Kakoli looked at her gravely.

"I am correcting my wrongs. This is my penance. Lord knows I don't deserve forgiveness, for all the evil that I've done."

To Rewa's shock, Kakoli got down on her knees in the courtyard and lay down in front of Rewa.

"I deserve the hell I am getting, Rewa, and maybe one day you can forgive me for what I did to you."

This felt like a crazy nightmare. Then, the memory of Tuku flooded Rewa's body. She shook away Davon's arm ran to Kakoli and pointed at Davon.

"Amma, that man, He is the one who killed Tuku."

Amma was calm.

"I know, Rewa, Davon has told me what happened. I know it was not his fault and I have forgiven him. Tuku was being controlled. I was aware of that."

"What?"

"You don't know the whole truth Rewa."

Rewa wanted to shake her Amma, but years of conditioning meant that she could not bring herself to touch her.

"Amma don't believe them. I don't know why they are doing this, and saying all these things, but tell them that they must be mistaken. Baba is not what they say he is. Amma! This man killed Tuku!"

"No Rewa, I killed Tuku," Amma said quietly, and sobbed.

"Tuku didn't deserve to die like this. I do. But not Tuku. He died because of me. I am so sorry."

"I don't understand Amma."

Kakoli looked at Davon and Oma.

"Did you tell her?"

They nodded.

Amma smirked. "You're still calling me Amma."

Amma stood up. Oma gave a signal and all the monks trooped out of the temple grounds to the market place behind. Ajoy stood there uncomfortably, Davon put his hand on his shoulder and led him away. The grounds in front of the temple emptied out. Only Rewa was left standing there with Amma.

Amma put her hands on her chest in a protective gesture and looked at Rewa in the eye.

"They have told you the truth Rewa, I am not your Amma, and Dabir is not your Baba."

"We are nothing to you. We are strangers, kidnappers, who took you away from your real family and kept you hidden. I know what Dabir did to your real family but while we were together, I never dared to ask, that was the first of the evil that I did to you."

Amma was speaking in a voice of steel.

"I met Dabir thirteen years ago, when I wanted to be a revolutionary, like so many educated women in Bengal. I was studying to be a doctor. Can you believe that? But I changed after I met Dabir. He was daring and brave and inspiring and I fell in love. He made me feel selfish. He made me *want* to sacrifice my petty personal ambitions for the country.

"And so, I did. I gave up everything for the revolution.

"But when I got pregnant with Tuku, Dabir disappeared. I was left to raise Tuku, alone. My family shunned me, I had nowhere to go. I found work as a maid, in Mughal Sarai. He came back two years later. This time he had a four-year-old child with him. You. He said you were an orphan but I knew he was lying. I was just so happy to have him back. So, I didn't say a word.

"A week later, he brought a cage for you because he said you were a violent child. I knew he was lying again.

"But again, I didn't say a word.

"He would give you medicines, *totkas* that would keep you asleep for days and weeks. And because of that, you would have fits and you would hurt yourself. I would clean you up, feed you, and give you those medicines again. He would be gone for days, weeks, months, and I would follow his instructions. I could have tried to find out what those totkas were, but I didn't.

"I didn't say a word.

"A year later I realized that he gave you those medicines to make you forget everything. Your name, where you were from, all your memories had to be gone. You became Rewa, I became Amma, and he was your Baba. The Baba, who finally let you out of the cage and you were so grateful for that.

"I hated taking care of you every day. Hated what I was doing to you and hated that you looked at me like a dog looks at their owner. Hated that you were grateful. I wanted to shake you sometimes, hurt you, harm you. I despised your innocence.

"But I didn't say a word.

"I fooled myself into thinking that I was making a family. Even though I knew that Dabir was with other women.

"Can you believe that in those first two years, I never once asked him who you were, why you were with us, what did he plan to do with you? Because I *wanted* to be fooled. I was devoted to him, like a slave, like a pet. I would do anything for him. Had he asked me even once, I would have gladly strangled you with my own bare hands just to prove to him how much he meant to me."

Rewa stared at Amma, horrified. Amma's words were rushing out of her, pouring as if her body couldn't contain them. Briming and spilling.

"Then, a couple of months before Kantha was born, he asked me to do something more terrible than anything I could have imagined. He wanted me to help him get more children like you and keep them in a cage too. You know what's worse? I helped him, I helped him get another child like you!

"I was burning up in guilt that I would be doing something so terrible, but I kept telling myself that we were a family. I was doing it for my husband. Then one night, I was standing by your cage, and you told me that Thakurma is dying. You said *my* mother is on fire. You in your cage, banging your head against the bars, bleeding and vomiting and screeching.

"I knew my evil had caught up with me. I knew it was a sign from God, a sign that I should repent and change. I had a chance to atone. But I didn't, Rewa I'm so sorry, but I didn't. Thakurma died four days later because of me."

Amma stopped sobbing.

"I couldn't be part of his plans anymore. I couldn't. So, for the first time in my life, I went against Dabir and I refused to put another child through what we made you go through. I gave that child away, and I refused to tell him where."

There was a long silence.

"I have never seen anyone that angry. I feared for our lives. He would have killed all of us that night. The family, that I had sacrificed everything for, was destroyed. That night he broke away from me forever, and he broke away from his child too. Tuku meant nothing to him and when Kantha was born a couple of months later, he cared even less for her. He just used them as and when he could.

"He only thought about you."

"You are part of his nefarious plan, that I never dared to understand. I stayed mute and compliant. I was unkind to you and ignored you. I buried his evil under my yearning for a family. And now, I have none. No Dabir, no family, nothing!

"If you have gotten away from his clutches Rewa, then you are fortunate. Stay away from Dabir and you will be safe."

She gathered herself and looked at Rewa.

"Rewa, I don't have the right to say this, but I have learnt that you must always speak what you feel. Because words that are unspoken, they don't just live in you. They swallow you, till all that's left are those very words, haunting you, consuming you, destroying you."

She looked at Rewa, red eyed but tearless.

"Please forgive me, Rewa, for what I did to you and for what I didn't do for you. I am so glad that I met you before I left. I came to Chittagong to meet Oma, and ask for her forgiveness as well. That's a story for some other time."

Kakoli sighed and looked at Rewa. For the first time in her life, Rewa saw love in her mother's eyes.

"I am leaving Chittagong with Kantha tonight. I suppose we will never meet again, but if you ever feel the need for a family. Come and find me. I promise you, my child. I will be the mother I couldn't be to you earlier."

CHAPTER 27

The Dushonus

Kakoli was crying silent tears as she trampled over the forest. In her left hand, the copper pot was open. With her right hand, she scooped the ashes and dispersed them over the plants and trees. This was the forest behind their last home. Tuku had been happy here. And now, he would lie here forever.

Rewa felt tears flow down her face as she walked respectfully behind. They were both praying for Tuku. The rest of the monks and Davon were all spread out over the forest. They held flowers in their hands, which they dispersed as a token.

Aleya and Kanan came up to Rewa and behind them panting, came little Fahim.

Fahim spoke up, "This is the woman who slapped you and kept you in a cage." Aleya and Kanan looked shocked. Fahim continued, "Tuku was only nice to you this week? He was always mean to you earlier."

"Can you see what is happening inside my head?" Rewa asked tentatively.

"Only if you speak in sentences. If you have pictures in your mind, then I can't catch them," Fahim chirruped.

"How is he doing that?" she asked Aleya.

"Well, he's your *Dushonu* isn't he?" Aleya said matter-of-factly. "That's what he's supposed to do. But only if you're somewhere close by."

"What's a Dushonu?" Rewa asked, wiping a tear from her cheek.

"A listener, someone who can hear the mind's voice. Three of us can hear your mind; while you listen to all the souls."

"Me?"

Kanan joined in.

"You're supposed to, but you're far from ready yet. We were sending you so strongly at Chakma, but you didn't hear, you didn't even look at us. Don't worry. Oma will train you. She taught me."

"She taught all of you?"

"Fahim didn't need to be taught. He was sending and receiving before he was even talking. He's the second most powerful one here."

"And who's the most powerful one?" Rewa looked expectantly at Aleya. All three of them stopped and looked at her strangely.

"You," they said, in unison.

Rewa felt her heart thud.

"Do you see deaths as well?" she asked slowly. Kanan grinned. "No, that's your job. We are just supposed to help you."

"Help me? Do what?"

"Well, Legend says that because you see deaths, you are the guardian of the door and you will control souls just before and after death. Those souls will be your Anthsena as well."

"Anthsena?"

Aleya laughed and said, "I think we're giving you too many terms to remember. Your army is the Anthsena. Which means last army. The last army that humans will ever need. Also, they are called 'Last army', because they will come to you before they are about to die, so you can use them at your command. Make them perform the last task of their life under your command."

"I will command an army?"

Kanan guffawed and then, was shushed by Aleya.

"Well, not yet," he whispered. "You have to study, like we have been, for years. Astrology, Fighting, Breathing. History. We've studied how your legend began. Where the protectors came from. We've studied ancient languages, so ancient that only god and his angel knows that language."

"Who's that?"

Fahim made an impatient sound.

"You, of course!"

Rewa began to feel her chest close up. She looked at Aleya and Kanan.

"So what can you do? Apart..."

Fahim looked at Aleya and said, "She wants to know if you have any powers?"

Aleya picked up a twig and swung it around.

"When I touch someone, I sometimes see what has happened to them that day. A few moments ago, maybe. But our main job is that as your Dushonus, we have to give you our *vitt*. Energy. That is sending. That is what happened, didn't it? After Chakma. We sent you and you started to change."

Kanan quipped.

"But you have to learn to receive soon. It's exhausting, looking at you. Our eyes hurt, by the way, when they turn white."

Fahim jumped over a log.

"She's scared of those white eyes."

Rewa began to wonder if she could stop Fahim from speaking out her sentences even before she had thought them out completely.

Kanan picked up a flower and looked at Aleya.

"Aleya's also the only one of us who knows whether someone can be a receiver. That is how he has chosen them."

He pointed towards the monks. Flashes of maroon could be seen across the thick trees as they moved towards Rewa's house.

"You chose them all?"

Aleya looked sheepish.

"Not all, I mean, Oma got Fahim, he just arrived one day as a baby and I knew the moment he came in, that he was a Dushonu. Then Kanan also picked out about three of them. And I picked the rest. The ones I picked stayed with us, the rest of them were sent back to the orphanage."

Kanan shrugged wryly.

"India is full of orphans it seems. My ancestors died during the Bombay famines. That's where I came from. Then there were riots in Mymensingh which is a city in the north, where Aleya's ancestors were labourers. His mother survived and travelled thousands of miles to Chittagong where she died and Aleya was begging on the streets. Then Indian mothers who were maids with British, Dutch, and French officers began to have children that looked white.

They were shunned by their own, and not accepted by the white people because they were also brown."

He pointed to a fair boy in the distance.

"Jeev's mother tried to kill him when he was rescued because he looked too white. They've come from all over the world, even Afghanistan. That's where we believe Fahim is from. Oma says more will come. According to the legend, wherever there is war, the Anthsena will come from there."

Fahim was looking at Rewa when he spoke.

"Aleya, she doesn't believe you at all. She thinks we all are mistaken."

Aleya smiled.

"How can we be? You say you saw people die when they came and touched you. So, you called them to you, earlier, but now after we *sent* you, you went up to the Mayor's wife on your own. So, now you're finding them. This is the legend. The Dushonus get together and the Ekaki leads them.

Ahead, Rewa saw the eight-foot wall of her home and was suddenly filled with sadness. Her family was shattered. Amma was a stranger, and from what these people were telling her, Baba was not only a stranger but also the man who had murdered her parents.

Could I have been so stupid? Why am I believing these people and this crazy legend?

"It's not a crazy legend," Fahim answered chirpily.

Aleya shook his head and grinned.

"Oma will lose her mind if she hears you say that. Her entire lineage has been about you and the Dushonus, you know?"

Kanan was the apparent tale teller. He began.

"The legend began from a valley in the mountains, Jatinga valley."

Fahim interrupted him,

"Birds go there to die. They just fly there, and fall out of the sky. Because there are whispers of dead souls that hang above the mountains as a mist."

Rewa stared at him to see if he was joking. Apparently, he wasn't. Kanan gave him a gentle shove and continued, "They say that when the Dushonus arrive at Jatinga, the birds will stop dying. And the whispers will stop."

Fahim stopped walking.

"So, let's go, *bhaiya*. To Jatinga. We can all go together now."

Kanan ignored him.

"Oma ancestors come from the secret caves in Jatinga. They say that those caves are so deep, you have to walk in the dark for eighteen days, before you arrive at the heart of the valley. And once you leave them, you can never find them again. Three hundred years ago, Oma's ancestors were told that they needed to leave the mountains and be prepared for the Ekaki. They left the valley and began to live between the area of Gandaridae—Varanasi to Chittagong. Each generation passed on your story to their children and told them to prepare themselves for when you would arrive. This was the only meaning and purpose of their lives. They had been instructed to wait. Wait till you were here.

"Fifteen years ago, on the fourth day of February, for the first time in hundreds of years, astrologers saw spots crossing the sun's surface. That was a sign that the Ekaki was ready to be born. That's when Oma's people spread all across the country looking for you. Every city, every village, every town to find where you were born," sighed Kanan.

"They knew you would be born to a peasant's family and you would not know your own divinity till you were four or five years old. After the age of five, the next two years were going to be hard for you, because you would see death and pain in the people around you. That would be when you would need Oma's guidance and the vitt of your Dushonus. By the time you were three years old, people around this area were already talking about this child goddess so Oma came to Chittagong and found you in a shack. And then, you were kidnapped. She lived in that shack for three more years, waiting for you to return. But the legend said that the Dushonus would find each other so she set about finding us."

They were approaching the door of her house.

Kanan lowered his voice.

"For nine years they have followed every story, every rumour, every astrologer searching cities and villages and towns, travelling thousands of miles. Looking for the most powerful girl in the world. You.

"The girl who can cheat death."

CHAPTER 28

Davon

Three boats carrying around fifteen soldiers of the New India Revolutionary Army, sailed through to the middle of the river and then began to drift apart in different directions. Five minutes later, they could no longer see each other. They would all make their own way to The British Club.

The next time these fifteen people met, would be after they heard the signal.

The signal.

Which would begin the whole operation, and was to be given by Peelo. This was the first time an operation such as this was going to be led by a woman.

Peelo would wait till the people at the party were sufficiently gorged and wined. She would make her way to the terrace and fire a shot in the air. Then, she would go down to the dining room and shoot the Mayor and the Governor at their table.

The terrace shot, strategically distant from the dining room, would not cause alarm, but would be heard both by the people in the forest and the team on the boat in the river.

If the security at the entrance *did* hear the shot, it wouldn't matter, they were the furthest from The British

Club house. Even if they did rush in, both the Forest team and the Boat house team would have already stormed the dining room and it would be too late. The revolution would have begun.

Dabir had made sure of that.

Riots and lootings would bring the city to its knees by the end of the night. He smiled grimly.

The news that the Lieutenant Governor and the Mayor had been slaughtered by the New India Revolutionary Army, would reverberate through the Empire.

Everything was going to plan.

Except for Rewa.

Dabir sat in the boat thinking furiously.

How did Rewa get that satchel?

***

The house was dying already. Although it had been empty for just three days, Kakoli walked through it blankly. She picked up nothing. She said nothing. She stood outside the door of the kitchen and then, she walked out without saying goodbye. The rest of the monks who were sitting outside the house, a hundred of them, watched her go towards the river. She disappeared into the forest.

Rewa watched her go, from the courtyard. Davon was standing next to her protectively. She looked at him carefully. Davon put his hands behind his back. The big strapping man was squirming.

"Who are you?" Rewa asked pointedly.

"I am Davon, Protect..."

"Stop please. Tell me really who you are."

"My Queen."

"Do not call me that."

He squirmed again.

Oma spoke up from the door. She was sitting on the floor, her bad leg stretched out. She was staring out into the forest and not looking at them.

"He's my grandson, the only one of my ancestors still alive. And from the looks of it, will be the last of the protectors since he hasn't married or has any children," she spat.

"You're her grandson?" Rewa was astounded.

"Yes."

"You work for the Mayor, as his spy?"

Davon smiled menacingly.

"Dabir told you that?"

Rewa nodded. Davon spoke evenly.

"Yes. Years ago, I decided that the best way to know what's happening in the British empire is to become a part of the empire. So, I became a spy for them. I began working for the Calcutta office, and would use their contacts and money to keep searching for you. After you were kidnapped, I came here to work with the Mayor, just so I could follow every lead, and use every source to keep looking for you."

Rewa digested the pride in his voice, and asked, "That day in Chakma, I heard you say, He's the one. Then you pulled out your pistol. You meant Dabir. How did you know he was the one?"

"The night he kidnapped you, He left behind a satchel, which had drawings, designs. He used the same designs to make pamphlets for the New Revolutionary Army. I recognised the designs. Oma had described him to me a thousand times after he had attacked her. I knew instantly, the moment I saw him that he was the one, who had taken you away. I wanted to cut him into pieces."

He shifted uncomfortably again.

"We thought he might have harmed you all these years."

Rewa thought of the cage Dabir had kept her in. Davon was looking at her in wonder when he said, "I...now that you're here, if you say so, I will not go after him. You're here, you're safe, that's all that matters."

Rewa turned and looked at the old woman, basking in the setting sun in the courtyard.

"Oma is..."

"My great grandmother."

"How old is she?"

"Nobody knows, but she says she's a hundred and ten years old. Her voice definitely sounds like it."

Rewa laughed. It was a beautiful sound. Davon looked at her, his eyes shining.

"You need to trust her. She will teach you. She's been waiting for you since before even I was born."

Rewa bit her lip. Davon understood.

"You are to call me Davon," he said bowing his head.

"Davon ji."

"Davon."

"Could it be possible, that you could be mistaken about this? That I'm not the one you're looking for?"

He smiled kindly and his light eyes lit up. He didn't answer.

"Can I ask you one more question?" Rewa asked.

"Yes, my Queen." He saw the look of disapproval on her face.

"You have to obey me, if I say so?" she asked firmly.

"Yes."

"Then please call me Rewa."

He nodded, his face twitching, as though he was very uncomfortable addressing her by her name. Finally, he spoke timidly, "Rewa."

Rewa grinned. "What I don't understand is that if Dabir can control and hypnotize everyone, how come he never did that to me?"

Davon smiled. "You're *the Ekaki*. He cannot control you at all, you are far too powerful for him. He must have tried and failed. You were also only a child so the only way to control you is to keep you captive and scared. But he could manipulate everyone around you."

"Two years ago, we reached a village near Dhaka, and found out that we had missed you by three days. When we spoke to the neighbours, they sounded dazed and confused. They were unable to remember any details about you or the rest of the family. Simple things like names and what you looked like. They tried to remember but they couldn't. That is when I knew that he had played with their minds."

Ajoy came to the door of the hut. He saw the two of them talking and went back out again. Davon looked at Rewa piercingly.

"This boy was with him at Chakma? His *revolutionary family*? Do you trust him?"

Rewa was taken aback.

Ajoy?

"Don't," Dabir said grimly. "They all belong to him. They are devoted to him. Their cause is not Hindustan. Their cause is Dabir."

"What are you going to do with me, now?" she asked.

"Do with you?" Davon stared at her, taken aback. "I... er... nothing. We're not going to *do* anything with you, my Queen. I will..."

"Please don't call me 'my Queen' and please don't say, 'you're going to serve me.' Please."

He stopped; this was exactly what he was going to say. He smiled. This was confusing. She was beginning to like the man she had hated so intensely.

Oma was looking at her, appraising her head to foot, with a smile on her old, wrinkled face. Rewa found it disconcerting.

She walked closer to her and asked, "If I am your Ekaki Oma...What am I supposed to do next?"

"You must learn to remember."

Oma stood up and took Rewa by the hand, out of the courtyard. The monks all straightened up in anticipation. Ajoy found himself pushed to the back, almost into the trees as the crowd began to flock towards the hut. They fanned out and settled on the little path outside. Oma and Rewa were facing the forest. Aleya, Kanan, and Fahim sat down cross-legged facing the congregation. Ajoy stared at the three boys in horror. Their eyes began to turn milky white. Rewa stood there in the center of the doorway.

Oma spread her arms out.

"Close your eyes my child. Just let your heart remember. These are not chants, these are the sounds of your soul. The universe knows them. You know them."

Ajoy staggered back. Everyone's lips were moving, but he couldn't hear anything. The woods were silent. As if all sound had been sucked out, yet Rewa was crying. Rewa was covering her ears as if someone was screaming. He wanted to run up to her and hold her. This was torture.

There was a sound.

A young monk from the crowd, was choking. Rewa began to scream

Stop! Stop! Please!

Rewa collapsed in Oma's arms.

***

"The universe began with a sound. The sound of *Om*. It was the sound of the universe creating itself. Then, they say, everything exploded into a million lights. Stars, planets, animals, plants and us each of us were created as a result of the sound. Now, each of us has a light, and a sound which we carry from the source. The Ekaki knows each melody. She knows the language of the soul, which is beyond words. The sound gets louder, when it's time to leave the earthly plane. And that's when she can hear it."

"She means, when we're about to die," Kanan said dryly. He mimicked a hanging —tongue sticking out, head on one side, eyes closed and hands acting like they're holding a noose. Oma glared at him and continued.

"The Ekaki hears the language when it becomes loud."

Kanan retorted, "Well, maybe not today," he smiled encouragingly. Rewa was still dizzy.

"Maybe not ever," she said weakly.

Oma was kind. "My child, this was just the first time. You will remember. Give it some time."

They were all sitting in the courtyard of the house, watching the sun go down in the west. There was a cool breeze. Oma had wrapped Rewa in a sheet, despite the burqa and the gloves, Rewa was cold. Aleya, Kanan sat next to her. Fahim played inside the house.

Ajoy sat away, staring at all of them as if in a dream. He did not know how to make sense of what he had just seen. He just wanted to get Rewa safe, away from all these people. He wanted to be home and he wanted the day and the night to be over.

Had Rewa forgotten? Today was the night of the attack. And he was here in this forest, in an abandoned hut. He wondered what Peelo must be doing at that moment. In a couple of hours, she, along with the rest of the soldiers would storm The British Club, and life as they knew it, would change for ever. But here he was, with these strange witches and wizards and black magic tantrics, God knows what. Doing strange things to Rewa.

Who is Rewa?

He was staring at her in wonder. He had seen her six days ago and she had been a pretty, quiet, scared little child and here she was being treated as some sort of cult Queen and witch.

What have we all gotten into?

A young monk stood by the door. He was the one who had choked earlier. He stood by the door. He was about ten years old, dark with small eyes. Ajoy guessed he was from the hills. Oma rasped, "Speak up child. What do you want?"

The boy looked frightened.

"I heard something. Something...she sent."

He pointed towards Rewa.

There was a long moment of silence. Aleya, and Kanan looked at each other and shrugged.

"We didn't receive anything from Jhara."

Davon stepped in behind the boy.

"What did she send my child?" Oma asked the boy.

"I heard the name Tukul. I heard these words—remember this night Rewa, because it starts here."

The boy looked terrified.

"I know the voice. It was *Rakshasuaru*."

There was a gasp. They were all staring at her. Oma, Davon, Kanan, and Aleya. For the first time, she saw fear in their eyes.

"I don't understand," Rewa muttered.

Oma's voice was trembling. "Did she look like Tukul?"

Rewa nodded and said quietly, "But Tukul is dead. I know that. She just led me to the shack."

Davon's eyes went wide. "Did she touch you?" His voice was hoarse. Rewa shook her head. Davon said ominously,

"She's here."

***

Two minutes later, a hundred and four monks, a man, a boy, a girl were hurrying towards the river. Four monks had placed Oma on a chair and were carrying her on that chair as they ran almost effortlessly. Everyone looked terrified.

Rewa ran up to Aleya. "What is going on?"

He looked at her grimly as they ran down the path.

"If you're an angel sent to earth to help the souls, don't you think that there would also be demons sent to stop you?"

CHAPTER 29

Death Is Destiny

As Rewa scurried down the trail towards the river, she realised that all them had formed a protective layer around her. She was surrounded by people who were running with her, but not touching her at all. She needed air. She needed to process all that had been happening to her. The three Dushonus were running with her, as she grabbed her burqa was coming under her feet.

Tukul was a demon.

What was I supposed to do?

Aleya said that she was sent here to help souls! Was she supposed to have helped the eight souls?

How?

But Baba said again and again, "Death is destiny."

Was that a lie?

Baba did you lie to me about that?

Could those people have been saved?

Then another thought struck her.

The attack at The British Club was about to happen!

24th September 1932.

Peelo would die tonight.

Suraj Roy would die tonight.

Eleanor would die tonight.

What if she could stop the attack?

What if she could save them?

Save Peelo? And Suraj Roy?

And maybe save hundreds of British officials at the British Club, and thousands across the city.

The whole throng was running towards the river. Rewa saw the green of the water reflecting the setting sun. Two massive boats magically appeared to be anchored near the river bank. Fahim, Kanan, and Aleya ran ahead, Rewa looked around to see where Ajoy was. He was trailing the whole group, stumbling, but keeping up. She wanted to talk to him urgently.

Suddenly, Rewa almost crashed into one of the boys. Davon had stopped. He turned around and put his hand up as a signal. Everyone stopped running. He looked straight at Rewa. He looked furious as he began striding towards Rewa. Rewa backed off in fear.

Davon came right up to her. His voice was loud, and seething.

"The New India Revolutionary Army is attacking The British Club? Why didn't you tell me?

Fahim's head appeared from behind Davon, sheepishly.

Rewa's heart sank. *Fahim!*

She almost screamed in frustration. Fahim had heard her mind. And now, Davon knew everything.

CHAPTER 30

The Gala Begins

By 8 p.m. the party was going well. The massive dining room was buzzing. Dinner was underway. The first course had been served. Under the oak staircase, the band played discreetly.

Richard was bored. The Lieutenant Governor Edward Bayley was a dreary man. He hated India, hated Calcutta, hated the humidity, hated the food, hated the people, hated the fact that he was there. There wasn't much that he didn't complain about.

Edward had the widest forehead Richard had ever seen and long hair straggling at the back of his head. With jowls that quivered every time he spoke, he gave the impression of being an old basset hound, especially with the greying moustache covering his lips and showing the whites of the foam of his drink.

He even spoke in a whine. Now three glasses of champagne down, he found it easier to complain about more things to Richard. He dipped into more cream and caviar.

"That ghastly Gandhi, I mean another hunger strike? I'm not surprised, the food here *is* mostly ghastly. I wouldn't want to eat it, but I'm more astounded that people still take his hunger strikes seriously. This time, it's been three days I believe."

"What is it about this time?" Richard asked, not really caring. This time the hunger strike was happening in Poona, clearly known across the country. He just wanted to keep the Lieutenant Governor talking till it was time to leave for home. He was worried for Eleanor.

"It's because of the Communal Award. One would suppose these idiots would be happy they're getting awards." Edward took a big sip of his champagne and continued.

"The PM, that MacDonald fellow, wanted to give awards for the lower castes, something called the communal award and Gandhi doesn't like it. Can't make up his mind that man. Keeps on blabbering about educating everyone. What about the entire lot of those untouchable fellows, don't they deserve an education? He's a fine one to talk, could afford to study in England, fat lot of good that did for him and for us. Entitled brats, all of them."

Richard was affronted at that. "They're pretty literate around here and around Calcutta, you know?" he said.

Edward smirked and said, "Well, of course they are, we brought them some culture and civilization, even some sport my dear man, but are they grateful about it? No! I mean we gave them a cricket team as well. Did you know the Indian team, so to speak, played us at the lords this year. Apparently, they lost by a hundred and fifty-eight runs or so."

He threw his head back and laughed.

"It wasn't even a contest. We might have just picked up that waitress and made her toss the ball around for us and we still would have won."

The waitress walked up to the table and replenished the Lieutenant Governor's glass discreetly and walked away.

Peelo looked at the clock.

The first course was served. The kitchen would soon be bringing the second course. It was quail so she imagined it would require some effort eating and that was when she intended to go to the terrace and give the signal.

The moment she came to Richard's table and smiled; Edward began to flirt with the waitress.

She was very pretty, young, and from her accent he gathered that she was well educated. Unlike the other girls who looked uncomfortable, the red skirt and blazer fitted her hips perfectly. She had small hips and a waist unlike so many Bengali women, but she had the sensual lips, dusky shiny skin, and big eyes, pulled back because of her hair being tied severely in a bun. She looked almost Burmese.

Edward smirked.

Peelo kept checking the antique grandfather clock under the staircase behind the band. She was aware that the Lieutenant Governor was watching her, so she played on. She began to walk a little more flirtatiously. Richard noticed and recoiled slightly. He stared out of the dining room into the gardens and stopped. He peered again.

Under one of the garden lights, in the distance, he was almost sure, he had seen two small boys. One of them bald, and one with long hair.

What?

He saw them for a second and then, they disappeared into the darkness.

***

The three teams were in position. Suraj Roy's team had reached mid river. Dabir's team was at the servant's gate of the British Club. Both had to enter the premises without alerting the security.

This was the weakest part of the plan.

Suraj Roy's team had to swim and reach the river path and walk their way up to the main Club House. Dabir's team had to scale the wall somewhere along the perimeter and hide in the lawns till Peelo gave the sign. Both teams had to accomplish this without being spotted. If anyone saw them and raised the alarm, it was over.

They had pondered and planned and plotted for years but had not been able to come up with any other plan to enter the British Club. They were relying on the fact that the New India Revolutionary Army had never before attacked civilian premises. This was against the 'rules'. No one would expect natives to even think of attacking this place.

Suraj and Dabir had both decided that rules and principles and *Ahimsa* was getting them nowhere. This was going to change the game completely. After tonight, the British would learn to never underestimate the New India Revolutionary Army. But first, they had to enter the place undetected.

At 7:30 p.m., Suraj and his men dived into the cold water and began to swim across the river to the boathouse.

At 7:30 p.m., Dabir's team began to scale the wall of The British Club.

The Mayor and his people had relaxed now. It had been three days since the stampede and nothing had happened since then. Suraj Roy and his people had run into the forest and according to all reports, had skuttled away to lick their wounds once again after their big recruitment drive, was a disaster. The Lieutenant Governor's visit had run smoothly the whole day. He had visited a few areas, given a few speeches and pompously paraded himself, more to the British contingent than the natives. There had been meetings with the Chittagong Business Council and tea with the British Army Generals.

Now they were all busy congratulating themselves on a job well done, and stuffing themselves on a feast they hadn't done anything to earn.

Suraj Roy and his four people emerged from the water, shivering and made their way up the path to the boat house. Inside, in one of the kayaks, Peelo had placed fresh clothes. Army clothes loaned by the *Gaddar*. In the same boat house, up the ladder on one of the high shelves above the water, were two pistols, four rifles, and a sack of ammunition. Gautam, before he was killed by Davon, had been filling up the sack slowly for over a couple of months. Now there was enough to mount a full-scale attack on the forty people dining, up the slope in the luxurious, magnificent dining hall.

They changed into dry clothes and made their way up the path to the row of bushes which hid them from The British Club, but they could see the terrace. They settled in.

Now it was up to Peelo.

***

Dabir and his people scaled the wall silently and after they landed in The British Club grounds, they stood for at least two minutes, listening intently. No alarm sounded, no one shouted. They could faintly hear the music playing in The British Club. They made their way in the dark. At one point, Dabir stopped and checked for a sign under a street lamp in the middle of the lawn. A tiny black arrow had been painted at the foot of the streetlamp weeks ago, it had faded but was still clearly pointing deeper into the dark lawns. After walking in the dark for another ten minutes, they came across another lamp with another arrow.

Gautam had done his job well. For a whole year, he had been recceing the premises and drawing these little directions for the team to follow.

You should have been here. Gautam.

Dabir gritted his teeth. This whole week had left him stripped bare. He had lost too much. He shook his head.

Not now.

They reached a clearing and a street lamp, with a large banyan tree which had now grown large enough to completely cover the lamp. It looked like a cave. Siddharth and Ashok both jumped up the tree. Two minutes later, Ashok yelled, "Here."

He lowered a heavy sack of four pistols each and rifles. Siddharth brought down another heavy sack of ammunition. Dabir smiled.

Gautam, who, would have been part of Dabir's team, had kept more weapons and ammunition for this team. They armed themselves and settled down under the tree.

Now they waited for Peelo.

***

Close by, in the lawns.

"I need to talk to him alone," said Rewa turning towards Ajoy, who looked mutinous and furious. He felt that the whole plan had been ridiculous from the start.

First of all, all the things she had just spoken about Dabir couldn't possibly be true. She had to be wrong about Dabir. He had known Dabir for years. Rewa had just spent the journey telling him that Dabir was a killer and had kidnapped Rewa and killed her parents. This did not make sense at all.

And he had so many questions that Rewa hadn't answered.

For example, who were these four Oma, and Aleya, Kanan, and Fahim? How did these people know Rewa? How had she ended up with them in the jungle? Why was she believing all this nonsense?

When Rewa said she wanted to go to The British Club and meet Dabir, Ajoy lost his temper.

"Are you crazy? Have you gone absolutely mad? They're going to shoot people there. They've been planning this for years and you're going to walk in there and just... speak...to Dabir? You'll be killed. Absolutely impossible. I forbid this. This is NOT going to happen; do you hear me?"

He had been screaming at Rewa, standing near the boats as the rest of the monks clambered on. Aleya and Kanan stood protectively behind Rewa.

Now an hour later. Ajoy and Rewa were stumbling around in the dark, in the lawns of The British Club. Rewa was leading him slowly, which was absurd, because she had never been here before.

What all has changed in the last two days? Ajoy thought.

The Rewa, he had met a week ago, to the Rewa he was following now, were two completely different people. She no longer flinched around people. She no longer looked like she was being hunted.

Her voice has changed.

Has she grown taller?

Or was she just standing differently? She used to have eyes that were haunted, now there was a glimmer of kindness in them.

And she smiled. He had only seen her cry or be pensive before. When he had agreed to come with her to The British Club, Rewa had smiled and his heart had begun to thump. He was happy.

What a word! Happy?

No, that was not at all what he felt. He felt light and he wanted to help her, please her. Anything.

It made him feel...

Yes, the word was happy.

The happiness was gone.

Rewa had led them to this spot.

They stood a distance from the banyan tree and in the light under the tree, they could see Dabir sitting on the floor with a rifle strapped on his shoulder and the other four men pacing, strolling and lounging around.

"I need to talk to him alone," said Rewa. This was not a good idea at all, thought Ajoy, and he was furious with himself that he could say or do nothing to stop this new self-assured Rewa.

Rewa walked towards the tree.

CHAPTER 31

Never Again

Dabir stood up; his mouth open.

Walking towards the banyan tree was Rewa.

"Rewa," his voice almost came out strangulated.

"How..?"

Rewa stood at the edge of the circle of light. The other four men stared at her. Dabir rushed towards her. She lifted her hand to stop him from touching her. Dabir noticed that but moved it aside and took her in his arms. His skin brushed against her cheek.

"I have been worried sick about you. Why are you here?"

He had never embraced Rewa like this before. She wanted to melt, but instead, she pushed against his chest, and stared at him.

"You touched me," Rewa said it silently, never letting her gaze shift from Dabir's eyes. "Don't you want to know what I saw? That's the reason right? That is the reason you kept me... isn't it?"

After a pause when neither one of them spoke, Rewa continued, "You're going to be fine tonight. No, you're not going to die. I saw nothing. You're safe."

Dabir stared at her, open-mouthed.

"Should I call you Baba, or should I call you Dabir?"

His eyes clouded and he looked at her disbelievingly.

"I think I will call you Dabir, after what Kakoli told me, because she asked me not to call her Amma anymore."

Dabir's jaw tightened and he gritted his teeth as he asked. "What did she tell you?"

"What's my real name Baba, wait..."

She walked up to him, "What's my real name, Dabir? Don't lie any more please. We both know that I can tell if a soul is telling me the truth or not."

She looked him deep in his eyes and said softly. "So... what's my real name Dabir? And what's the name of my mother and father? My parents, whom you murdered. You did murder them? Didn't you?"

Dabir was silent.

"It's Jhara, Dabir. Not the name you gave me. After you stole me away from my family when I was just a child."

She was shaking but she spoke calmly, "You killed them, stole me away, kept me in a cage. Just tell me why?"

The other men who had been looking at them discretely, began to look uncomfortable because Rewa was getting louder.

"I loved you so much, I wouldn't believe it when Amma told me. You who told me about freedom and loyalty and the country and the revolution. Why did you preach when you were doing all those things to me...I was just a child? Tell me why? And I will leave...You can continue with your grand revolution. I just want to know why you would do such a thing?"

"Why?" he finally answered.

He had a bitter smile on his face.

"You speak as if I did something so terrible. I did not do anything different than what was done to me. What else should I have done, turned over and died? I was prepared to die, but then I asked myself the same question."

"Why?"

"Do you know what it feels to have lost everything? And then when you learn to live with that, to lose everything for the second time! Everything."

"Your land, your money, your family, your history, taken away from you, eroded. Wiped out by these bloody goras. We were rich landowners, we had acres and acres of land, forests belonging to us, we were considered the lords of our villages. People used to clear the street and stand by the side when my grandfather walked into town. Priests used to wait in temples, till we showed up, before they began their pujas. We used to have twenty-five servants; my grandfather told me. But where did I grow up? In the corner of a dirty, oily, printing press. I was a mechanic in a printing press, even before I could grow a moustache. Sleeping on the floor, under the machine, outside in the courtyard, out on the streets. Like a beggar. This was what our life had become. OUR LIFE!

"I joined the revolution to fight for my country and for my people and live and breathe a life free of these goras. I became part of a new family, all people like me, who wanted liberty, who wanted freedom, who wanted their life back, the way it had been before these *firangs* showed up. Like how my grandfather told me it used to be. And what happened?

"Suraj laid down arms and went into jail, as calmly as that. Imprisoned for years. Manoj died at Kaala Paani and I was on the run, except that I had been shot, had been left to die and this time I have nowhere left to go to.

"Once again, I had lost everything. They raided my home; The printing press was demolished and my grandfather was killed.

"I became a beggar again. Me, who belonged to the race of the most educated people in the world, now begging off white tourists in Guwahati. I was finished, I was alone and sick in an abandoned shack in the mountains. I wanted to die. And I asked the same question, why?

"Then, I heard about this girl who can cheat death.

"And I finally got the answer.

"To win this time. To get back everything that I had been cheated of. I knew that this time I was going to get everything I wanted, for me.

"So, I got better and stronger. I had gone to the mountains to die. I swear I had. But I *didn't* die. And the reason was you. I spent two years in Jatinga valley, studying about you, studying about your powers, how to find you, where to find you. I began praying, meditating, training. I have learnt things about the human mind that no one has learnt in hundreds of years. I could do things no one could do. Then, I came for you.

"You think I did something evil to you?

"When I found you, I saved you.

"I saved you from those people who were going to make you a performing monkey. Your parents? They were already telling the whole world about this wonder girl. Did you know that people were paying them to come see you? They were turning you into a public spectacle. What did they think you were? A tourist attraction? *I* saved you from that life. I fed you, clothed you, taught you. And you think *you* had a rough time?

"I didn't lie to you about that Rewa. I meant it. Now it is our turn to rule the world.

"We are going to cheat death. Together, we are invincible. This is all for you and for me. Everyone can go to hell."

Rewa had expected to be devastated, instead she found herself pitying him. How alone, how desperate, how angry, how scared, how greedy, and terrified he was.

She spoke slowly, "Baba, Are you not even a little bit sorry? For what you did to my parents? For what you did to me after you kidnapped me?"

He had the grace to look ashamed as she continued to speak softly, "And you really think, 'we' will be a team after I found out all these things?"

Dabir signalled his men. In a second, they had grabbed Rewa's gloved arms and were dragging her up to Dabir.

"You think I will give you a choice? Tonight, it's my turn. I do not have the patience to convince you or cajole you."

He looked at Azim and Harshall who were holding Rewa's arms.

"Take off her gloves."

CHAPTER 32

It's Time

Peelo looked at the clock. It was 8:30 p.m.

In the great dining hall of the British Club, the Mayor and the Lieutenant Governor had finished their second course and downed two bottles of champagne. Edward seemed happier than he had seemed all day, and Richard looked more and more exhausted. The band had gotten raucous and the diners louder. Thank god, there were no women apart from the waitresses. The noise would have been deafening. The other girls were getting the hand of serving.

It's time!

Peelo discreetly slipped out of the dining room, pushed open the heavy wooden doors, walked down the wide corridor which was decorated like a museum—photographs and memorabilia of the Raj and of various British Club events displayed on one side and cheap imitation paintings of Cornwall Sea, Big Ben, Tower of London all adorned the other side of the corridor. The faded carpet muffled her block heels as Peelo made her way down the long passage.

She climbed the stairs up to the second floor and then made her way across the huge library—completely empty at this hour. At the end of the library, a door opened up to a terrace.

She stepped onto a dusty terrace, just one lamp above the door leaving the rest of the sprawling terrace in darkness. The entire terrace was covered with potted plants of various shapes, sizes, and smells. Someone had watered them untidily, leaving mud marks all over the floor. Towards the parapet twenty steps away on her right, was a large green pot on a wooden stool. Peelo smiled to herself, "Now!" she said aloud.

Walking to the green pot she put her hand under the stool and reached for something.

What?

She rummaged in the dark; the sack, containing a pistol and a rifle had disappeared.

She had checked this afternoon. It had been right here. She began to sweat.

No! No! No!

She knelt down and peered under the pot. It had to be here. Could it be the wrong pot?

No. this was it. It had been here. There was no other green pot like this. That is why Gautam had chosen it.

She got up on to her feet, her heart thumping.

Then she saw.

Shoe marks. On the muddy terrace. These weren't from her block heels.

She hadn't paid attention before. Someone else had been here.

"NO!" she shouted.

Someone had come up to the terrace and found her weapons.

She looked out towards the dark lawns on one side, and on the other side towards the river path. Both teams would be in position now, waiting for her signal. They would be waiting for her shot. But her pistol and rifle both were gone.

Peelo turned and ran out of the terrace, through the library. Back to the top of the staircase.

There must be a pistol somewhere or something that she could shoot with. Anything. Anything that would make a loud sound.

The band! The drums? Would they be loud enough?

She could grab a drum and bring it up to the terrace. Would it be loud enough for both teams to hear?

She racked her brains as she stood at the top of the staircase, thinking, when she realized something.

The band had gone silent!

She ran down the staircase, down the wide corridor, back into the dining room. She pushed open the big wooden doors to the dining room and stood there in complete shock.

The dining room was completely empty.

* * *

Suraj Roy and his four soldiers were cramped under the bushes. They had been waiting for almost an hour now. Waiting for Peelo to give the shot. The dinner would be over in an hour. They had to act now.

Where was Peelo?

Was there a reason she hadn't given the signal? Had she been caught? Or maybe she hadn't been able to slip out and go to the terrace, or maybe it wasn't safe yet for the teams to get into position and enter The British Club.

How long were they supposed to wait?

Suraj turned to the three men all curled up under the bushes with him. Aswanii, was most uncomfortable hidden on the floor. He was fidgeting and trying to keep his legs from falling asleep.

"Tskk..."

Suraj made a noise. Aswanii was sweating profusely. Suraj saw how uncomfortable he was and nodded. At Suraj's signal he stood up and looked across at The British Club. The dining room was up the path about a thousand yards away from them.

Then they all noticed together.

"Where's the music?" Aswanii said.

One by one, Suraj and the other two stood up. The dining room was completely silent.

"What?" Suraj shouted.

Thick curtains had been drawn across the dining room full length glass windows. They couldn't see anything inside.

***

Ajoy stood in the darkness in complete and utter bewilderment. He had let Rewa go ahead and talk to Dabir. Now the four men with Dabir had caught Rewa and were ripping off the gloves from her hands. He couldn't stand there anymore. He rushed forward.

"Dabir bhai, what are you doing? Have you gone mad?"

Dabir looked almost mildly perturbed on seeing Ajoy.

"I thought so."

He signalled to Ashok who jumped on Ajoy and caught his arms behind before Ajoy could reach Rewa.

"Dabir bhai, what is this? What has happened to you?" Ajoy wasn't even struggling. He was too taken aback to really struggle. And Dabir wasn't paying any attention to him.

He was stared intensely at Rewa and spoke to her softly, hissing, "The gloves are off. All four of them have touched you. Tell me now. Which one of them is going to die tonight? I know you saw something."

He walked up to her slowly. Azim and Harshal held her arms, while Siddharth and Ashok held Ajoy's hands. Neither Ajoy nor Rewa were struggling.

Dabir walked up to Harshall. "Is he going to die tonight? Tomorrow?"

Then he touched Azim on the shoulder. "Is it Azim? When? Next week?"

Then Siddharth. "Siddharth? Or Ashok? Don't try to lie to me. I know you *saw* it?"

Ashok, Siddharth, Harshall, and Azim didn't flinch. They stood straight, silent, grim and stiff.

Ajoy begged them. "Ashok bhai, Siddharth bhai, let me go. Let go my arm, I just want to talk to Dabir bhai."

It was like speaking to a rock. Their eyes were dark and they weren't blinking. They were in a sort of trance. Ashok didn't move, he didn't look at Ajoy. It was like he hadn't heard Ajoy at all. Rewa recognized the look.

Tuku!

Tuku had looked like that in the jungle when he had attacked Davon's men.

Ajoy was now shouting at each one of the men. They did not even acknowledge him. Any struggle was futile. Both Rewa and Ajoy turned to Dabir.

"See?" Dabir said and shrugged. "I spent years studying how to do this. I even tried with you Rewa, but now tell me," he hissed again. "Which one of them... will die tonight."

"Are you worried about them? Don't be? We are all revolutionaries. We're all ready for death."

"Just tell me, Rewa, It's not a big deal. I just want to show you *something.*"

Rewa was looking at him in terror. She cast a look at one of the men—Ashok, almost apologetically. Ashok, who was holding Ajoy, stared ahead.

"Aah! its Ashok, is it? See? It's okay. You don't need to get dramatic about it. As long as it's not you or me, it's okay."

Then Dabir stopped and thought of something and turned to Rewa. He looked at Rewa with his eyes wide as if he had realized something. He smiled.

It was the scariest smile they had ever seen.

"How Rewa?" he said almost kindly. "How does he die?"

Rewa looked down towards her feet. She couldn't bring herself to speak. No one moved for a few seconds.

"Aah, now I get it." Dabir said.

Dabir walked two steps towards Ashok, took out a knife and slashed it across Ashok's throat. Blood poured out of his neck as Ashok grabbed his neck frantically. Blood splashed over Ajoy's shirt who backed away, gagging.

Dabir caught Ashok as he tumbled to the ground. Then he lay him down and stood up. Ashok's eyes were wide and in shock. He was no longer in a trance and his legs were kicking as he clawed at his neck and stared up at Dabir in disbelief. Dabir watched him flailing on the ground.

"Is that what you saw Rewa?"

Rewa nodded numbly.

Dabir wiped the knife and stood up. He looked up towards The British Club House terrace.

Peelo still hadn't given the signal.

CHAPTER 33

The Dining Room

The British Club house dining room, at the British Club, had glass windows on both sides; during the day, one side offered a beautiful view of the serene river path sloping down to the river on the west side. On the east side, you could see the gravel road and then the sprawling green lush lawns. It was considered one of the most spectacular views of Chittagong.

At night functions, the row of lights lighting the river path gave it a fairy tale glow of luxury, and on the other side, the lawns looked exotic with just a few streetlamps sporadically lighting up circles of trees. The light from the dining room usually spilled on both sides and made it look like the only party in the world.

Right now, thick curtains had been drawn inside the dining room. The music had gone silent. Suraj Roy and his team couldn't hear anything.

What was happening? Had Peelo been caught?

The party had been going on full swing a few minutes ago. Where did they all go? The guests, the staff, the band, everything was silent and hidden by the thick maroon curtains. Suraj needed to make a quick decision.

Had the plan been discovered? Then the people inside would be attempting to get away. They would either rush towards their vehicles and call the security from the main gate. Any minute now, someone would be running from the main hall to call the guards in.

"Aswanii. You stay here and if anyone runs out of there, shoot. The rest follow me."

Suraj and two others ran up the path, instead of running towards the entrance towards the dining room, he led them all by the west side of the building and to the back. He stopped.

All the vehicles were still there.

They were all still inside The British Club.

Suraj made a quick estimate. There would be about sixty people who were still somewhere in the building. The question was where?

***

Azim and Siddharth had moved Ashok's body to the back of the tree away from the light. They were leaning against a tree, Ajoy sitting on the floor in between them.

Rewa and Dabir sat separately. Dabir looked at Rewa sadly and asked, "Why did you come here tonight, Beta?"

Rewa was startled. *Beta?*

Shaking her head, she replied, "I thought you...were a different person."

There was a moment of silence.

"I'm not, Rewa. I'm just someone who will not lose again."

"How is this winning..." She stopped herself from adding "Baba". She bit her lip. Dabir noticed and smiled to himself.

"What do you think is going to happen tonight?" Dabir asked.

"You're going to murder all the Britishers inside including the Mayor and The Lieutenant Governor. Then, riots will begin and thousands will die all across the city."

"I didn't come up with that plan alone, Rewa." Dabir explained like a teacher in a class. "This is the revolution. With or without me, this was going to happen. These goras deserve all the blood shed they get. Didn't I teach you about Jallianwala Bagh?"

"The riots across the city? What about that?"

"Rewa, how am I responsible for them?"

"Maybe not, but how do *you* win?"

He smiled, "Finally, you asked the right question."

Dabir leaned forward and spoke, "The revolution was going to happen anyway. If not tonight, then any other night, and any other way. The difference is what I'm going to do after. When I'm done here, with the Mayor and the Lieutenant Governor dead, news will spread of the new warrior leader. The leader of the New India Revolutionary Army. Suraj Roy was happy to go to jail and 'die for the people' and do everything for the Hindustanis." Dabir spat. "'The new leader" Dabir pointed to himself, "will organize Chittagong, then Dhakka and then all of Bengal. I will rule them."

Rewa stared disbelievingly.

"Why not? We've been ruled by thugs and foreigners for seven hundred years? This time they will be ruled by an Indian— strong, fearless, educated and most important immortal. A ruler who cannot be defeated and cannot die. Touch me now."

He stretched out his hand and grabbed hers.

"You see? I won't die tonight and I won't die any other night. You will be there to tell me if ever you *see* anything."

"But..." Rewa couldn't formulate the words. Then she finally asked. "What if I do *see* something happening somewhere?"

He smirked, "Then, I won't go there."

Rewa was aghast. She spoke slowly, "Death is destiny?"

"For everyone else, but me."

She looked across at Ajoy, and the other two.

"And Peelo?"

Dabir looked exasperated. "What is wrong with you Rewa? You've seen deaths before. You know what happens. Why are so worried about Peelo?

Rewa was stared in his eyes. "She loves you."

"So?"

"She's pregnant with your baby."

Dabir sucked in his teeth. He looked thunderstruck.

It was another two minutes before he spoke again.

"Did you see her death?"

Rewa nodded.

"Then, there is nothing I can do about it."

"You'll let her die? Because you want to be the king?"

He looked at her, mildly surprised. He smiled.

"Tell me Rewa, if the reason was different, would you be okay with her death?"

***

When Peelo left the dining room and went to the terrace to find her gun, Davon had sprung into action. He had been hiding in the lobby of The British Club, when she went up the stairs. The man at the reception didn't stop him as he ran into the dining room. He recognised Davon as the Mayor's bodyguard. When Davon threw open the doors of the dining room, the crowds began to grow silent. Someone said loudly.

"That's a native, isn't it?"

They began to murmur amongst each other as Davon ran up to Richard's table. Richard glared up at Davon.

"What are you doing here?" he retorted. "Leave please." Edward was staring at Davon and Richard could sense the disdain in his demeanour. Davon handed a note to Richard. Richard read the note and his stomach caved.

The New India Revolutionary Army is coming to attack The British Club right now. Your waitress is one of them. Do not look at her at all. When I give the signal, take the Lieutenant Governor and the guests to the basement, through the kitchen."

Richard began to sweat instantly.

The British Club! Why hadn't he thought of that. They had been very detailed about the itinerary for the governor and extra stringent about the security all day. Once they had traversed the whole city, he had relaxed.

This was a masterstroke by the New India Revolutionary Army. If they attacked The British Club and killed them all today, the Raj would never recover from this blow. The aftershocks would be felt all over the world. They had survived the 1857 mutiny, the skirmishes across Bengal. They wouldn't survive this. This wasn't going to be just a terrorist attack; this would be the start of a coup.

Richard clutched the note and looked up at Davon wide-eyed. Davon put a calming hand on his shoulder. Richard nodded that he had understood. Davon walked up to the band leader and whispered in his ear. Then, he left the room abruptly. Richard sprang into action.

He tersely announced that there was a rumour of some revolutionaries headed to The British Club and that they had to vacate the room in two minutes. Then, he grabbed a tipsy Lieutenant Governor unsteady on his feet and told him to follow him. Four officials of the Governor's security who had been enjoying the dinner as well, jumped up and led the governor out the doors, into the messy kitchen and down the stairs. Richard led the way. Miraculously, everyone followed quickly and without creating any pandemonium. The band, the bar tender, and the waitresses fell in line and briskly left the dining room.

Davon waited till they had left. He was staring out towards the lawns. He had not guessed about Suraj Roy's team coming up from the river. He quickly ran across the room pulling the heavy curtains across the windows. It took him about a minute before the windows were completely covered by the curtains. He stood behind one of the curtains and took out the pistol and the rifle that he had found under the green pot at the terrace.

The dining room was empty and the entire process had taken less than two minutes.

He waited for the girl to return.

CHAPTER 34

Ajoy

Peelo appeared at the edge of the circle of light under the banyan tree. She stopped when she saw Rewa and Ajoy with Dabir and the rest of them.

"Ajoy?!" she called out.

Ajoy got up to run to her, Azim grabbed his arm. Dabir rushed up to her.

"What happened? Why are you here? Why didn't you give the signal?"

Peelo was breathless. She had run all the way from The British Club to the tree and it had taken her five minutes to reach them.

"I need weapons. They know. I don't know how, but they know. Someone found out and took my weapons."

Rewa perked up.

Davon.

It had to be Davon; he doesn't miss a trick.

Peelo reached towards the bag of weapons as she kept on talking rapidly. "They're hiding! They're in the basement. They're all there but now they're armed. Someone has my pistol and my rifle."

She took the bag from Dabir and took out a pistol and a knife. She put the knife in her jacket pocket. The skirt had no pockets so she held the pistol in her hand.

Dabir took charge instantly.

"Azim, take Rewa and Ajoy to the river, take any boat from the boat house and leave right now."

Ajoy began to struggle and shout.

"Peelo, stop him. Stop this. Dabir bhai, please!!"

Peelo stared at Ajoy trying to make up her mind.

Siddharth pulled out a rope from his bag and began tying Rewa's hands behind her back, she didn't put up a struggle at all. Then, as Harshall held Ajoy's arms behind his back, Siddharth tied him up as well. Ajoy kept struggling and shouting. Azim slapped him hard across his face. Peelo cried out.

Dabir held her hand, "It's okay, Peelo," he looked at Azim and warned, "Azim. Behave yourself!"

Then, Dabir turned to the others.

"Siddharth, Harshall, there's no time. Get to The British Club now, wait in the dining room, Peelo and I will follow. But be ready. If you see someone before we reach you, shoot them. Don't wait. Shoot."

Siddharth and Harshall slung their rifles and the bags of ammunition on their shoulders. They held their pistols and ran out into the darkness. Azim began to drag Rewa and Ajoy. Suddenly Dabir said,

"Stop. Leave Rewa. Just take Ajoy. I will need Rewa at The British Club."

Rewa knew what he was thinking. He wanted her to touch people hiding inside The British Club and tell them if they were going to die tonight. It was going to be a cruel grisly game. He would tell them to their face, that they were going to die, before he killed them. She wanted to cry.

Ajoy struggled desperately. "No! No! Peelo stop him. He's crazy. You don't know what all he's done. He just killed Ashok. Peelo. Stop him."

Ajoy screamed as Azim tried to drag him away. "I will not leave without Rewa, I won't leave her here with this mad man. Peelo, Peelo, HELP!"

He began shrieking wildly and fell to the ground, kicking Azim furiously.

Dabir acted like he hadn't heard anything that Ajoy had said. Slinging his rifle across his shoulder he grabbed Peelo's arm. Peelo turned to Dabir wide eyed. He grabbed Peelo by the shoulders.

"Focus, Peelo, *focus* on what we have to do."

They stared at each other for a moment. Then Dabir stepped back. Peelo turned towards them slowly. Azim, who had been dragging Ajoy, stopped and stepped away. Ajoy scrambled to his feet. His arms were tied behind his back so he leaned against the tree and stood up.

It happened slowly.

From her right jacket pocket, Peelo took out the knife. She took three swift steps and thrust the knife in her brother Ajoy's abdomen. Then she stabbed him again. And again.

Rewa was silent for a moment before she began wailing.

***

There was a sound of a shot from the lobby of The British Club.

Davon stepped out from behind the curtain. He knew it was a warning shot. Someone was coming towards the dining room. The girl had come in ten minutes ago, looked at the empty room and run away again. She must have gone to get her comrades. The dining room doors had the ancient big bolt that was nailed to one side of the wall and had to be laid across both the doors to bolt them. He ran and let down the big bolt and placed it across the doors.

He had a pistol in one hand and a rifle on his shoulder and a bag of ammunition on his other shoulder. He had no idea how many of these revolutionaries were coming through the lobby, how well armed they were. He wasn't going to last more than five minutes.

He heard the sound of running feet over the carpet. They were coming towards the dining room. In a minute they would slam against those doors. He was alone.

Then, two men, the Lieutenant Governor's guards came running across from the kitchen towards Davon. They were both tall strong Irish men and they were shouting instructions to Davon who couldn't understand their accent at all. Thank god they had their pistols in their hands.

Someone slammed against the Oak doors. They realized it was bolted. They slammed against it again. The bolt held. More shouts from the other side. It sounded like three or four people on the other side of the door. They shoved and slammed against the door, a couple of times with no result. Someone shouted some instructions and then they ran away from the door.

There was silence.

He stepped back. He thought for a moment, before he understood what was happening.

He slowly turned to the windows.

They're coming from the glass windows. But which side?

Davon and the two Irishmen fanned out. All three chose separate tables and scrambled underneath facing the glass windows. Davon chose the east side, the river side. The other two chose the glass facing the lawns.

They still had advantages. It looked like there were about four revolutionaries outside and three men inside. The three inside would be under the table and hidden from view and be able to shoot at whoever came in through the glass windows. They cocked their pistols and grew silent.

Then suddenly the whole Club house went dark.

Richard Henley, the Mayor, and Ben Hardgrave the Manager of the British Club and three other men were making their way silently across the kitchen towards the dining room. The kitchen was messy, all signs of preparations in process. A party abandoned. Half piled serving dishes on various stations. Empty dishes piled next to sinks. Food strewn on the floor. Water tap dripping. Napkins crumpled near the door. Had the guests seen the state of the kitchen, they wouldn't have enjoyed the meal as much.

Richard grabbed an open bottle of wine on one of the tables and took a big sip and spat it out. It tasted like tap water. The wine was warm. He looked across a table and saw a half bottle of whiskey. He opened it and took a swig. His chest burned, and he shook his head violently. His thoughts full of Eleanor.

How ironic, he thought, that he would die first, when this morning, he had been so cruel and cold about her death. Here he was, walking across the kitchen holding two massive kitchen knives in both hands, and Eleanor was lying in her bed, probably breathing her last.

One of the men from Edward's contingent, a spindly, pasty thirty-year-old man called Charles who had just arrived from England a week ago, was mumbling as he crept behind

Richard. The knife in his right hand looked almost comical. Charles was from the British Civil Service; he looked like his most exerting physical activity would have been watching cricket on a Sunday afternoon. He kept mumbling, "Why are they so angry about the sign outside?"

Richard stopped, confused, when he realized that Charles was referring to the sign, 'Dogs and Indians Not Allowed'.

Charles continued to mumble, "I mean, we don't allow women in The British Club either. It's not personal."

Richard stared at him.

They made their way to the dining room.

Before they could open the connecting doors, the entire Club house went dark.

***

Rewa was numb.

When Peelo had stabbed Ajoy, and Rewa had watched Ajoy's stunned expression, before he had collapsed to the ground—his eyes were open and vacant, staring at nothing in particular. He lay on his back. A tear trickled down from his eye into his ear. The dimple on his cheek surfaced. Was he smiling?

The wails were so loud, and Rewa realised that they were coming from her. Peelo was standing a foot away from where Ajoy lay. She turned to Dabir, her eyes unnaturally bright.

Peelo was smiling, begging for his approval, her face was shining. She put her hands on Dabir's chest, like a child.

She's in a trance.

Rewa found herself gagging. She turned around and threw up. What was going to happen when Peelo realized what she had done. What Dabir had made her do.

Then with another shock, she remembered that the realization would never come. Peelo was going to die tonight. She would die oblivious about three deaths—her brother, her unborn child, and herself.

Dabir held Peelo's hands to his chest.

"Now go. I'll follow."

Peelo grinned.

It was the most grotesque sight Rewa had ever seen, then Peelo turned around, cocked her pistol and ran out into the darkness.

She hadn't even turned around to look at Ajoy.

Then the lamp above them switched off. The woods turned dark.

***

Suraj was furious and panicked. Peelo hadn't given the signal. They had all known it was a suicide mission, they hadn't ever discussed abandoning the mission and retreating, they had been so fervid about their purpose and so bloated by the thought of their own sacrifice that these possibilities hadn't been covered. Dabir had said, time and time again, that this was a foolproof plan. Obviously, it wasn't. Something had gone wrong.

He looked at his team. Aswanii and the men had quickly lit three torches and were holding the flames above their heads. In the light, Suraj saw their eyes, flaming as well. He turned towards them and squared his shoulders.

They understood.

Aswanii shouted, "*Inquilab Zindabad*!"

All four of them shouted 'Inquilab Zindabad' and rushed towards the dark Club house.

CHAPTER 35

Death is Destiny

I should have touched him.
I should have just grabbed his hand.
Then I would have known.
I should have stopped Peelo.
Oma said that when they're about to die, they will find me.
Is that what happened?
Did I kill Ajoy?
No, it was Peelo.
How could she do this?
Her own brother?
How could she?
I had seven days. Seven days with Ajoy.
I didn't touch him once in seven days.
I would have seen it.
How could I have not seen it?
Death is destiny.
I could have saved you Ajoy.
Death is destiny
I could have saved you.
DEATH IS DESTINY.
NO... I don't care anymore!!
Ajoy.

In the dark. In the shimmering moon light trickling through the branches of the tree. A tingling sensation crawled down Rewa's back. Like a cold wind swishing up her legs. Goosebumps appeared at the back of her neck and she shivered as her entire body huddled on the floor. She was sitting curled up, her knees to her chest, when something compelled her to look up.

She turned to Ajoy. His body lay a few feet away, his arms thrown by his side. She crept closer to his face.

He was smiling.

He was looking at Rewa. She was on her knees crawling towards him, when his eyes blanked out.

Rewa had the strangest feeling. Joy surged through her body. She felt like she was being lit from within. Like something was burning, right in the centre of her chest.

Ajoy was leaving. He was leaving this world.

Like a whiff of something, he was drifting through the air, passing her by.

His spirit has a perfume!

His body was on the floor, but Ajoy was floating. She couldn't see it; she could feel it. She found herself crying and smiling at the same time.

***

In the dining room, Davon and the two Irishmen hid under their tables, waiting silently. Richard and four other men stepped out from the kitchen and stood in the dark. Richard thought he saw someone under the tables.

"Davon?" he whispered.

Davon asked in response, "Who turned off the lights?"

Ben answered in response. "One of my guys.

Davon saw that they were five of them standing by the kitchen door, fully exposed to anyone who came in from the windows. "Get back down to the basement. Where's the Governor?"

"Hiding!"

A moment later someone shattered the glass windows of the dining room on the west side. But no one came in.

Everyone in the room stood poised, waiting.

The smell hit them first. Someone had set fire to the curtains in the dining room. Then, they saw the smoke.

The bottom of the curtains was on fire. The room was not dark now, the Mayor and his men could clearly be seen in the flicker of the fire.

Another glass was shattered on the other side of the room and the curtain lit. When Davon turned to the east side, a man behind him threw the lit torch into the room, jumped through the curtains into the dining room shooting his pistol.

One of the Irishmen picked up a plate from the table and sent it flying into his face. The man toppled and his pistol fell, but there was another man coming in behind him.

He came in crawling and sat on his knee. He aimed the rifle and shot the Irishman in the face. The Irishman's face exploded even though he was still standing, another plate in his left hand, his pistol in his right hand. He hadn't even aimed to use it. He hovered for a second, and then fell on his back.

Davon, from under the table, fired at the shooting man. He missed as the man leapt across the tables to unlock the dining room doors.

The man hadn't seen Richard and Ben. Richard charged at him with his knife, Ben charged at him with a just a blood curdling war cry, but before they could reach him, Davon stood up from under the table and took aim, and shot the man in the back. The man running towards Richard, spread his arms up in the air and crashed to the ground.

The sound of glass breaking from both the sides and shots ringing from the curtains. Two more revolutionaries were setting fire to the curtains and coming in from the windows.

I am counting four! Two of them are dead.

Davon thought, as he, Richard, Ben and the one Irishman ran back through the kitchen doors, back towards the basement.

Davon had an idea. He left them, took a chance, and ran to unbolt the Dining room doors. The corridor was empty.

Good. They were all outside.

He needed to call the police. His first instinct had been to save the people in the dining room and hide them. But now he had to figure out how to get them out of here. The blood bath that the revolutionaries had planned had been averted, for now.

The British Club had one telephone in the main office of The British Club manager, it was one of the twenty-two telephones that existed in Chittagong in 1932. It was a matter of great prestige that The British Club had a telephone, but it rarely worked.

Behind him he heard two shots from the dining room and a triumphant shout. The Irish man had shot someone. Another one of them was down.

Four came in and three dead!

As he ran to the lobby, he saw three revolutionaries come running in through the wide entrance from the lawns. One of them holding a torch in his hand.

Seven!

They hadn't seen him in the dark corridor, he kneeled and fired. A loud scream, and one of them tumbled down clutching his left knee and began wailing.

Seven, four down!

The other man dived behind him and the third one, the one with the torch turned around and ran back into the garden, leaving them all in the dark.

So much for bravery, thought Davon.

Then he understood that the man hadn't run out because he had feared Davon, instead he had run out because he had heard the bell.

A big vehicle was coming up the driveway, approaching The British Club house. It was full of armed men, and one of them clanging a loud bell furiously. The police had arrived.

***

A few minutes earlier, outside The British Club grounds, almost a mile away, Jaidev had had enough of waiting. The four revolutionaries were hiding in the trees in the dark, cramped by the side of the road, a couple of hundred yards away from The British Club entrance.

Right next to massive gates on the right, a sign 'Dogs and Indians Not Allowed.' They could barely see the sign from where they hid, but they could see that the six, armed guards were still at their spot. It was a big night at The British Club so they were highly alert.

According to the plan, they should have heard the shots of the other two teams attacking the dining room and should have abandoned their spot to run inside.

This should have happened an hour ago.

Peelo had been in charge of the signal. The signal hadn't come, and any minute now, the dinner party would be over and the guests would leave. That would be the end of this raid.

It was now or never. Jaidev was impatient and restless. He was going to burn that sign right now and die in the process. Let the other teams' plans go to hell.

This was his moment and he wasn't going to lose it. He looked at the rest of his team grimly. They all knew what he was thinking. He was going to storm The British Club and they would not let him do this alone, they would all go with him. They probably would be shot even before they approached the gates, but this was their mission and they were ready. The four of them looked at each other and braced themselves. They slung their rifles and their bags over their shoulders.

Just when they were about to step out on to the road, they heard the bell of the police van.

'It's started,' Jaidev said gravely.

Hannan, one of the men looked stricken.

"The police? Now what do we do. They weren't supposed to be informed till we were inside."

Jaidev stared around the group. "Doesn't matter anymore. We do what we were destined to do. The revolution has to begin tonight," he said softly. "Inqilab Zindabad."

They grinned at each other and waited in the dark for the Police van to pass them by on the way to The British Club.

***

In the lobby of The British Club, Aswanii was down, he had been shot in the knee, and Raquib was with him. Suraj ran out of The British Club onto the gravel path. holding the torch in his hand, running towards the sound of the ringing.

The police are here? How?

He could see the van driving up towards the parking space. They hadn't yet seen the curtains on fire. They didn't know about the attack in the dining room. The dining room windows on his right were shattered, and the curtains on fire.

He began whispering, "Inquilab zindabad!"

Then the whisper turned into a howl.

Suraj cocked his pistol, dropped the torch on the path, and ran towards the dining room window. He was shrieking like a wild animal as he jumped in. Richard, Ben, and two other men were caught completely off guard. They had heard shots from the lobby and were making their way cautiously towards the corridor. Their backs were to the dining room, when Suraj Roy began shooting at the figures he could see, shouting 'Inquilab Zindabad' continuously.

A lit torch was on the floor and the curtains were now fully on fire, flames licking the table covers in the room.

Two men who had reached the corridor went down, before they realized that someone had come in from behind. The Irishman ducked behind one of the wooden doors and began shooting at Suraj. Suraj leapt over the tables shrieking when he tripped and fell over one of the revolutionaries lying dead on the dining room floor. His pistol went clanging on the wooden floor. He scrambled towards it.

Then, Davon came flying back through the corridor to the dining room. He ducked behind the other wooden door and began shooting at Suraj. Before Suraj could retrieve the pistol, Police men stumbled in from the window from the lake side. They were six of them, all aiming at Suraj.

He began shrieking 'Inquilab Zindabad' like a madman.

CHAPTER 36

Dogs and Indians Not Allowed

Mudassar and Shoaib, the security guards stationed at the main entrance of the British Club, were staring in at the gates towards the main club house building when they were attacked from behind. It was their fourth month as security guards at The British Club and they were supposed to wait for just one more hour. The Mayor was going to leave early surely with the Governor and they would be able to go home.

But something strange was happening inside The British Club house.

Five minutes ago, The British Club had gone dark. None of the six guards outside had noticed that. They had continued to stand at attention and walk up and down the road.

Then, they had heard some shots from inside The British Club and the ringing bell of the Police van coming from the city, both at the same time. Mudassar pushed open the massive iron gates and let the van in. The other four security guards had run behind the Police van towards The British Club building.

Mudassar and Shoaib were staring at the darkened club building, when they heard the cries behind them. Four men with rifles and lit torches emerged from the darkness of the road, shouting,

'Inquilab Zindabad.'

Mudassar didn't have time to react. He was shot in the chest and Shoaib ran down the gravel path into the lawns, screaming for his life.

Jaidev stood there a wide grin on his face. The other three roared at the sight of Shoaib scuttling in the dark.

So easy?

Jaidev walked slowly towards the sign.

"Dogs And Indians Not Allowed."

It was made of wood.

Good, it would catch fire easily.

It was actually a very amateur sign. For a second Jaidev thought of the beautiful calligraphy that Dabir did for them. Hannan handed him a tin, Jaidev began tossing kerosene on the sign. He lit it with a torch. It didn't catch fire. He laughed and swore. He looked at the other members of his team. Two them grinned, picked up their heavy sacks of ammunitions and ran into The British Club tottering under the weight.

Jaidev tried to light the sign again. Hannan helped him by holding up the sign. When it finally lit, they looked at each other. Eyes shining, they grinned.

They were throwing back their heads and laughing when Shoaib the guard, creeping back from the lawns towards the main gate, and shot them both.

***

Suraj was bleeding. He had been shot in the arm, but he had managed to escape.

Two of Jaidev's team members had arrived at the right time, covered him, by shooting at the police. Suraj scrambled from the dining room floor and ran towards the lawns. The policemen on the lake side, overturned the dining room tables and began shooting at them from behind the tables.

One the lawn side, two of Suraj's men went down, shot by the policemen who had just driven in. Suraj didn't look back and ran towards the banyan tree. He needed to find Dabir.

***

Davon and the Irishman sat at both sides of the large dining room wooden doors waiting. They had almost run out of bullets. Davon called out frantically over the shots.

"Richard!"

"Here"

Richard was kneeling behind the Irishman.

"I'm fine. Ben's been shot."

The Irishman was saying something and pointing frantically towards the lobby. Davon couldn't understand a word. He turned towards the lobby.

Running towards them, in a red skirt, and a red coat, on block heels and shrieking incoherently was Peelo!

The waitress!

That's what the Irishman was shouting.

She was charging at them, with a pistol in her hand and firing indiscriminately in their direction.

Both Davon and the Irishman stood up and shot.

Peelo tumbled on the ground screaming piteously.

***

The entire grounds of The British Club were dark. The only part of the dark lawns that had some light coming from it now, was the banyan tree lit by a fire torch. Suraj scrambled towards the light. He didn't notice Rewa sitting curled up next to the tree trunk.

Rewa saw him enter the light.

She closed her eyes and began to rock herself gently.

"Dabir. What are you still doing here?"

Suraj was holding up his injured arm and almost shouting in terror. "Someone called the Police. Peelo didn't give the signal. We've lost Aswanii, and Jaidev and Siddharth and Harshall. We need you. Let's go, give me a pistol."

He ran towards a sack on the ground. He found one and got up.

"Come Dabir."

Dabir said softly, "No."

Suraj stopped.

Now.

Rewa hid her head in her knees.

It's now.

Suraj walked up to Dabir, he looked at him kindly. Tears glistening in his eyes.

"Dabir, don't lose it. This is for freedom. This is for Hindustan. Don't be scared. I'm with you. I'll be with you till the end."

Dabir looked at him, he was crying.

"I'm not scared dada."

Suraj put his hands on Dabir's shoulders.

Rewa cringed on the floor. She was rocking herself and moaning.

No Dabir, No Baba, Don't!

As tears began to spill down Dabir's cheeks, his face froze in determination.

"This *is* the end, dada."

Suraj Roy hadn't noticed the knife in Dabir's right hand. Dabir shrugged off Suraj's hand from his shoulder. He lifted his right hand high in the air and then caught the knife with both hands and plunged it deep into Suraj's chest. The sound that came from Suraj was more like a sigh than a scream.

CHAPTER 37

Remember

My name is Rewa, I am fourteen years old. I was kidnapped by a man, who killed my parents. Stolen from my own life, because this man wanted a girl who could help him cheat death.

I was drugged and kept in a cage. I forgot my name, who I was, where I came from. I became a slave. Nothing better than an animal.

I forgot that I was loved by someone. I forgot that I was special, not because I had some power, I was loved because I was someone's child.

He wanted to cheat death?

Because when I touch someone and they are about to die, I see their death in my head. He wanted to cheat his death, because I see the when, the where, the how, and the who—and he wanted that power for himself. This man travelled hundreds of miles to snatch a child from their family. He didn't care about them, or her. His need was larger. A man who had lost everything. "Twice," he said. He didn't understand loss at all.

His loss was bigger than anyone else's loss. His misery demanded greater sacrifice from the rest of the world. His sorrow demanded that he now lived at the expense of the whole world. That he lived and ruled, when everyone else should die.

Cheat death?

How can I possibly cheat death? Everyone around me is dead because of me.

Ajoy is dead,

Tuku is dead,

Suraj Roy is dead.

Ashok is dead.

Peelo will die soon.

But I am alive. Still.

Seven days ago, when Peelo came to our house, I saw a young girl, pregnant with my Baba's baby, a teacher, who wanted to help change the destiny of Hindustan. A girl who had lost her family but had still managed to educate herself and her brother. She understood loss.

I had felt love for the first time as a physical thrust in my body. Love, inexplicable, desperate, hallucinatory.

She was devoted to Dabir, he was everything to her. Her body, her soul, breathed love for Dabir. He had saved her, taught her, inspired her, changed her, loved her body and consumed her soul.

But for all the wonders that she had to offer this world, he had seen none, yet he had used her till she was vacant. Now she was a body, with a mind that was lost. At his bidding, she had killed her only living family, Ajoy, and she would die herself soon, before this nightmare of a night would be over. Peelo was empty, soulless, less than a slave, she would do his bidding till her death.

And so, will I?

What happens after tonight?

What happens to me? Will I escape that cage?

Did I ever escape that cage?

I trusted Dabir and now I will spend the rest of my life as the slave? Because I can cheat death? This worthless skin. This horrible, leather coating on my body, that only kills or seeks death.

I am Rewa the cannibal!

Come to me everyone, let me watch your death, let me suck your life and spit it out like a witch.

I am Rewa. I am fourteen years old and I am the devil!!

A voice inside her said, "Remember Jhara, remember."

Her breathing slowed down.

She remembered.

The lights came on—inside The British Club, and under the Banyan tree. Dabir sat by Suraj Roy's body, his tears falling on the dirt of the floor, he didn't bother wiping his face.

Peelo limped into the light, pistol in her hand, her hand bloody. Azim was behind her.

Dabir?" she called out. Her left hip had been shot and blood had trickled down her legs. Her hand, her shoes, her face was all covered in blood. She leaned against the tree. Azim tried to help her, but she shrugged away his hands. Dabir looked at both of them and saw disaster and defeat.

He stood up.

"Siddharth? Harshall? Aswanii?

Peelo didn't say anything. Azim shook his head. Dabir heaved a sigh. He picked up a pistol. Slung a round of ammunition on his shoulder. He turned to Rewa. All three of them fell back, their mouths open, their eyes wide in terror.

Rewa was floating in the air.

Her feet were six inches off the ground.

She made no sound. She was shining.

Her arms were outstretched. Her toes pointed. Her hair open and blowing.

She was looking at them, her eyes piercing, wide. They had turned milky white.

Rewa was flying.

Azim turned tail and ran into the night.

Dabir didn't panic. From the floor he picked up a rope and caught one of Rewa's outstretched hands and tied a knot around it. Then he began to pull. Rewa found her feet touching the ground and she balanced herself, and then followed him without resisting. Her eyes became her normal colour again.

Dabir hurried in front of The British Club, the fire had spread across the dining room, the staff and the waitresses were running in with buckets and throwing water. There was no sound of any shooting. No one had noticed Dabir dragging the girl away.

The 'revolution' had died in only twenty minutes.

His team was dead.

They had relied on the element of surprise, and those crucial few minutes when the guests had emptied the dining room had destroyed the operation.

But he was still undefeatable and he would still be the new leader of the New India Revolutionary Army. He had Rewa.

He hurried down the river path with Rewa a step behind.

Dabir stopped and Rewa bumped into him.

Then she heard it too.

Ringing through the silent night, across the lush garden, in the air, was an eerie haunting sound, a ghostly siren, an ululating chanting song. Children, singing.

A strange song, in an ancient language. The song resounded everywhere. From the darkness of lawns, from the river path, from behind The British Club house. A few voices at first, then ten, then fifty and then hundreds of voices, chanting and singing.

Rewa felt her mind clear and her heart lift, she began to sing.

She knew the words!

She didn't know what it was, what the song meant, but she knew the words and the melody. She knew how she had to shape her mouth and tongue differently to sing this song of centuries past. She knew how to bring the sound from the back of her throat and how to brace her chest to let the air breath through the song. She was crying and singing at the same time.

Then, through the darkness, sounds.

Pattering of feet.

Approaching. They had heard Rewa and were coming to her.

Dabir's eyes widened in fear.

From behind the trees, and bushes, from far across the whole garden, the song becoming louder as they came closer and closer.

Children. Boys!

They poured out from all over the garden, charging towards Dabir and Rewa. There must have been over a hundred and they were storming towards the two of them.

Led by Aleya, Kanan, and Fahim!

Dabir took one look at the horde and began to drag Rewa down the river path. He stopped. Coming up from the river path was another group of determined boys wearing the same maroon monk uniform. In the dark, a singing army, swarming towards the two. Dabir had nowhere to run.

Then, from the midst of the swarm. A creature in a red saree, bent, grotesquely, wheezing and rasping, surprisingly fast for the fact that she was limping, Oma doddered up with startling alacrity and smashed her staff across Dabir's face. She turned to Rewa with a grin on her face.

"Don't you dare touch her."

Aleya laughed at the pointlessness of her declaration after Dabir had already blacked out on the floor. He looked at Rewa still laughing, "We heard you. All of us. At the same time."

"But you got here so soon?" Rewa's eyes were wide.

"You .... flew?"

Kanan burst out laughing. "No, we knew you had come to The British Club, but Fahim had been hearing your thoughts for a long time. He was the one who told Oma."

Oma siddled up to Rewa and patted her head. "I gave them hell, that they let you go alone. Don't you do that ever again. Please!"

Rewa gave her a tight hug.

Aleya continued, "So, we were already close by, when you started to send us your thoughts."

Kanan walked up to her, "How did you do that so suddenly?"

"I .. don't know. I just heard someone say '*remember*'. So, I remembered how to do it."

Kanan was looking around. "Where's Ajoy?"

Rewa's face fell. But before she could speak. They heard a shot. Peelo stood at the top of the river path, pistol in her hand.

"Dabir!" she shouted.

Then she realised what she had done.

Up from inside The British Club, they began to hear sounds of people who had heard the shot and were running down the gravel towards them.

There were a hundred kids spread across the path.

Rewa closed her eyes.

"Hide. Don't make a sound."

She whispered and sent it out to the sky.

She saw her words float through the air till they disappeared into the wind.

All the boys 'heard' Rewa clearly.

By the time she looked down, all the boys had disappeared from the path. A hundred of them had vanished into the bushes and trees and under the stony path.

They made their way silently away from the river path up to the lawns. Their job was done. They had found Rewa. They began to creep into the gardens.

Rewa felt Kanan's hand on hers as he tugged her away. Suddenly the entire river path was completely empty, but for Peelo running down towards Dabir who was staggering as he stood up.

She grabbed his hands and looked at him desperately. "Dabir, they're coming."

She was crying. Dabir looked her in the eyes. "You know what to do."

He ran down the path towards the river, leaving Peelo alone, standing on top of a rock, weeping.

"I love you," she whispered to no one. Dabir was too far down the path to hear her.

She had never told him about their baby.

She heard a splash. Dabir had dived into the river.

Rewa watched Peelo from the darkness.

This is what she had seen when Peelo had touched her that day. This is the agony she had felt. The abject misery of losing everything.

Peelo turned and wailed into the night. She took out a pill from her pocket and put it in her mouth. Then she turned to the three police men who were coming down the path towards her and she began shooting at them. The three police men heard the shots and scrambled for cover. From the cover they shot blindly in her direction. Peelo kept shooting till she thought Dabir must be a safe distance now. She took one last look at the river, and she stood up and screamed, "Inquilab Zindabad!"

A shot threw her off the rock she was standing on, she tumbled down the path and rolled away. There was silence.

Rameshwar, one of the Policemen got up and looked down the path. He couldn't see anything in the dark.

"Is she dead?"

"Must be," the other policeman answered.

"Shall we go look for her?"

"Na. Let's go back. This place is scary. Did you hear the... the ghosts?

"What?"

"Ghosts of children singing."

"What ghosts? What children? What are you talking about?"

"I heard them," the third Policeman walked up to the other two. "There were some children chanting or singing. Must have been on the boat on the river. But this place is supposed to be haunted."

Rameshwar dismissed them as complete idiots.

"I was inside trying to douse the fire and I heard nothing. Stupid fools you both are. Come. Let's go back in. The Mayor and the Governor are leaving. Let's go and salute them."

Rewa left the boys on the path and ran down to where Peelo had fallen. Peelo was lying in an awkward position. Her right shoulder had a bullet wound and the arm lay open as if she was welcoming someone. Her head was thrown back and her left arm had twisted under her back. Her red skirt now torn was bloody from her hip wound. Her eyes were wide and she was coughing.

She saw Rewa and she began to weep.

Her mouth drooled. She tried lifting her head but couldn't. She was trying to say something. Rewa knelt next to her and *heard* the words.

Please forgive me,

Please forgive me, I didn't mean to hurt you. Ajoy.

I didn't know what I was doing. He made me do it.

Forgive me for all my sins. Forgive him for what he made me do. Am I actually saying these words?

Wasn't this the prayer we hated Ajoy?

Ajoy, can you hear me?

Even at this moment I'm making jokes...

Ma was right...we are idiots.

I am an idiot.

Rewa knelt down next to Peelo. She prepared herself.

She looked up into the sky and began an ancient wordless chant.

The monks were slowly walking towards the main gate of The British Club, when Fahim said slowly.

"The Ekaki is here."

The Dushonus left the monks and stood by the side in a circle. They held hands. Their eyes began to turn milky white.

From the wind, and the dust and the specks of rain, a mist began to form above where Peelo lay. Leaves floated up above her body, flying like birds. Whispers from the trees became a chant. Rewa looked up at the mist as it began to take a shape. Leaves, rain and pieces of torn cloth, stalks and stems from the garden, began to fly and take shape. Peelo was sobbing and blood was seeping out of her mouth. She looked at Rewa.

Rewa's eyes were milky white.

Peelo looked at the shape and recognised it.

"Ajoy," she said.

Peelo's face softened. The shape floated over Peelo like floating on a surface of a lake.

For a whole minute, the world turned silent. Then the shape evaporated. Peelo turned to Rewa.

Rewa saw her eyes cloud over. She felt her sorrow, her desolation, her remorse, and then her gratitude. Rewa saw colours, flashes, visible only to her, blinding her for a second. Her body and lungs filled up with light. She felt porous, like everything in her body had dissolved into the air and water and drifted away tenderly.

Peelo was leaving.

She was happy. She was gone.

Aleya, Kanan, and Fahim were standing and waiting on the gravel path as Rewa appeared in the darkness alone and trudged towards them. She was no longer wearing her head scarf or gloves. Fahim ran up to her and caught her arm.

"Now can we call you Jhara?"

When he touched her, the shock hit her in her gut. She came crashing down. She felt her head spin. Rewa had to sit down.

This can't be true. NO! NO! NO!

Oh God!

The moon was high up in the sky and in the moonlight, she saw Oma, Aleya, Kanan and Fahim standing and looking at her anxiously. She saw the guilt in Oma's face. Rewa looked at Fahim and thought, *"Is it too late?*

***

"She's still alive, but I'm afraid... not long now. Dr Martin looked anxiously at Richard, "I heard there was an attack at the British Club?"

"Yes, but I'm okay. They tried to storm The British Club. Some communists, I think."

Richard had rushed home, as soon as he had ensured that The Lieutenant Governor was safe on his way to his hotel. He had rushed up the stairs to the bedroom and Dr Martin had told him, rather gravely, that though Eleanor was still breathing, she was sinking and could probably not hear anything or anyone at all. She had been given heavy doses of morphine and would hopefully go peacefully in the night. This morning Richard had taken the information coldly, but now his heart was bursting as he looked at Eleanor, lying helpless on her bed. Mouth open and gasping to breath.

"Thank you, Doctor. Can you leave us now?"

Davon took the doctor aside and led him out of the room. He shut the door discreetly. Richard knelt next to Eleanor and tenderly patted her head. He had so much to say, but nothing came out of his mouth.

I'm so sorry my darling.

So sorry, I failed you in every way. I have been so selfish. With Daniel gone, you needed me and I wasn't there. It was always about me.

I thought I was being brave. I wasn't.

I was hiding. Hiding from your grief, hiding from the truth. I thought if I could keep functioning, I could somehow lie to myself that there was hope, that there was some sort of justice out there for us. That Daniel would come back.

But what kind of justice could exist for us in this world. Look at what we have done to this country and to this world. Look at what I've done to you, my darling. The arrogance that such things couldn't happen to me or to you. That we were somehow exempt.

I let you drown, you took my share of the sorrow and drowned in it alone.

I love you. I'm so, so sorry. Please forgive me. Go in peace my love, go in peace.

The door opened. And Richard said without looking up.

"Can you please let me have some privacy. Please!" He turned towards the door frowning.

At the door.

An Indian girl, standing there in the silhouette. Dark, and tall. Her hair was open and flowing in the wind. She was wearing a dirty and tattered burqa.

Her face.

He had never seen a face like that before.

When he described her later on, all he could say was, her face was so bright, that his eyes began to burn almost instantly. She was aglow. She was full of love. He felt her joy and her tenderness melt his body from a distance. His eyes began to water, he had to keep looking away. She stood at the threshold of the room.

She smiled; he felt his knees buckle. She walked up to him and turned to look at Eleanor. It was then that he noticed the small boy walking behind the girl. The boy was staring at everything intently. He had blue eyes. Richard stepped away from the bed.

Rewa leaned forward and kissed Eleanor's forehead. She whispered. "He's here. He's come home. Wake up."

Richard didn't understand.

Rewa looked up at him as she said, "Daniel's home."

CHAPTER 38

Daniel's Home

The little boy. With the blue eyes!

He smiled at Richard.

Richard wanted to die.

Daniel!

It was Daniel.

How had he not recognized him? He was darker. He would have been mistaken for a Pashtuni or a Kashmiri. He was dressed in a maroon monk-like pant suit. Richard could have easily missed him on the street. He looked like a tiny north Indian boy.

Hadn't he seen monks like this roaming around in the bazaar hundreds of times? Last week he had seen some near his office. Had he given him a coin? Or had he brushed him away. Richard couldn't remember. Pain cruised through his body.

Oh god, could he have met Daniel on the street and walked away?

The Indian girl helped the boy climb on the bed. The boy sat next to Eleanor's head. He touched her forehead.

Richard recognized the curve at the top of the lips, under the nose, they were so like Eleanor's. He recognized the shape of the chin. He recognized the texture and colour of his hair. It was brown and though friends and family had told Richard that Daniel would eventually turn blonde like his mother, Richard had known that wasn't going to happen. And now here he was Daniel, with brown hair. He moved towards the boy and then stopped abruptly.

Was this Daniel?

Oh god, but how? How tonight? How here?

Who is this girl?

His heart was beating as he looked at the boy again.

Am I so desperate for a miracle? What if this isn't Daniel? This bloody country is full of maniacs and con artists!

He racked his brains for some sort of identifying feature, anything that would prove this was Daniel. He couldn't come up with anything.

Then Eleanor opened her eyes. And smiled.

My darling son, my Daniel. You're home. I thought I would never see you again. Every minute without you has been a lifetime of wretchedness.

You're home.

You're home.

I couldn't believe that I was alive without you. Every breath, I was hurt because you were away from me. Every thought I had was so full of torment. I couldn't hold you and kiss you. I hated the world for being alive, for carrying on as if losing you didn't matter to anyone. I would cry that the universe hadn't stopped functioning when you were gone. How could it be?

Sometimes I hated myself for loving you so much. In all of eternity I only had a few months with you. How could it be that it hurt so much to lose you? And then I hated myself for thinking like that. Please forgive me. Just know that I have loved you so much that I have nothing else in my body. My blood, my heart, my soul, my flesh, is love.

I want you to know that I will never leave your side. I will always be there with you. Do not spend a moment thinking about me when I'm gone. Live your life, find your loves, make your mistakes, be brave, be fearless, be good and kind and happy. Hold on to the people you have and forget those who leave. Do not remember me with sadness. I was alive then, to bring you to this world and I am alive now because I was waiting to see you one more time before I go.

Through millions of years, through millions of lives, I will always know in my soul that love means you.

Daniel.

I will never forget you.

I love you.

Thank you.

My darling son.

Thank you for being my son.

Thank you for coming back to me.

My Daniel.

Goodbye, my love.

Rewa stepped out of the Mayor's mansion on to the veranda and walked down the path towards the river. In the distance she saw the boathouse and smiled for a second, thinking that this was the very spot from where Amma and Dabir had kidnapped Daniel and now he was back home. Finally.

The morning sun was rising in the east, coming over the mountains glistening in orange over the river. Her face was wet with tears. Davon followed her down the path as she walked to the water's edge.

She spoke without turning, and she spoke without looking at him, "Seven years ago, when I was still in the cage, Dabir wanted to get 'The Dushonus' together for himself. He had already kidnapped me and then he made Amma work here, in the Mayor's house as a maid. As Pushpa. She kidnapped Daniel with his help and brought him to the village. But she couldn't bring herself to keep the child. Oma already was running the 'school' in the city, so Amma went to her, told her everything and left the baby with her. She managed some courage and never told Dabir where she had left the baby, and he nearly killed her for that, but he couldn't find the baby boy after that, and we kept moving because he was trying to keep me hidden."

"Oma raised the boy in the school as Fahim. Today when Fahim touched me, I saw everything. I remembered that I had *seen* him when I had touched the Mayor's wife that night. I brought him here, just in time."

Davon was silent, he knew what was coming.

"Tell me," Rewa asked quietly, "Did you know that he was Daniel? Or did Oma hide it from you?"

"We both knew."

She turned to him, "And yet you worked here with the Mayor for years, claiming to look for his son. You saw that his wife was dying, and you kept her away from her child. You were willing to let her die? Heartbroken? Why?"

Davon looked at her sorrowfully. "Please forgive me. Please. I had no choice."

"Why?"

"Daniel had been missing for a few months, when your Amma left him with us. I could have gone and given Daniel to them, but I knew the moment they got Daniel, they would have taken him off to England instantly."

Rewa was dumbfounded.

Davon was looking for her helplessly.

"Don't you see? He *had* to stay here. He *had* to wait here."

Rewa couldn't believe her ears. Davon pleaded.

"Our legend said that only if our three Dushonus were together, would the queen, the Listener, come to them. If they had taken Daniel and gone to England, we would have never found you. We had to keep them together. Even now, do you know what you have done? You brought him here and now he's with his father. Richard will leave for England and take Daniel with him. What will happen to the Dushonus? They are supposed to be here for you. Its destiny, my queen, we did it all for you."

"You did it for me?"

"Yes, my Queen, for you."

She stepped back and looked at him, anger and revulsion written all over her face.

"I am no longer your Queen."

Davon staggered as if he had been slapped.

"I banish you from my side." Rewa said calmly.

"No!"

"I banish you as my protector, as my servant. I banish you and I banish Oma. I will not have anything to do with your 'family' or your 'people' who have been waiting for me for generations. I am done with you."

Davon began to cry piteously as he fell to his knees.

Rewa said mercilessly. "You are no better than Dabir. You know, he said something to me last night. He said, if the reasons are different, than is it alright to kill someone? No, it isn't. Your reasons for destroying their lives..."

She pointed towards the Mayor's house.

"...Do not make what you did, right. You think you deserve forgiveness and Dabir needs to be damned because your *reasons* are better? Both of you only think about yourselves. 'Your' legend, 'your' queen. You never once thought of the child and the mother?"

Davon was on the floor, on his knees his head bowed, begging for forgiveness. As Rewa walked away. He looked up, tears streaming down his cheeks. He looked devastated.

"My Queen, I am so sorry. I was a fool. I was scared and desperate after we lost you. I wanted to do anything to bring you to us, safe and sound. And I know what I did, what we did was unforgivable."

He steadied himself as he stood.

"If I am to be banished, then that is what I deserve my queen.

"My destiny is serving you. And I will always do that.

"Wherever you may go, whatever you do. I will always be a breath away. You will never see me, but you will feel me. No harm will come to you, you will need for nothing. I will always serve you. You are my queen, and I will wait for the day you call for me.

"If I have to wait for centuries for you to forgive me. So be it."

CHAPTER 39

The Boatman's Song

Rewa stood next to the river, alone and silent.

A boat glided across the river, the boatmen was singing a rather mournful song, to his solitary passenger, a young girl, but Rewa couldn't hear the words in the distance.

She sensed the two of them approach. Aleya and Kanan.

They came and stood by her. Aleya sat on the bank and dipped his feet in the water. Kanan began picking up stones and throwing them further into the river.

No words please. Rewa looked at them pointedly.

Both of them understood. They communicated silently.

Kanan looked at her.

You're leaving.

Yes.

Aleya joined in the silent conversation.

Because you're angry?

No.

Kanan looked accusatory.

Fahim is going to go to England now. He'll be gone forever.

Rewa understood that she had broken the Dushonus by bringing Daniel home. Kanan was resentful.

No. He will be back.

How do you know?

He will be back. Not soon, but one day, Fahim will be back with us.

But what about The Dushonus?

Rewa waited for a moment.

There is time.

Aleya turned his gaze around from the river to the mansion.

Davon is inside looking at you like a hawk.

Kanan grinned.

You think he won't follow you?

Rewa smiled.

He will. But he will learn not to.

Kanan looked at her disapprovingly.

What about the demon you met in the forest, aren't you afraid?

Rewa thought for a second.

Not yet. She'll come for me. But not yet.

Do you want us to come with you? Wherever you are going?

No.

Why not?

Rewa sighed. She pointed to the man in the boat, singing, as he glided across the river.

That man thinks he has an old mother in a village. He hasn't seen her in ten years. He thinks she's alive, but she died last month. I can see her. She's saying something to him, but he cannot hear.

The girl in his boat is seventeen years old and she's pregnant but she doesn't know it yet. Her husband died in Lahore, two months ago. I can see him too. She thinks she's going to join him next week. She will be killed on her way to Lahore. The baby too.

I want to tell her husband what is going to happen, but he can't hear me as well.

Why is this happening?

Both Aleyah and Kanan said nothing.

Do you know that the strangest world approaches? A world at war. At war with its own capacity to shine. A world so cruel, yet so beautiful that no one will know how to live in it. Cities will be bursting at the seams and people living in them, will be dying to die. In the next hundred years, we will see things that will make no sense at all. Everyone will be able to see everything in the world, yet they will not be able to reach out and touch the heart of someone standing right next to them. Everyone will have everything or they will want to have everything, but in the end, they will have nothing at all, except hate and decay and loneliness. Rage bursting out of each of them like a torrent.

Aleya stood up and stepped back till he and Kanan were standing next to each other.

What has happened to you? He asked silently.

Rewa turned to look at them.

I don't know. I can see and hear and feel so much that my eyes and my heart is burning. Everyone up there in that mansion, you both, Davon, the cook in the kitchen making tea. The people across the river, I can't even count as many, but I can hear all of them. I have their hurt in me like a fever right now. All I know is that I have been chosen to see and feel all of this. You both have known about your powers for a while, but can you answer me as to why me? What are we supposed to do?

She looked towards the mansion in the distance.

I don't trust anyone anymore. I need to know for myself.

Aleya got up and dusted his pants.

And we can't come with you?

Rewa shook her head firmly.

No. I don't know myself what I'm going to do.

Rewa thought of Amma and the last thing she had said to Rewa.

"If you ever feel the need for a family. Come find me and Kantha. I promise you, my child. I will be the mother I couldn't be to you."

She felt homesick. It felt like she had been homeless and roofless her entire life. Amma had not been a kind mother, but right now all she longed for, was something familiar. All she had known was gone. With Amma this time, it would seem real and honest, with no secrets. She thought of how Kantha hadn't even looked back at her, the last time she had seen her at the village.

She looked up at the sun, which was now a foot above the mountains and a flock of birds flew across the orange orb.

Maybe she would go to Jatinga Valley, where the birds fall.

Where the story of The Dushonus began.

Don't go alone. Kanan communicated with her resentfully. *The Dushonus are supposed to go together. You won't forget you're one of us, will you?*

Rewa burst out laughing at that. Aleya looked at her with affection.

Will you come back? You know that we can hear you, right? So, we can find you if we want.

Rewa's smile faded.

"That's something that I have to find a cure for. You all can hear a bit too much of what I'm thinking."

This time she spoke out loud. Then Kanan spoke out loud too.

"Don't be stupid. What if something happens to you and you need us. Please be sensible, and careful and..."

He looked serious.

"...Don't die or anything."

"Don't worry about that." Rewa grabbed his hand and then she grabbed Aleya's hand.

"See?" she said, smiling.

"The Dushonus will be alive for at least two hundred years."

Epilogue

I am Jhara.

I am the Ekaki.

I am the guardian of the door. The whisperer of the souls.

I came to earth to help souls.

This is what I learnt when Ajoy, Peelo, and Eleanor left the world last night.

Mine is not a war for power.

This is a prayer.

When souls are leaving this earth, I will bring them love and peace.

Life is hard. It is pain, loss, hurt, regret, shattered dreams, loneliness, judgement, fear, and sorrow.

But it is love.

It is gratitude. Life is the people you love and life is the words you didn't say to them when you could have.

Life is the time that you didn't get to spend with them and you wished you had. It is the hurt and pain you wished you hadn't caused them.

Life is the moment you look someone in the eyes and say "I love you so much. I am so grateful that I had *this* life, and *this* moment with you. Thank you."

The world needs to say that.

The world needs someone to listen to these words, that beat in your heart before your heart stops beating.

When your time will come, I will hear you.

Glossary

1. Bangla – Refers to both, the language (aka as Bengali) and the people living in West Bengal, Bangladesh, Tripura, and parts of Assam.
2. Beedi – A thin cigarette commonly wrapped in a tendu leaf, tied with a string or adhesive at one end.
3. Burqa – A loose, enveloping garment for women that covers the face and body.
4. Bushirt – A loose-fitting cotton shirt with patch pockets.
5. Chamra – A slang used for skin. Skin of an animal or human.
6. Charpoi – A traditional woven bed. The word "charpai/ charpoi" is a compound of "char" meaning four and "pai" meaning footed.
7. Dada – Big brother.
8. Didi – Sister.
9. Dushonus – Translates to "two spirits".
10. Ekaki – In the Sanskrit language, it means alone, or solitary. Here, according to the legend, it means the 'Solitary Queen of souls'.
11. Firangs – Foreigners.

12. Gamcha – A piece of cloth used to wrap around the head or neck. It is a much smaller cloth as compared to a Turban.

13. Gora Saheb – British Gentleman.

14. Goras – The British.

15. Inquilab Zindabad – The famous slogan was one of the rallying cries of the Indian independence movement, and can be translated as "Long Live Revolution".

16. Jholi – cloth bag

17. Kulfi – Iced candy.

18. Macch diye ja / Meccho bhoot. – A legend about the fish who eats ghosts lurking near ponds and rivers. Supposedly, it also captures and eats humans. These ghosts ask passerby humans to give them some fish to eat, and then they hunt them as prey.

19. Macchardani – Mosquito net.

20. Mirgi – Epilepsy.

21. Mocher jhol – A spicy gravy made with local fish.

22. Paisa – Indian coins.

23. Patra – Banana leaf used to serve food.

24. Petni – Woman who is possessed by a ghost or an evil spirit.

25. Rajnigandhas – White, night blooming flowers with a sweet smell.

26. Rakshasuaru – The most evil and powerful demon of all. A female demon.

27. Shaundesh – Bengali sweets.
28. Thakurma, Thakurda – Grandmother and Grandfather.
29. Tonga – A light two-wheeled vehicle used in rural areas of India. It is usually pulled by a horse.
30. Zamindar – Land owner.

Acknowledgements

How writers become writers is an unfathomable, unexplainable phenomenon.

Events happen disconnectedly; and then it is left to the writers to trace the events back to their origins, and try to make sense of the why and the how.

I began to write very early on, I think around eleven or twelve years of age and I didn't think much of it till years later. And now with this book stepping into the world, I have been trying to understand the trajectory of its birth.

Thank you, mom for encouraging me to buy Enid Blyton books instead of just comics at the Delhi Railway Station when I was traveling to Calcutta. Thank you for building that huge bookcase under the window in our bedroom, where your Wilbur Smith novels nestled against my Hardy Boys books. It began there.

Thank you, Vaneeta Bhogal, Anuradha Wadhera, and Simi Kashyap, for actually reading my childish novels at the age of thirteen and remembering them years later. Maybe you should share the blame.

Thank you, TJ, for those long discussions sitting on the railway track behind your home, in the freezing North Indian winter with a cup of chai—discussing Thomas Hardy, or Ayn Rand (which I totally didn't understand then). Thank you for putting my quotes at the top of your desk and embarrassing me. Thank you for those eight-hour long journeys from Ludhiana to Delhi and scouring Connaught place and Khan Market bookstores for strange titles no one had even heard of. You opened more worlds for me than anyone else in my life.

Thank you, Pinky, and Ravi for the support when no one knew what the hell I wanted to do with my life. I love you, sis.

Thank you, my dearest darling family. Supriti, for reading my novel and asking me frustratingly piercing questions and then, making me rewrite and redraft and then, rewrite again.

Also, thank you for lending me lots of money. I will pay you back, very soon. Nyah for being smarter, kinder, more intelligent, and insightful than I give you credit for. And for being my critical audience. The loves of my life.

Thank you, Terence, for publishing those terrible scripts that I wrote for your shows, on the billfold. Maybe you shouldn't have given me that ego boost. This is on you.

Thank you, Angela, for being our angel, our superheroine, and our screaming tree all in one. Family forever.

Thank you, Sarosh Bharucha, for being the first one to read this book. That meant more to me than I can ever say. So, we'll just get drunk instead.

Thank you, Nidhi Kaushik, for all your hard work.

Thank you, the incredible team at Nu Voice Press—Tanvi, Kevin, Navya, Archita, Vedika, and Leslie.

And thank you, my dear reader, who is reading this right now.

P.S. – You have spent money on this book.

Wow! I promise you a cup of coffee wherever we meet, if you are carrying a copy in your hand.

About the Author

Harssh A Singh is an actor, writer, and an award-winning radio host. He has been involved in the performing arts his entire life. He won numerous awards as a radio host, before he branched into theatre and films as an actor.

He has worked with some of the best directors in the world including Mira Nair, Anurag Kashyap, Anubhav Sinha, Feroz Abbas Khan, Kabir Khan, Atul Kumar, John McTigue, Melly Still and many more.

Some of his films include *Raman Raghav 2.0, Kabir Singh, Thappad,* and *Pippa*. His web shows include *Mumbai Diaries – Season one and two, Rocket Boys Season two,* and *Special Ops.*

He also has a YouTube channel called "An Actor's Review", dedicated to films, acting, and entertainment.

He has, at various times in his life, been a lab technician, an aerobics and dance instructor, a dancer, and a singer in a rock band.

This is his debut novel.